BY CHARLIE PRICE

DEAD
INVESTIGATION

DEAD
INVESTIGATION

CHARLIE PRICE

FARRAR STRAUS GIROUX · NEW YORK

Farrar Straus Giroux Books for Young Readers
175 Fifth Avenue, New York 10010

Printed in the United States of America
First edition, 2015
10 9 8 7 6 5 4 3 2 1

macteenbooks.com

Library of Congress Cataloging-in-Publication Data
Price, Charlie, author.
    Dead investigation / Charlie Price. — First edition.
        pages cm
    Sequel to: Dead connection.
    Summary: Since the affair of the murdered cheerleader, seventeen-year-old Murray has moved into the lawnmower shed at the town cemetery, where he is close to the dead that he talks to and considers friends—but the caretaker's daughter, Pearl, wants him to use his gift to find a homeless man who seems to have disappeared, and may have been murdered by someone who is hunting the homeless.
    ISBN 978-0-374-30227-6 (hardcover)
    ISBN 978-0-374-30228-3 (e-book)
    1. Psychics—Juvenile fiction.   2. Spirits—Juvenile fiction.
3. Murder—Investigation—Juvenile fiction.   4. Cemeteries—Juvenile fiction.   5. Paranormal fiction.   [1. Psychics—Fiction.   2. Spirits—Fiction.   3. Murder—Fiction.   4. Supernatural—Fiction.
5. Cemeteries—Fiction.   6. Homeless persons—Fiction.]   I. Title.

PZ7.P92477Dei 2015
813.6—dc23
[Fic]
                                                    2015007180

Our books may be purchased in bulk for promotional, educational, or business use. Please contact your local bookseller or the Macmillan Corporate and Premium Sales Department at (800) 221-7945 ext. 5442 or by e-mail at MacmillanSpecialMarkets@macmillan.com.

To the Fairhope Center for the Writing Arts
and the city of Fairhope, Alabama, for their
commitment to the arts, continuous inspiration,
and extraordinary people

DEAD
INVESTIGATION

Living in the cemetery lawnmower shed turned out pretty well. Murray had gotten used to the uninsulated prefab and its peculiarities. Sure, the concrete floor leached warmth from anything that touched it and the place reeked of motor oil and industrial cleaners. The window rattled when a city bus passed on the street. The little hut was an iceberg during cold spells, and yes, its seams made an eerie whistle when the wind gusted. Nonetheless, it had only one serious drawback.

The shed sat atop a foundation that had been mistakenly poured eighty or ninety years ago over an old woman's grave, and she complained nonstop to anyone who'd listen. It was enough to drive a person crazy.

If you parked the riding mower under the front utility shelf, there was room in back for a cot and a milk crate that held a battery lantern so you could read yourself to sleep. Murray preferred it to home and was very grateful to Pearl for suggesting it, and to her dad, the cemetery caretaker, for making it available.

Saturday morning was chilly but not shivery. Murray washed his face in a metal basin, put on jeans and pulled a hoodie over his sweatshirt, grabbed an apple from the grocery bag he kept on the tool bench. Breakfast. He'd get something at 7-Eleven for lunch. Candy bar, orange, something easy. What was cheap and built muscles? A banana? Murray noticed his T-shirts were tighter. But he wasn't fat. He might be getting some muscles. Made him wonder why. All the walking he did? Genes from whoever his father had been?

And he'd grown taller in the last few months. He could

tell because his pants were too short. Time to visit Salvation Army. And his face? Pimples were rare now. His messy hair almost fit current styles. His nose was still too big, but his face wasn't actually frightening. No horns. No fangs. Girls looked at him sometimes.

In February nothing needed mowing, but there was always trash to be bagged, stuff that visitors left behind, plus cups and wrappers the wind blew in off the street. Murray was picking a fast food sack out of the hedge at the cemetery's north border when he heard somebody jogging through the leaves and downed branches behind him. Unusual. Most people were somber and dignified in cemeteries. He looked up and was surprised to see Pearl. Ordinarily she was quiet. She'd been known to sneak up and startle him just to watch him jump. So . . . in a rush today. Why?

Pearl didn't seem like a cemetery caretaker's daughter. Her skin wasn't pale green, her head didn't do three-sixties. She looked . . . well, gingery blond hair, tight curls, a decent face that didn't need makeup; medium tall, a girl jock with muscles and the start of a figure. Actually, Murray thought she looked kind of pretty. But dangerous. Smart and stubborn. Went after what she wanted like a torpedo. Could get you to do things you'd rather not. Murray braced himself.

"Hey, Ghostbuster. I need your help."

"I'm busy."

"You'd rather pick up trash than talk to me?"

"Um . . ." At least half the time Pearl came around she had something she wanted Murray to do that was borderline risky. He'd learned to be careful about what he agreed to. "What kind of help?"

"Your special thing. Like the others." Pearl held out a dirty wool stocking cap.

Murray didn't get it. "What others?"

"Others with the gift. Clairvoyants."

Murray stepped back onto the garbage bag and heard it rip. "Dang it, Pearl, don't use that . . . I don't . . . Leave me alone."

"You just probably haven't tried it before." She pushed the cap toward him. "They hold something that the person wears or handles a lot and they get information."

"What information?"

"Tell me where to find that down-and-out guy who walks around outside the gate all the time."

"Try outside the gate."

Pearl stuck out her tongue. Glared. "I have stuff for him."

"Uh, why?" Murray couldn't imagine.

"You know the ratty sleeping bag he carries? Dad and I got him a new one and a coat and some canned meat. I'm pretty sure he sleeps up in these hedges sometimes."

Murray nodded. Both Pearl and Janochek did kind things for people all the time. Murray was one of them. "Okay, I'll tell him."

"Have you seen him lately?"

Murray tried to remember. "Probably not for a week. Ask at the mission."

"I did. Nothing. They didn't recognize him."

"How would they? You don't even know his name, right?"

"That big red bump on his forehead? Like an infected boil? Pretty hard to miss. They said they'd never met him."

"Yeah, so, what could I do? I'll tell him you have stuff when I run into him."

"No, you could actually find him." Pearl held out the stocking cap again.

"You're nuts. Even if that's really his, you want me to read the label and tell you where he bought it or something?"

She stuck the cap out closer to his hand. "Just hold it and tell me what comes to you."

Where do you even start with a request like that? Murray had never done anything like it. Would never do anything like it. Felt queasy just thinking about touching the smelly thing.

"I've been reading," Pearl said, rummaging in her backpack like she was searching for a book. "Clairvoyants can hold somebody's favorite pen and know where they're hiding."

Murray retreated another step, hearing paper and cans crunch under his feet.

Pearl shook her head, pursed her lips. "Don't be such a pussy. Give it a shot."

The last time Murray had helped Pearl he got shot, literally. Spent days in a hospital and got hauled into the police station to explain how the two of them found a missing cheerleader's body. And then, somebody talked. Maybe a cop told his family at dinner or a reporter leaked it. Something. Somehow. The story got around school that Murray Kiefer thinks he can talk to dead people. He went from being a mostly invisible loser to a well-known certifiable wacko.

Big problem: it was true. He *was* friends with a lot of dead people, and he learned things from them. The cheerleader, for example. "A lot happens in your last second. You're so mad that you're dying, and so scared, but there's also this relief . . . and it hits you all at once like lightning. I couldn't say anything quick enough before I was gone."

Maybe Murray could have guessed the fear and anger part, but relief? That was a surprise . . . and then it wasn't. Living is probably hard for everybody.

"When you realize it's really the end, everything gets clear," Blessed Daughter told him. "In that moment I knew who I really loved and who I didn't, what I was proud of and what I wasn't. It was surprising. I loved my dog as much as I loved my parents. I don't know why. Riley was always bouncy and happy. Didn't understand how quick I was dying away. I didn't have to watch his face crumple."

As far as Murray could tell, Blessed was as sharp and sensible as a lot of adults even though she had died of a brain tumor when she was only eleven.

"And the school grades I worked so hard for? I was prouder of my swimming medal, 'cause they said the tumor would wreck my swimming but I made the team anyway. And I won a fifty-yard backstroke before the cancer messed my timing."

His older friend, Dearly Beloved, told him she didn't miss her family very much. "It was back in the fifties. Mom and Dad mostly paid attention to my brothers. 'Stay a virgin till you're married.' That and 'Wear clean underwear when you go to town' was the only advice I ever got. I wish now I'd moved out before the darn car accident."

Dearly had gone through the windshield when her date hit a tree.

"When I croaked, what I missed was the life I'd saved money for. I'd earned enough to bus to San Francisco. I thought if I winked and smiled I could maybe get a job at a bookstore in North Beach."

Dearly was lighthearted, and wise for her twenty-five years. Almost like a mother to Murray.

"Don't worry about me and the others," she said. "The grave isn't uncomfortable or cold or anything. Really, you don't even feel it."

That was good news, because Murray couldn't imagine being an adult. What would he do? He didn't drive, didn't have money, couldn't think of a job he could hold except caretaking this cemetery, and Janochek already had that. So Murray was pretty much ready to die. He had his tombstone picked out, charcoal granite with silvery flecks. He was paying for it by keeping the lawns and hedges and grave sites free of trash. And he had his words:

Murray Kiefer
May 12, 1997–
Friend to the Deceased

He knew he'd miss Pearl and Janochek. That's why he hadn't died yet. Well . . . and there was one more reason. He was happy in the cemetery. Mostly. Except it had started again. Voices. People he didn't know and wasn't talking to. Moaning. Mumbling. Hurting. East, just past the back fence, probably on the hill between the rodeo grounds and the rear hedge. He'd heard them last week and again this morning when he was picking up trash. More than one person at the same time. That hadn't happened before. He knew they were dead. But they were outside the cemetery. Not his people.

SHERIFF'S DEPARTMENT

His son's birthday was drawing nearer, this day, a month from now. Deputy Roman Gates sat apart from his peers, quiet and reflective during the morning briefing. At the head of the room, the duty sergeant straddled a corner of the desk beside the county map and read from his clipboard without so much as a hello or good morning.

Petty crimes were mostly confined to Cypress Street, five blocks on either side of the freeway. Convenience store / gas stations open all night and vulnerable. Next, a DUI chase ending when the fifty-seven-year-old local realtor fled the wrecked car and made a run for it but was easily apprehended when she staggered unclothed into a barbed wire fence. That got Gates's attention because he knew the woman. Played blackjack with her at the local casino during the time he'd burned down his marriage and job with the gambling.

Main news: a third home robbery in the Garden Tract. To date, total property losses were under two thousand dollars, but if this pattern continued there was a high probability that a homeowner or family friend or, god forbid, a child return- ing from school would interrupt the burglary, and injury or death could result. Riverton Police Department was currently busy with a heroin sting operation involving a local gang and La EME Mexican Mafia from the San Diego area, so the Sheriff's Department drew Garden Tract responsibility and Gates was lead investigator.

As the briefing drew to a close, the community liaison asked for a minute. A stocky gray-haired woman named Pitt- man made eye contact with each of the five officers present before speaking. "Both Good Hope Mission and Faith Be Saved House have repeatedly contacted me about missing homeless people. Lately they believe the numbers are increasing. I know this is easy to dismiss. I know many of the homeless are transient, and I also know this population has been a low priority in the community for years. Chamber of Commerce, city council, county supes all have economic and political pressure to downplay the number of Riverton's homeless along with the social and medical problems they present."

The woman looked at a manila folder she held under her arm as if she was considering reading from it.

A relatively new female deputy used the pause to respond. "No way we're ignoring the homeless. The majority in shelters? Decent folks, horrible life. Bad upbringing, bad education, bad breaks. Just saying. We get it. We look out for them. But the troublemakers? Maybe 25 percent? We bust them day-in, day-out for petty crap and they're free before dark. No jail room. I'm not sure what else we're supposed to do."

Gates had not personally met this woman deputy, never heard her speak before. Built like a fullback. He thought her name was Faraday. She was a recent hire from Alameda County, where he guessed they knew a thing or two about street people and poverty. Anyway, he agreed with her. Was glad she spoke up.

Pittman nodded, acknowledging the woman's point. Moved on. "There's a disturbing thread to the recent reports. At least three of the missing had jobs within support agencies, had a motel room or low-income apartment. They disappeared for no discernible reason. Agency staff is concerned someone could be targeting these people and that possibly several less visible homeless have similarly vanished with no one to report it."

She stopped for a deep breath, more like a sigh, and once again made eye contact with each deputy. "I know this is not a glamorous concept. Some may feel that Riverton would be better off if all the homeless vanished or moved to another town. I'm sure that viewpoint isn't shared by the officers in this room, and I'm asking you to begin paying more attention to the library, parks, and shopping centers where transients and dispossessed tend to congregate. Particularly, whether an individual or group of predators might be monitoring them."

Now the woman opened the folder, ran a finger down a typed page, and stopped near the bottom. Looked up and continued. "Recently a local homeless man's gone missing. David Payne. Before his life fell apart he was an auditor and financial planner for an engineering firm here in town. The mission reports the disappearances of its other clients have increased since that event. They believe it is possible a person or persons is . . ." She stopped and swallowed.

Gates got the impression the woman didn't want to say the words that had entered her mind.

"They're wondering if someone might be hunting these homeless for sport."

DEADWEIGHT

When Murray turned the corner on Continental Street and walked through the main gate, the cemetery looked empty—no funerals, no families, Janochek off working somewhere. That was good. A chance to meet some of the new kids nearer the street without being interrupted. In the west section, three rows over, a plaque marked a fresh site. A boy he hadn't met. He sat in front of the marker. Relaxed into a long breath. Read the information.

MALIK FEATHERS

SEPTEMBER 23, 1994 — JANUARY 24, 2014

GATHERED TO THE LORD

Murray introduced himself and the guy piped right up like they knew each other.

"Shoulda knowed better to ride with no white boys. I'm front seat, drifting on tar, new stuff from L.A. They just plain drunk. We highballing 'cross the river get on 5. I'm slayin' on the water an' the moon an' shit and Bobby slides the damn Chevy off the road, down some hill, and we bangin' into shit and my door flies open and I'm out an' the damn car rolls over me. You believe that? Nineteen, got a damn job, and Feathers is gone. Not a scratch on nobody else."

Murray pushed back from Feathers's gravestone. Couldn't think of anything to say. *Thanks for telling me* seemed dumb . . . *Oh.* He scooted forward again and touched the headstone. "It's not so bad here. Hang in there." He leaned back again. *Hang in there?* That was totally lame.

Getting to know someone brand-new was hard because nobody young wanted to be dead. Except maybe the new suicide. Murray hadn't met him yet. Maybe he didn't want a friend. Right?

"Hey, Ghoulbrain, I think I figured it out."

Murray knew it was Pearl without turning around. Wished he'd heard her footsteps. Hated being surprised.

"Who's that?" She sat beside him, breathing hard like she'd been running.

Murray didn't say anything. Pearl could read the plaque if she was really interested. He, on the other hand, was trying to concentrate.

"Will you hold the old guy's cap?"

"I told you no. Give it a rest."

"Want to hear my theory?"

"No."

"Did you see *21 Grams*?"

Murray had no idea what she was talking about.

"The movie? About how much the soul weighs?"

God, the girl could be irritating.

"I don't watch movies." Pearl knew that. And soul? He had no idea what to think about that word.

"So people weigh twenty-one grams less when they die. Mass has energy and that's the weight of the energy. A guy measured it. But what if that's not all the energy? What if that's just the energy that leaves? What if there's still energy remaining and that's what you're reading when you talk with the dead? What if some of our soul's energy sticks to things we touch and sometimes clairvoyants can access it?"

"God loves a duck!" Murray whirled on her, borrowing

one of her father's favorite expressions. "That's . . ." He couldn't find the right word. Ridiculous? He settled on "just plain nuts."

"Wait—"

"I'm not reading energy. I don't even know what that means. I don't know anything about a soul. Dead people talk and I hear them. It's as simple as that."

"You're fooling yourself. Nobody else hears them. Explain that."

"There's nothing to explain."

"Dad even says you're clairvoyant."

"He's being nice. That's a fancy word for crazy."

"Come on, Murray. You're not dense. You wonder what's going on." Murray pushed himself to his feet and jogged away toward the cemetery gate. He wasn't going to have this conversation. She wouldn't believe him, had never believed him.

Deputy Gates caught Pittman, the community liaison, on her way to the parking lot. "Mission admin might be watching too much television."

"Got your attention."

"But why hunting? Why not random hate crimes, or rape, or even gang initiations?"

"I talked to several agency staff," the woman said, tapping the file. "The missing told no one they were leaving, took no belongings. Several had worked for months to achieve their jobs and benefits. A few made pocket money by begging around town. Fifteen dollars was a good day, so robberies gone wrong doesn't make any sense."

Gates, thinking along with her, couldn't see a useful pattern.

Pittman pulled her coat collar closer together against the chill February wind. "What's the predator's motive? Not money. Probably not sex. Kidnapping a workforce? That's an even crazier idea. If it's different predators, why would each one hide the body after killing? Only someone who didn't want law enforcement to notice the extent or the method of his crimes would go to the trouble. With no payoff or discernible purpose for the disappearances, serial killing or sport hunting were the only things the staff could think of. Otherwise, the vanishings make no sense at all."

Gates considered how pistol sales had skyrocketed in the county after all those movie theater and school shootings in the national headlines. He knew local men had been taking both marksmanship classes and private training in outdoor armed engagement. What if one of these men was practicing with live targets, or perhaps taking it on himself to reduce the number of homeless in Riverton?

"What can you tell me about this Payne?" Gates asked, wishing he'd put on his own coat before rushing outside.

"I met him at the mission. Nice man, soft-spoken, self-effacing. His counselor told me Payne was the first exec fired from his company in last year's building downturn. Apparently that started a chain reaction, the man's marriage, home, money, all down the drain within a few months."

"Not bitter? No chip on his shoulder? Not likely to start a fight?"

"More like deflated. If he'd ever had any confidence, it was missing in action. That's part of why it's hard to understand. The Payne I met wasn't likely to provoke anybody. He was barely comfortable with eye contact. More, he was supposedly getting back on track, training the mission's peer-client staff. He had no reason to take off." Pittman shook her head, frustrated, gave a quick look toward her car like she was ready to leave.

"What about family?" Gates asked, himself ready to get indoors. "Couldn't they help? Send him someplace for a fresh start?"

"From what I understand, wife had a substitute waiting in the wings. Local contractor. She and her daughter moved in with him almost immediately."

* * *

Once back inside, Gates poured a coffee and carried the brimming cup across the squad room to his desk. Sat to find the interview sheets he'd requested on the Garden Tract robberies. Before he began reading, made a mental note to visit the mission himself. Get his information firsthand.

Murray spat out a stream of swear words he'd learned from his mother as he strode north on Continental toward the river. Down a steep trail to the gravel bank, throwing rocks at the water, he was still furious.

Pearl wants to know how he can talk with the dead? He was screwed. Murray had seen her in action. When the girl got her teeth in something, a tractor couldn't pull her off, so this wasn't going away. Explain? Murray wouldn't know where to begin. You don't force someone to tell you why they're insane. They just are.

Somebody who thought they could hear dead people talking, sooner or later their brain would blow up . . . It happened to a girl at school last year. She'd been accepted to Yale and she was in Latin class, taking her senior final, and she tore up her exam and walked to the whiteboard and wrote Satan Is God and began yelling that everybody was going to hell and bacteria was eating them . . . It was horrible. Murray was in the hall when the police took her away.

He couldn't stand to think about what talking to the dead meant. He knew what it meant. Made it hard for him to breathe. Like somebody had strapped a bomb to your chest and you could hear it ticking.

Dearly Beloved and Blessed Daughter and Edwin were his friends, and you talk to your friends. Enough said. But he had to get along with Pearl because she held the keys to his kingdom. Janochek's one child. If she set her mind to it, she could make Murray's life miserable.

He did know this: the dead were kinder than most kids

at school. Murray could be dead people's friend. Nobody else could. He knew it was beyond weird, but he had kind of a duty.

Let Pearl explain that if she's so smart.

Before he left the river Murray had an idea. Couldn't believe he hadn't thought of it before. The library. Look it up. See what the experts said about hearing dead voices.

It took Murray thirty minutes to walk to the library because he took a detour south of the new City Services complex to pass by his mom's house in an area known as "The Hood." Less expensive homes, more drugs, more break-ins, but at least it was pretty with its old trees and proximity to the river. His mom lived on a fairly busy street called Freebridge, a two-bedroom house, white paint peeling and trim faded from forest green to a dull gray. As he neared, a large red sedan passed him and stopped in front.

His mom opened the passenger door and stepped onto the sidewalk wearing a copper-colored track outfit and bright white runners. *What the—?* Murray had never seen her in anything like that before. The big car's brake lights flashed, the engine shut off, and the driver's door opened, allowing a lanky man in a cream-colored velour running suit to lever himself out. He rested his elbows on the roof and paused to smile at Murray's mom, shaking his head like he couldn't believe his luck.

His mom returned the smile, curtsied, and saw Murray gaping at her from a few feet down the sidewalk. "Murray, sweetie pie, how nice to see you!" She strode toward him with open arms. "You've met Howard, haven't you?" she asked, nodding back over her shoulder as she walked. "He is the nicest man and he's a lawyer!"

Murray didn't run in time and got crushed in her embrace.

"Come meet him, darling, and let me fix you some lunch."

Murray relaxed, waiting until she released him. Lunch. At four-thirty in the afternoon. Like she did it all the time. He could see the man continuing to lean on his car, probably not sure what to make of this spectacle. Murray would bet dollars to donuts that his mom had never mentioned she had a son.

She relaxed her hug and grasped him by the shoulders. "I swear, every time I look at you you've grown an inch."

Murray took a quick step back and twisted easily away. "Got to run, Mom. I'm late for—"

"Honey, he's defending me, and he's not charging a thing!"

Murray hustled out of hearing distance before she could tell him more. At the end of the block he glanced back to see his mom and the slim man walking arm in arm toward her front door.

He smiled in spite of himself. His mom was a chameleon, matching her colors and habits to fit the guy she was near. He was glad he didn't have to live at her house anymore. His mom was a mess. Most of the time she was either bonging or flirting with some new guy she was trying to impress. Murray lost track of their names. It never lasted. Guys got tired of her pretty quick, and that was sad. It showed you that sex doesn't solve anything. It showed no matter what you do for someone, you can't make them love you.

At the library, the parking lot was full and people sat in the sun on benches near the front door. Murray pulled his wallet from his pocket, ready to get out his card until he saw that all the computers were busy. He wound up asking the woman at the info desk where he could find a large dictionary.

Second floor. Reference. He sat at one of the bigger books, gave his area a quick scan to make sure no one could see what he was looking up. Page 414. *Clairvoyance*: "Having or claiming to have the power of seeing or knowing beyond the range of ordinary perception." The roots of the word related to seeing clearly. That wasn't so bad, but the book looked pretty old.

A newer book had *College* in the title. That might be more useful. "The supposed power of seeing in the mind things that exist beyond the realm of normal senses." Supposed power? Uh-oh. Was this clairvoyant thing real or was Murray just making it up?

Across the room he saw a girl get up from a computer and go downstairs. He gave the second-floor librarian his card, sat at the vacated machine, and typed in his library password. When he reached a search engine, he typed "clairvoyance." Wikipedia was the first reference. Clairvoyance was defined similarly to the dictionaries. But the next sentence . . . "Claims for the existence of paranormal and psychic abilities such as <u>clairvoyance</u> have not been supported by scientific evidence published in peer-reviewed journals . . . The existence of the paranormal is not accepted by the scientific community. Parapsychology, including the study of clairvoyance, is an example of <u>pseudoscience</u>."

Not accepted. Pseudo. Murray's stomach rolled. *Certified psycho.* Murray hurried down the stairs and out the front entrance. Stopped by the yucca bushes at the edge of the parking lot, bent to his knees to get his breath. It was as bad as he'd feared. Worse, since everybody seemed to know clairvoyance was a crock except him and his friends. He heard footsteps behind him—someone going to her car, or coming to help him? He straightened and hustled toward the sculpture garden. No one should see him like this.

There, a metal bench on the edge of the walkway faced east, away from the library. Murray sat to gather himself. He wasn't sure he understood exactly what the words meant that had set him off, but he understood the gist. Pseudo. False. The voices weren't real. Weren't real. That thought robbed him of the will to move.

Janochek was wrong, and somehow Murray had always known it. The truth? Murray was a lonely pathetic dope who tricked himself and imagined he could talk to dead people. He buried his head in his hands, went over the things that had happened a couple of months ago.

Last year, November to be exact, Pearl found out Murray could talk to dead people. She spied on him and badgered him until he admitted it. It was a weak moment. As much as he liked her, he wished he hadn't caved. Big mistake. He told her he was hearing a voice he couldn't explain. Said it sounded like a girl crying.

Murray tried to backtrack, tried to recant, but Pearl was relentless. She got her way. She usually did. Nosy pushy bratty beautiful—no, scratch the beautiful—Pearl made him pinpoint the voice's location. Murray felt sorry for the weeping dead girl but he didn't want to get involved. He knew it would give people more ammunition to use against him, more reasons to think he was deranged.

Anyway, about two months ago on New Year's Eve, Pearl dug the girl up where Murray'd located her grave and solved the kidnapping. Found Nikki Parker, the local cheerleader who'd been killed and hidden in a plot not a hundred feet from the cemetery lawnmower shed.

Pearl and Murray told her father, Janochek, the cemetery caretaker, and he'd called the police. As a result, the police later said Mr. Janochek discovered the body. That was okay. The caretaker should get the credit. Police kept Murray and Pearl pretty much out of it because they were juveniles. What a word. Sounded like some kind of alligator.

ANNIVERSARY

Sheriff's deputy Roman Gates rolled the squad car out of the parking area and headed north to Garden Avenue, where he swung a right on Florence. This was the upscale neighborhood known as the Garden Tract, where there'd been all the home property thefts during the past week. Gates was betting a son with a drug habit, broke and temporarily living back home. Parents working or oblivious.

The first robbery was probably simple opportunity. Probably close to the young man's home. The next ones would be farther away, both to mislead and to reduce the level of neighbor awareness. Gates combed roads and alleys in an eight-block radius of the initial crime site, looking for a slow-moving beater car or a scruffy young pedestrian with a roving eye.

As he drove he thought about his own son. Next month was his only child's birthday. Twenty. Would probably be playing spring ball at a college. Probably studying communications. Probably dating a cute athletic girl who loved to hike. Probably. If he were alive.

Dwelling on his son's imagined future was hard to avoid. There were so many reminders. Work: overdoses or arrests for cocaine and heroin. Newspaper: local sports articles, photos of teens at school activities. Gates's rage ignited. Against every oath he'd ever taken, he would kill the person who'd sold his boy the drugs . . . but the coroner had ruled suicide.

Had his son really intended to kill himself? Was that the boy's goodbye to a life he believed hopeless? Ashamed of his father who'd become a gambling addict, destroyed his marriage, ruined his family, lost everything, and wound up publicly humiliated as a prisoner in his own jail? His mother, fled with no forwarding. Gates knew his son had been scalded by those events. Hurt, furious, did the boy make a quick decision he couldn't undo? A wave of shame took Gates's breath. Some thoughts could stop a heart.

Gates knew he was lucky to finally get his old job back. Demotion from lieutenant to investigator was fair. He parked the cruiser in a paved area off East Street facing the highway 44 on-ramp. Yahoos often raced along that stretch like the Daytona 500. Barely three weeks ago a boy had died close by when his friend's speeding car flew out of control on the 44 to 5 connector.

Gates opened the car door, hauled himself outside, and half sat on the front fender. Saw wispy contrails across a faded sky. Not a bird, not a squirrel, not a moth. Nothing but the distant hum of traffic. Where Gates had parked, he was a stone's throw from Forest Grove cemetery. Janochek and his daughter and that strange kid, Kiefer. Gates would never have found the murdered cheerleader without Kiefer's help. Did he believe the boy had located Nikki Parker's body because he'd "heard" the dead girl crying? Janochek was nobody's fool and he believed. But how could it be possible to hear from the dead?

In the moment of wondering, a thought surfaced. Made Gates flinch. What if Kiefer could talk to his dead son—ask him whether the overdose was an accident? The rush of feelings made Gates dizzy. Was it even ethical? Ask a police informant for a personal favor? He rubbed his eyes, rubbed the back of his neck. Took a deep breath, knowing he might never be able to bury that thought deeply enough to forget it.

Murray sat on the bench till the sun slipped behind the western mountains and the air became seriously chilly. He had considered the new information from every direction. Finally decided there wasn't so much to get upset about. Experts didn't understand talking with the dead any better than he did. Just because they couldn't explain it or figure out how to study it didn't mean that Murray's conversations weren't real. They were. Unless . . . he was imagining everything. Murray Kiefer, slightly nuts, so lonely he might be making it up. Wanting someone to talk to, he invents that the dead are talking back to him. Invents conversations. Forgets he's making it all up and actually believes it. Pitiful, but possible.

But damn it, he didn't make up the cheerleader's voice. He didn't know her, hadn't even met her. And he didn't make up people like Edwin. The kid died of polio. Murray didn't think he had ever heard of polio till Edwin told him about it. Bottom line? Even if he was delusional, at least he had friends.

When Pearl asked him again, he'd tell her he'd done research. The result? He didn't know what was going on and no one else did either. Hearing the girl crying? He simply couldn't explain that. Nobody could. And he would admit that the Nikki Parker thing could have some different explanation. Like maybe he'd noticed the fresh grave and wondered about it. Maybe Murray'd heard the guy digging the night he buried her but didn't make anything of it. Forgot about it. Whatever, there was probably something real that explained finding the body, even if he didn't know what it was.

The whole thing was a mystery, and life and love and death have lots of mysteries. That's the way it is.

Maybe Pearl would have mercy on him. Maybe she'd feel embarrassed that she'd been pressing him so hard and would back off before she pushed him all the way round the bend. If she'd ease off, everything would be fine. Really, who cared? Nobody but her. Nobody but her and the dead.

There was no sugarcoating it, Murray wasn't going to stop. The dead needed him. That was obvious. And sometimes they were surprising, amazing even. Didn't exactly have to worry about what people thought of them, right? But some of the dead were unsettled. Not resting in peace. Had things that bothered them. You can see how frustrating that would be. Stuck in the ground but still having troubles.

Murray was embarrassed to admit it, but he was afraid of the dead who were the most upset. As soon as he talked to them, they wanted him to fix something from their past life, and usually he didn't want to. All those feelings? He could comfort the dead, but he couldn't deal with the living. They were too mean. Sad cases, a lot of them.

Back at the cemetery, on his way to talk with Edwin, Murray noticed a new grave. He didn't have time to check if it was a kid who needed visiting, but he'd come back later. Right now he needed some advice, or the thing Janochek sometimes talked to Pearl about, perspective. A different viewpoint.

Murray spoke as soon as he'd sat and touched Edwin's headstone. "Why do you think we can talk to each other?"

"Uh, we like each other?"

"No, I mean, am I clairvoyant?"

"I thought you were Protestant."

"Damn it, I'm serious."

"Maybe if you told me what this is about."

"Pearl knows I talk with dead people and wants me to find a missing guy because she says I have a gift."

"I don't get it."

"She says I'm clairvoyant, and Janochek thinks so, too, and I looked it up and it says it's false science. So, how can you and I talk? What's going on to make that possible?"

"I'm not following you. We talk because we're friends. We talk because you visit me. Uh, you think living people and dead people shouldn't talk? You think dead people don't talk? Who am I?"

"Edwin."

"We have a winner!"

"But you're dead!"

"You want me to shut up?"

"No! Crap! I just want to understand what's going on."

"I think you should ask somebody else. I spent all that time in the iron lung and I never really even understood polio. I'm just glad you found me . . . buddies."

"What happens to you when I'm not here?"

"Nothing."

"What do you mean?"

"Murr, the square root of nothing is nothing."

CLASSMATING

The new grave was on the far south side near the 44 border, a little out of the way, and Murray hadn't noticed it until he'd gone to talk with Edwin the last time. The funeral must have taken place when he'd been in school. Murray sat carefully, respectfully, and reached out to touch. Read the name and got a surprise.

SANDRAY VANCE
AUGUST 24, 1997 — JANUARY 28, 2014
ALWAYS LOVING, ALWAYS LOVED

Sandray. The junior from Endeavor High across town who'd gotten killed at home. The whole gun argument had once again divided classmates. Murray's school vibrated with the girl's death. And he'd seen her, at a couple of sports assemblies. She was so . . . what word would do her justice? He'd asked the person next to him, *Who's the girl at the front of the dance team?* A girl behind him answered—Sandray Vance. That's all he knew. He'd never spoken to her. And then she got killed, and when he heard about it, it seemed like such a waste. Why always the best ones?

And now she was buried in his cemetery! How cool was that?

"Hey. You go to Endeavor?"

"Did."

"Dance team at the rallies?"

"Did."

"So what happened?"

"I died."

"I can see that . . . How?"

"It's a long stupid story."

"I got time."

"Who are you?"

"Murray. I saw your routines."

"You go to Endeavor?"

"Sierra, but you came to our assemblies a couple of times."

"You played ball?"

"No. They wouldn't want me."

"Why not?"

Murray sat back and took his hands off the metal marker. He didn't want to get into that. When he put his hands on the plaque again there was no connection at all. No reception, no transmission. Silence. *Is she mad at me?* Gradually he felt the slight tingle, heard the familiar soft hiss like a PA system coming on.

"Sandray's a pretty name."

Nothing.

"So what happened. How'd you get killed?"

"You didn't answer my question," she said.

"Uh . . ."

"Don't be a child."

"I'm seventeen." Murray tried to think of a response to why he didn't play sports that wouldn't make him seem like a loser. "Okay, I'm not super coordinated and I haven't played on any teams. You probably wouldn't know me, even if we'd gone to the same school. My mom got in trouble with . . . I guess I usually keep to myself." He could feel the tingle step up a notch like the girl was really listening.

She was quiet for a moment more. Trying to imagine him? She moved on. "I've been here a couple of weeks."

"Yeah, the ground is pretty fresh."

"I wanted to be cremated but nobody listened."

Murray was surprised. Hadn't met anyone who wanted to go that route. He guessed that the girl thought burning was a greener method. This correctness stuff never ended.

She went on, "My uncle Jake, Dad's youngest brother, got back from Afghanistan a while ago. It was pretty hard on him and he's been acting kind of strange."

Murray could imagine. War would change a person.

"Anyway, he's been angry, jumpy, yells a lot . . . god, it's so crazy . . ."

Murray relaxed. Patient.

"He's been staying with his ex-girlfriend's family, and he got in a big argument and they threw him out. He came to our house blitzed and raging about them and the Vets clinic, and everything. I was upstairs in my room, working on trig, and he was so loud I could hear him. Dad must have said something like calm down or be cool and Jake completely lost it. Started screaming. He had a pistol and he was firing it into the ceiling. Didn't know I was above him. And he got me. Twice. One under the arm and the other through my leg and up into my body. I knew he didn't mean to. I wanted to tell him. Tell my dad . . . but I died before anyone found me."

What do you say to something like that? "Jeez, that's . . . awful." It reminded him. "I got shot last year but it didn't kill me."

"Where?"

"Here. About fifty yards over toward the street. A drunk."

"No. Chest? Arm?"

"Side. I was lucky. Missed everything major."

"Really lucky. Even if he hadn't nicked my heart I would have probably bled out with the leg thing. Never thought I'd die like that. From a bullet."

"I'm sorry," Murray said. "You were so lively, so pretty." He looked away from the headstone, remembering. "You had great moves—" The hiss ceased like someone had pulled a plug. No energy. Nothing but silence. "I'm sorry," Murray said, feeling like an idiot. Great moves would be pretty hard to hear if you were dead. Newly dead. "I'm really sorry." But he was talking to a bronze metal plaque.

Before school the next day, Murray stopped by Feathers's marker. Got a surprise.

"Who the hell are you?"

No one had challenged him before. It was sort of shocking. *Who else sits in front of your stone and touches it?* "Um, Murray" was all he could think of.

"Yeah, so?"

"Uh . . ."

"What ya got?"

"What do you mean? . . . News?"

"I need news like I need 'nother hole in the head. You got a forty?"

Murray snorted, couldn't help himself. "You can't drink. You're dead."

"Tell me something I don't know, Eisenstein."

"What do you want?"

"You got a girl?"

Murray nodded. "Matter of fact I do." He got up. *Let's see how you get along with Pearl.*

Deputy Roman Gates wedged his pickup into a parking spot, far corner of the sheriff's compound. Crossing the blacktop to the office, he was momentarily distracted when a bedraggled man approached.

"I done stuff you wouldn't believe," the man said. "You ought to lock me up."

Gates believed jail might look like a pretty good option if he was in the man's torn shoes. Gates tried to imagine how he would feel wearing the same clothes day after day, no shower. The older fellow was filthy, raised red sore on his forehead, grimy windbreaker, stained wool sport coat worn like a blanket. He stopped, asked the man if people he knew were disappearing.

"Disappeared a long time ago. Piss on 'em."

Gates didn't want to pursue that. "I mean recently. Other people in the life you're living."

The man stared at Gates. "Yeah. Call this living?"

"I heard street folks are going missing. Know anything about that?"

"Happens all the time."

"More than usual lately?"

The man studied Gates's name tag as if he might want to file a complaint for harassment. "There something you're not telling me?"

"I'm not . . ." Gates looked away for a moment, uncertain what to say. "If you're usually careful, be more careful."

The man shook his head. "I don't got enough trouble . . ."

Gates made sure the man knew about food and bed at

Good Hope and Faith. Gave the guy an orange and the cheese crackers from his lunch sack. That exchange made him a couple of minutes late to the morning briefing, where he caught something about a fight at the skateboard park.

He got focused in time to hear about the hit-and-run on Old Alturas Road—victim hospitalized. Two armed robberies: ShopMart on Churn Creek and FastGas on Placer—less than a hundred dollars each and no one hurt. The only vandalism was spray-painting, poorly drawn but nonetheless obscene pictures, on the girls' gym at Redwood Middle School.

Duty sergeant's closing words, an admonition. "Still a wolf in the Garden, Mr. Gates. Make us proud."

Gates checked his desk for new messages or further interview sheets. None. He half filled the to-go cup he'd brought from home with the bitter dregs from the squad room pot and grabbed his vest and a clipboard so he could jot notes as he drove. Down the steps and into the parking lot, he saw the homeless man was still there, now following a young deputy toward the coroner's office. Maybe safer, but probably not the kind of accommodation the man was hoping for.

His second full day of his patrol of the Garden Tract was no more effective than the first. From today's briefing, Gates knew there had been another robbery in the area. Conclusion? So far he was a waste of taxpayers' money. And gasoline. What had he missed? He'd been looking for a male in dark clothing, sixteen to thirty-five. Slender because it would be easier to get in and out of houses without knocking things over or making too much noise. Caucasian because that was this neighborhood's predominant race. Hadn't seen a one.

What had he seen? Nothing, nobody . . . except three or four people, housewives or parents or college students walking their dogs. That didn't fit a robbery—tie your pet outside while you burgle? Nope. His assumptions about the thief had probably been wrong. In what way?

He parked at one of his favorite places, the driving range on the Sierra River, and watched families of geese puttering around, squabbling with inland seagulls. Wildlife, water, and beautiful country helped him think. He had planned to re-imagine the robberies: the way a particular house would be chosen, perhaps a different suspect profile; but his mind drifted back to Pittman and the recently missing homeless. Was sport hunting completely off the mark?

Peggy Duheen, a friend of his, social worker at County Mental Health, had told him he was lucky to have an "unconscious process." Said it helped his investigations. Gates hoped she was right. Or maybe occasionally he just got lucky. Someday he would ask Duheen what the hell an unconscious process was.

"You've been avoiding me." Pearl stood blocking the shed. One hand on her hip, the other clutching the stocking cap down by her side.

Not a good sign. "Uh, no. You've been gone a lot."

"Softball tryouts. I made the team. The homeless guy's still a no-show."

"Maybe he moved on. They do. All the time."

"Maybe something happened to him."

He brushed past her and went inside, not wanting to argue where Janochek might see them.

She came through the door and turned over an empty bucket to sit on. "Nobody will help."

"Maybe because it's not really a problem. There's a million explanations why you haven't seen him again."

"If somebody you knew was missing would you just ignore it?"

Uh-oh. This was exactly the way Pearl had pressured him into locating the cheerleader's body. "Look," he said, "this kind of thing, this clairvoyant crap, just makes people think I'm getting crazier."

"So it's all about you. You really don't care that an older man, a guy who's weak and pretty helpless, might be in trouble."

"Pearl, you're making all this up. It's not about this guy you don't even know. It's about you and proving you're a good person."

Pearl reddened, eyes narrowed.

"Besides," Murray said, sitting on the cot, holding its edges. "Bad news."

Pearl waited.

"I did some research. Clairvoyance is a pseudoscience. You know what that means?"

Pearl's frown became a grimace.

"It means there's no such thing. Like I told you before, I'm nuts."

Muscles in her jaw compressed. She was up so fast the cap dropped and the bucket tipped over. "So my dad's a dope or a liar?"

"No, I—"

"You're a coward! You've got something that could help people and you're so . . . gutless you won't even figure out how to use it."

"I know how to use it. I help my frien—"

"They're dead, you moron! They don't need help. The living do. You helped Nikki's family find their daughter. You do something good like that and then you crawl back in your grave? Spend your life in a goddamn lawnmower shed? I don't know what I ever saw in you."

This time she was the one who stormed away.

Murray shuddered. Like having a cannon go off in front of you. Pearl was so hair-trigger. Impossible to reason with. But he thought about what she'd said.

Mr. Janochek was a wonderful man. Neither a fool nor a liar. Maybe he was just too optimistic. He'd said Murray was clairvoyant to protect Murray. To shield him from being a suspect. To keep him from being hurt by the rough police interrogation. And Janochek had believed Murray was onto something about the missing girl that deserved to be followed up. Janochek thought clairvoyance explained how Murray could get information about the dead. The nice man had probably never looked the word up.

Had Murray made a mistake? More likely him than Mr. Janochek. Murray would go back to the library. Maybe he hadn't understood the concept. No matter what explained it, Janochek was right. Murray did talk with the dead. Just part of being crazy. And one other thing. The voices outside the cemetery were getting louder. Harder to ignore.

It was happening again. He couldn't believe it, didn't want to believe it, but he was involved. Stuck knowing something he shouldn't be able to know, stuck with exposing his . . . his what? Gift? Curse? Letting people see he was abnormal or nuts. He couldn't just shut up about it? Sure he could. But what if he did and then the voices got even louder and began following him and driving him so crazy they had to come and take him away?

Pearl was convinced her touch-the-cap idea was a good one. Over dinner the same day she decided to ask her dad. Wouldn't he think it was possible? She waited till he was a couple of bites into his turkey, bacon, Jarlsberg, serrano, and tomato triple-decker.

"I've been thinking," she began.

Janochek paused with the sandwich halfway to his mouth. Put it back on his plate and turned to look at her. In his experience, her ideas sometimes required his very careful attention. He could never predict what mischief might grow from Pearl's cogitations.

Pearl noted his concern. "No. Seriously, what if dead things or even ordinary objects in our world contain bits of information? Maybe electro-chemical charges or patterns on the surface like, um, old fingerprints. Like stains from strong emotions that are created when we're freaked out. Uh, like something could seep through our pores and get left behind when horrible things happen?" She paused and looked away, thinking. "Say a playground near where the Hiroshima bomb hit—couldn't someone like Murray walk around there and still hear the screams? Or a rock that was used to hurt someone—couldn't there be a remainder of the person's noise and pain on its surface?"

Janochek was dumbstruck. *Good god, what's my daughter doing now?* "Hell in a horsecart, girl, where do you come up with these notions? Murray? Horror films? YouTube? I've never heard of such a thing. Never. What brought this up?"

"Well, we talked about different kinds of energy in

science class and I started wondering how come Murray hears new voices sometimes, even when he doesn't really want to?"

"Life is . . . strange, honey. Mysterious. Why do the atoms in our bodies combine and hold together to become a person? And after we die, those atoms disperse back into the universe. There's so many things beyond our current understanding." Janochek knew he was in over his head. He should probably just listen.

"You know, I asked Murray to touch the cap I found that belonged to the homeless guy who used to sleep around here. The guy we bought the coat and sleeping bag for?"

"The guy's cap? The knit thing?"

"He wouldn't. Even though I told him clairvoyers can do that sort of thing. You know, touch somebody's favorite ballpoint and tell where they're hiding?"

Janochek felt like he'd missed the first hundred miles of highway on this particular trip. "Hold on. Um, you asked Murray to touch a cap so he could tell you where the man that's probably been sleeping around here a few nights has gone, so you could give the old fellow the things we bought?"

"Yeah. And then I keep wondering how Murray could have heard Nikki Parker crying and moaning when he walks past hundreds of graves every day and doesn't hear those things. And I thought, maybe it's the pain. Maybe it sticks somehow. Maybe that's what he's sensitive to. And I wondered if other whatever-you-call-'ems with that special talent could detect that kind of pain? What, um, circumstances might make it possible? And remember the film we watched a couple of weeks ago? *21 Grams*?"

Movie? Janochek barely paid attention to the films they

watched together at home. It was just a chance to sit quietly next to his daughter and enjoy one of the simple pleasures of fatherhood. He tried to regain a purchase on her original question.

"Wait. Wait! You're asking whether a clairvoyant person can pick up on someone else's pain, uh, in the form of an electro-chemical energy trace substance created during a traumatic event? This whatever-it-is might adhere to people's bodies or to inanimate objects they touch? Could a clairvoyant perceive such residual energy?"

That rewording was pretty complicated, but as she mulled it over, Pearl thought it might be what she'd meant. "Yeah, uh, maybe. Probably," she said, encouraged that her father had taken her question seriously.

Janochek glanced over at his computer as if he needed a reference library for this discussion. "The paranormal . . . er, clairvoyance is one aspect of paranormal phenomema. Lots of people, absolutely normal people, swear they have seen and/or heard a ghost. I think the main theory about ghosts is that they've got some kind of unfinished business and they're dislocated in time."

"Do you believe in ghosts?" Pearl asked, wondering how her dad got interested in the first place.

"I've never seen one," Janochek said. "Caretaking a cemetery? Could get pretty distracting."

Pearl thought about that. Smiled.

"Anyway," he went on, "phenomena appearing or speaking is not so unusual, but Murray's degree of clairvoyant ability is clearly special. There's some evidence that people with this gift can touch an object owned or loved by a missing person and develop information that contributes to his or her location. I think it's hit-or-miss. The clairvoyant doesn't necessarily know what impression is accurate and what's not."

"So Murray might get something if he held the cap?" Pearl was nodding as if she knew she'd been right.

"Unlikely I think, but who knows? 'Might' is probably the operative word." Janochek sighed. "So, an emotionally charged secretion that leaves a trace? Pretty esoteric, girl. Pretty darn creative. Makes me think you should apply the quality of this thinking to your academic subjects."

"Dad, jeez—"

"Eat your supper, honey, and I'll try to think of someone I can ask. Sounds like a question for Stephen Hawking, but maybe I'll start with Siri."

"Don't bother. She said she doesn't know." Pearl resumed eating. "Just think about it," she said. "Acorns become oaks, you know."

"Yes, and a grain of sand becomes a pearl or an irritant," Janochek said, pressing his palm against his forehead. "In this case, salad and turkey become a second baseman. Eat your food."

WORKING ON THE RAILROAD

That afternoon Deputy Gates was stopped at a downtown railroad crossing, waiting for whatever the train crews did during their twenty-minute road blocks. Repaint old boxcars? Lay new track? Finish a hand of pinochle, give the brakeman a pedicure? He decided to wait it out; decided not to set a bad example by turning on his flashers and driving down the sidewalk to get out of the traffic jam. He took the cruiser out of gear and let his mind idle along with the engine. He could see it wasn't just blocked cars of course. Pedestrians were stacked up waiting to cross.

Two men in dark suits and flashy ties, lawyers, he bet. Tall brunette in a smart wool suit and high heels? Another lawyer probably. Teenage girl pushing a baby carriage. A knot of boys joking and shoving, popping on and off their skateboards. An older woman carrying a stack of books home from the lib—

Now he was thinking about the robberies.

Had he considered a boy on a skateboard? Cover a lot of territory, quick getaway? No. But he hadn't seen any that he could remember, either. So why? An image slid into place. Each day he'd patrolled he *had* seen someone. The same someone. And he'd paid her no mind. A young woman pushing a baby carriage. How would a thief transport stolen items without arousing suspicion? Gates hit the flasher to exit the jam. Time for another pass through the Garden Tract.

*   *   *

He pulled to a stop beside the young woman he'd barely noticed on these streets for a few days now. Got out of the car taking his keys and radio.

"Good morning, officer."

"Hello, miss. I have a question."

"Sure, just don't wake my baby."

"Do you know that there's been several home break-ins, thefts in this area the last couple of weeks?

"Really? No. No idea."

"Do you live in this area?"

"Just visiting my folks. They wanted to meet Justin before I took a new job in the city."

"I'd like to meet Justin, too. Don't wake him. Just pull back the cov—"

The carriage hit Gates in the leg, barely missing his groin, and the girl was running. Gates, in his late forties, limping now, gave chase. Caught her. Eventually. Because two blocks away she tripped on a curb and knocked herself silly.

"Will it scar?" she asked. "My chin?" Looking up at him, seeming hardly more than a child.

At the next morning's briefing, Gates got a handshake and smiles for what his sergeant called a missed carriage of justice.

The newer part of the cemetery faced Continental Street and took up three or four acres. The wrought-iron front gate was right in the middle of this western boundary, so the main entry road went through and up a gradual hill past the lawn-mower shed, all the way to Janochek's workshop and cottage. Another narrow walkway went farther east from there to the top of the ridge and the rear boundary. There, on the edge of the bluff, a tall hedge and fence separated the graveyard from the rodeo grounds below, the convention center, and the river beyond.

Murray stood at the hedge on the cemetery side of the fence and listened to the voices. They didn't really make any sense. Weren't telling him any story, just groaning and mournful. He could understand that. He would be miserable, too, if someone buried him with other people, hidden on a hill, undiscovered, lost, and forgotten.

Maybe he should look for a broken corner of fence, slip down the hill. Find them. Talk to them. Ask them what they wanted. Maybe. But then what? He couldn't think what he'd do next that wouldn't get him in a ton of trouble.

Less than a quarter mile in from the street, another narrow paved walkway ran north and south, separating the newer from the older part where they'd been burying people for over a hundred years.

Murray's best friends Dearly and Blessed and Edwin were in the older part, and he still talked to them but not as much.

Not since he'd been making new friends with the kids who'd lived during the time he himself had been alive. Kids who might understand what his life was like? Not bloody likely. *Oh, your mom's a prostitute, too. Yeah, I know, small world.*

It was cool that Sandray was the same age, same grade. Pearl was a freshman. Murray rarely encountered her at school and had hardly seen her lately since softball started. Pearl was obnoxious and bullheaded and could be the most annoying person he'd ever met. On the other hand she was strong and bright and funny, and could look so great with her curls and her prankster smile.

He had to admit, he'd thought about what she'd be like for a girlfriend. He knew she sort of liked him, at least as a friend, but she was a couple of years younger, and Janochek's daughter. That was a minefield. Murray couldn't afford to make a mistake there—hurt Pearl's feelings and wind up getting kicked out of the cemetery. Janochek was almost like a father to him, but he wouldn't stand for any mess-up that involved Pearl. If Janochek was forced to choose, Murray would be history.

So if he ever wanted a girlfriend, Pearl wouldn't do. Too risky. Too difficult. Really, Murray had never given girls this much thought. An actual girlfriend? How would that work? What would they do? He could . . . bring her to the cemetery? Introduce her to his dead friends? He smiled in spite of himself. Even if he liked somebody, and even if, against all odds, they liked him, it was hopeless. *Dead-end street.*

But Sandray . . . maybe she'd like him pretty well if she got to know him better. She was really attractive and probably really smart.

Walking to her grave, Murray couldn't believe what he'd just done. *You want to feel like a complete idiot? Wash your face and comb your hair before you go talk with a person who's dead and buried. Not like they know whether you're spiffed up!* Murray didn't actually see the dead; he imagined what they looked like and he supposed they did the same. With Sandray, he didn't have to make much up. Reddish-bronze hair, lively eyes, little bit of a curve to her nose that made the end cute as a gumdrop. He remembered her white teeth and great smile. Wow. Guess he'd noticed her more than he'd realized, because he could keep going: tan arms, great legs! Right down to her feet in white runners. He was feeling tingly before he even reached the grave.

He sat carefully, close to her marker, where he could hold it comfortably. "Were you born in Riverton?"

"Hey. Maury? Why?"

"Murray. Just curious. My mom moved up from San Leandro when I was barely two. But I've been here since."

"I was born in Cheyenne. My dad was the curator of the museum there. Got hired to come to California nine or ten years ago and work for the city doing kind of the same thing."

"Wyoming? Lots of cowboys?"

"I was eight when we moved. I didn't really notice unless I was out with my family Friday or Saturday nights. Then there'd be pickups and loud radios, guys standing around the sidewalks outside honky-tonks."

"Country-western music? We have some of those downtown."

"Jimmy's Rodeo Club. I've never been in."

"You're too young, right?"

"Maybe not. You know Carla? Stacy Hill? They go to your school. They get their look-good on and go about anyplace. I was going to try it."

"Wow. What would you do?"

She laughed. "See if a guy would buy me a drink? I don't know. Flirt? When I drink a little I really like to dance—"

The sound went off again. Murray had never experienced a dead person disengaging so immediately, so completely. He thought regular friends who'd been dead for a fairly long time were glad for his company. Maybe their painful feelings weren't so fresh. Murray wondered if that's what Sandray's cutting off was about. Getting real sad, real quick.

Bruce couldn't stop talking, hadn't been able to sleep the last few nights. Well, he probably could if he wanted to. Other residents were complaining but screw them. He had ideas. Good ideas. He could organize them later, now he needed to say them before he forgot.

He'd found all these great clothes just a few blocks away at Progressive People Thrift Store. Great clothes! Colors you wouldn't believe, and cheap! He bought so many shirts they were hard to carry. And fleece up the wazoo. Good for warm or cold. And a rain what-do-you-call-it? Polo? Ponto? Something like that, and some shoes and scarves—he could always use scarves—and another short-brim if he lost the one he was wearing and a Yankee's cap 'cause everybody liked the Yankees, and a great belt that was a little small but he could put a chain on it and make it longer, and sweaters that he didn't like but he was going to give them to the old couple that always sat on the couch by the front window. And a couple of pictures for his room, a red car one and something else . . . a mountain? Yeah. And god he was hungry. And he could use another bag of that new medicine. Slip him back from fifth gear into neutral for a couple of hours.

The problem with regular medication was that most of it didn't work. At least not for special people. And he was one of the few people that didn't like alcohol. Not even that lemonade stuff. He'd been fighting this battle for years and nobody, *nobody*, understood. Especially not his father. His dad was a nice enough guy, but he wanted Bruce to be like other people. And his doc was nice enough, too, but really, the lady just wanted to dull Bruce out. Take out the creative spikes. In a word, zombify him. Well, hello! The world wasn't exactly slow. Like today, put these clothes in his room, go to a movie, get a taco at whatever that place was, get a donut, meet some people, and tonight, catch some music? Go for a swim? Hitch to Chico and meet some babes?

Bruce walked in the Sadler House door with his armload of clothes and immediately got in an argument with the Petrushkins on the front couch. They were trying to pretend they didn't want the sweaters he'd dumped in their laps. That's another thing Bruce couldn't stand. Ingrates.

The manager of the Sadler House where Bruce had his room called Mental Health. The phone call was referred to a psychiatric social worker, Peggy Duheen, who had wound up with Bruce on her caseload when his prior social worker went to work for the Veterans Clinic across town.

"Duheen."

"This is Bobby at the Sadler. You better get down here or get somebody down here before there's a fight."

"Who is it this time?"

"Guy who's been calling himself Springsteen but the name is Simmons, Bruce. He's on a jag. Definitely off the meds. I mean he's always kind of hypo—"

"Hyper?"

"Yeah. Mile a minute. Goofy. Today? Got about twelve layers of clothes on—"

"Right. I'll be there as soon as I can. No actual fighting, right?"

"Not yet."

Gates finished the written report on the robbery arrest and had just set it in the "Out" tray, when his desk phone rang. Dispatch. Would he take a call from Peggy Duheen, County social worker? Sure.

Duheen, a sometimes colleague, asked him to help her make a Mental Health client pickup. It was common procedure to get an officer assist on mentally ill patients who might behave unpredictably, possibly dangerously. Duheen and Gates enjoyed each other's company and worked together whenever possible at Mental Health interdepartmental treatment planning sessions and client community contacts.

Sheriff's Department was only a quarter mile from the psych unit. Gates met her in front of the hospital. She hopped in the cruiser and brought him up to speed.

"We're going to the Sadler House. Bruce. Robert Barry Compton's friend from the Parker case?"

"Wacky kid," Gates recalled. "Donut fiend. Never seemed very dangerous. Drugs?" he asked.

"I don't know," she said. "More likely he got to feeling pretty good and thought he didn't need his meds anymore. Common for bipolar."

"He was mostly solid last fall when I was doing things with him and Compton." Gates smiled. "Where is Mr. Robert Barry Compton, by the way?"

"Kind of a success story. Got stable on his meds and

moved to a halfway house near his mother in Corning. Tehama County is covering him now."

Gates smiled, glad to hear it. "So what do you want to do when we get there?"

"I was hoping you'd talk to him. You know him better. Get him to ride with us to a crisis appointment back at the clinic. Doc'll see him there."

"Copy. I'll do it if I don't get pulled by dispatch."

They rode in silence till they were stopped by a traffic light on Cypress.

"You want to do something one of these days?" Gates asked, staring straight ahead.

Duheen knew she was blushing. She reviewed her recent behavior. Had she been obvious? And what was the right response? Thought you'd never ask? Maybe? Love to? Better not since we're sort of co-workers?

"I didn't mean to make you uncomfortable," he said, moving forward on the green light.

Duheen still couldn't think of the right thing to say. *Is that a yes?*

CONSULTATION

Murray wondered about Sandray's disconnections. And more, did the dead actually talk to each other? Did they get to know other dead in the same cemetery? Or did they just know about each other from his own side of the conversation? Dearly knew about Edwin and Blessed but possibly only because he told her about them. If they couldn't talk to each other, then they needed somebody like him as a go-between. Was he the only one? Were the rest of the dead so lonely they could hardly stand it? That was scary. Murray could imagine if he killed himself there might not be anyone else to talk to. Forever.

He needed a consultation from an old friend.

Dearly Beloved had a good head on her shoulders. Murray plopped down in front of her. "Got time for a question?"

"Hi, darlin'. Nothing but. Speaking of, long time no see."

"Yeah, my bad. I've been welcoming people in the newer section. Seems like more kids almost every day. Like Feathers? You met him?"

"Hon, it doesn't work like that. We know who we knew in our life. And you. You tell me about Blessed and I imagine her, but I don't know her. Your world grows, ours stays the same."

Murray listened carefully for a note of sadness but didn't hear it. Had Dearly made her peace with death? He was curious but was afraid to ask. All those feelings.

"Your question?"

"Uh, there's a new girl I've been talking to . . . Sandray . . .

same year as me, different school. How cool is that?" Murray had an uncomfortable thought. Do the dead get jealous?

Dearly waited.

He plodded on. "Sometimes when we're talking everything goes dead." *Brainless!* "I mean the energy disappears and I don't feel any connection at all. Do you know what causes that?"

"Not sure, sweetie. So it's like she withdraws? I guess that's possible. Want me to try it?"

Murray nodded. *Moron!* Like she could see him. Why was he so nervous about this? "Please," he said.

Silence followed but the faint electric hum didn't go away.

"Nope, we're connected," he said, not disappointed but still puzzled.

"Yeah, I could feel it. Of course I'm grateful for it. I love your company. Always."

Murray felt the same way. Dearly had been a dependable friend.

"I don't know, hon, maybe it's new. Like a tiny speck of evolution or something. Or maybe it only disconnects if she really needs it to. Maybe she hangs up if she gets desperate for privacy . . . if she gets overwhelmed."

Yeah. That was kind of what Murray had been guessing. He wished the voices he'd been hearing up at the hedge would disconnect completely.

Bruce could see right away this was going to be tricky. He'd resisted a deputy before and wound up in jail. They took all your stuff and locked you up with a bunch of losers and lunatics. Not a good conversation in the bunch. A few of them got in your grille wanting to prove something. He didn't need that. He decided to go along with the woman and what's-his-name and make this as brief as possible.

"Your car smells like urp," he said to the officer's back.

"Sorry," Gates said. "Probably needs a cleaning. We'll be there in five minutes and you can get out."

Bruce thought he'd have to burn these clothes when he got back. Luckily, he had plenty more, and if he needed to, he could go shopping this afternoon.

"This is a waste of time," Bruce commented, scooting forward slightly to command better attention.

"Well, I'm remembering the last time you stopped your meds you wound up at Heritage Oaks in Sacramento. For about three weeks," Duheen said, turning partway around.

"Yeah, I had the flu, but I'm fine this time. Feeling great. Got some new clothes, new meds."

"Well, something's not too great. Manager says you can't stop talking, you're arguing with people in the lobby."

"Like he's qualified? Got his head in his butt." Bruce patted himself on the shoulder. "I'm great." Should he tell Duheen about his new medical discovery—powder works better than pills? Bruce was torn. He wanted her to know that she was making a mistake, that he didn't need any help. The Petrushkins needed help, and the other poor chumps in his hotel. But you couldn't trust these doctor people. They want everything quiet. Better living through boredom. Plus, good sniff is hard to find. What if she messed with his supply? But she was a professional. She should know. "Skag works great." *Oops.* Did he say that? His brain needed to shut up.

"Where do you get this new med?" Duheen asked, not turning around, casual tone of voice, like she was just making conversation.

"No place," he said, feeling back in control. He got it from his pal Tuffy, who got it from— No, Bruce would be quiet now. "So, like, I don't need anything. I'm fine," he said, not noticing he was still talking. "I'm cooperating." He figured this would throw her off the track. "Remember that," he said, admonishing her, wagging his finger at her back. "You say. I do. That's me all over."

Duheen craned around to look at him again, saw Bruce was practically vibrating; knees up and down like a sewing machine, chewing his lip, scratching his head, zipping his jacket up and down. "I'm glad you feel that way," she told the young man. Was he using heroin to take an occasional break from his mania? A good bet.

Bruce didn't like her looking at him. She'd hand him over to that Dr. Mendella . . . Madonna? Filipina woman that talked like a butler and looked like an actress? A smile and she got him to do anything. Yeah, yeah, pop some pills. Okay, no prob. A pill wouldn't knock him off the track. It's NASCAR, baby! Just a pit stop and be home by dark. Miles to go before I sleep! Somebody said that.

Duheen stood with Gates in the Mental Health building's outpatient corridor while Bruce went in the psychiatrist's office. "Skag works great," she said, shaking her head.

"Can it interfere with his regular medication?" Gates asked, wondering if heroin was as damaging as meth.

"I told Dr. Mendoza before Bruce went in. She'll assess that."

"You think Bruce buys it on the street?" Gates asked.

"Who'd sell it to him? Some friend probably," Duheen said, looking down the hall past Gates as if she could spot a likely culprit.

"Last year when I spent some time with him and Compton, Bruce was good at meeting people," Gates said. He remembered taking Bruce and Compton to fast food and donut shops, hoping to find out if they knew anything about Nikki Parker's kidnapping. Bruce stopped at each table and talked with every person he saw. Couldn't seem to stop himself.

"Yeah, well, now he's more full-blown manic," Duheen said. "Most people would steer clear of him."

"So possibly someone he's known for a while. Somebody at Sadler House?" Gates asked, thinking out loud.

"Good guess," Duheen said. "Don't ask him now. That would raise his anxiety and boost him even further out."

"Don't worry," Gates said. "I'll be subtle."

"I suppose that's statistically possible," Duheen said, "though my observations fail to confirm it."

COURTING

Murray couldn't get Sandray out of his mind. When she was good she was . . . uh, good, and when she was bad she was radio-silence. And she was so pretty. Really, he couldn't help but wonder if she liked him. Did she have a boyfriend? He had no idea.

"Hey. I got an A minus on a pop quiz today," he told her for openers.

"How come you can hear me?"

"A girlfriend of mine's been asking me that same question."

"Girlfriend?"

"Uh, girl comma friend. This place's caretaker? His daughter, Pearl."

"When did she die?"

"No." Murray smiled at the thought that he had a friend who was living. "Not dead. She's a freshman. At Sierra. Kind of a jock. Basketball, softball."

"My boyfriend played basketball for you guys. Kevin. Point guard."

"Kevin . . ." That answered Murray's earlier boyfriend question. He was caught off guard by a wave of disappointment.

"Kearns. You go to games?"

"No."

"The lead in last year's spring drama?"

"Uh—"

"God, don't you do anything?"

"I work . . . help around here."

"Anyway, ex-boyfriend."

Yes! Murray was afraid to ask what happened and get another disconnect.

"We broke up the week before."

"Before you were shot?"

"Duh. He'd been slithering around with Marcia Nuñez. Finally got around to telling me. Know her?"

Murray started to shake his head. Stopped. "Aronson's class? Sits by the window?"

"How would I know?"

Right. "That's, uh . . ."

"I saw her. She's pretty but she's a bitch. She knew we were going out. Who are you going with?"

"Um, no one. I'm pretty busy."

"Busy."

"I, uh, talk to people."

"Other dead people?"

Even the dead don't believe me.

Sandray snorted. "That's totally unglued."

Who to ask? Murray chose Edwin first.

"Hear you got a girlfriend" was the first thing out of Edwin's mouth.

"Who told you?"

"Bud, it's all you talk about lately. Strange name for a girl. More like a fish."

"Yeah, well. Hey, I have a question."

"Shoot. Can't hurt me."

"Seriously." Murray waited for a minute for Edwin to settle down. "Uh, do you think there's such a thing as ghosts?"

That wrecked it. Brought another cascade of laughter.

"Come on! Do you?"

"Can't say I've thought about it."

"Did you ever see one?"

"Heard about them. Never seen one."

"Do you think they're real?"

"I don't think so."

"How can you say that when you and I are having a conversation and you're dead?"

"Good point. But I can say any damn thing I want and that's one of the few good things about *being* dead." Edwin shifted back to his more serious tone. "But why? What's the deal?"

"If you wanted a ghost, could you just summon one?"

"You're not going to tell me what this is about, are you?"

Murray swallowed. But hey, this was Edwin. Who else could he say this to?

"I was wondering, if Sandray was a ghost, uh, couldn't she and I go places together? Do things?"

The duty sergeant was last to arrive in the briefing room, strode to the front desk holding a newspaper in one hand and a wad of something in the other. It wasn't just the raw-sunburn color of his face and neck or even the ramrod quality of his posture as he stood feet apart in a position the military called parade rest. Gates could feel heat coming off the man as if something had pushed him beyond his occasional realm of vile mood and into the country of nuclear meltdown.

"Today's *Sacramento Bee*," the man said, giving the newspaper a single shake that would have broken a chicken's neck. "Front page article," he added, throwing a fistful of confettied newsprint at the seated deputies.

No one moved, the whole room on full-alert. Duty sergeant was not known for his love of journalism but this was over the top. Would he light the paper on fire? Draw his service revolver and blow a hole through it?

"Riverton law enforcement officers made top five. *In the nation!* But don't line up for your merit badges yet." The man started to pace in front of the desk, stopped, and again faced the room.

Gates liked the duty sergeant. Liked his rough humor in the face of a slow-growing bladder cancer that had taken him off patrol and put him in the office for his remaining months. In the last year the man had gone from a doughy two hundred pounds to a hard-ridged hundred and forty. His eyes had grown paler, more the color of icebergs than sky.

"We have risen to fifth in the country . . . the entire country . . . with this year's increase in violent crime. Practically lead the United States in law enforcement incompetence." He stopped, surveyed the room, giving each man a full moment's stare. "That's it, ladies," he said. "Read the goddamned board for the morning report. I'll be in the bathroom scrubbing the shit off my uniform."

Sobering news. No one left the room with a smile.

The bulletin board had the usual. Hit-and-run driver took out a fire hydrant on Shasta Street, a block from the RPD station. Windows broken at HILo Liquors on California. Thief made off with multiple pints and a roll of lottery tickets.

A female bicycle rider hit a rut on Parkview and flew through an oncoming car windshield, narrowly missing the teenage driver. The human cannonball scored a .28, three and a half times the legal intoxication limit on the subsequent blood alcohol test. Minor miracle; only broke her nose and shoulder and provided conclusive evidence you never forget how to ride a bike.

Carjack at an all-night gas station on Hilltop. Young Caucasian man with a tire iron. Purse snatching at knifepoint outside of Macy's. These, the kinds of things that drive up your violent crime statistics.

Gates took the cruiser and went on patrol. Maybe he could actually stop something *before* it happened.

Not today. The morning patrol was relatively uneventful. A no-injury fender bender at the intersection of Canyon and Happy Valley Road. Both drivers actually civil. A status contact on an elderly man in a trailer just off China Gulch

Drive. Daughter frantic, trailer locked, father not answering the phone. Gates got no response till he hit the doorframe with his flashlight and gave the small wooden porch a hard kick. Heard footsteps.

The door was opened by a rumpled elderly man with a sheepish expression. "I lost my hearing aids," he said. "I was afraid to tell her. She paid a month's salary on the little buggers."

Gates stopped by Don's Eats for a corned beef sandwich and was back at his desk by noon-thirty. Sat to find two nine-by-twelve manila envelopes sitting on his calendar. Paper-clipped to the envelopes, a newspaper folded to an article marked with yellow highlights: "Broken down by agency, the second-largest number of unsolved murders was in the jurisdiction of the Sierra County Sheriff's Office, which had thirteen." A handwritten note scribbled across the body of the article: "Let's do something about this."

Gates stood to survey other desks. Several had copies of what could be the same newspaper beside a similar envelope, cardboard box, or tagged weapon. Okay. Gates understood and it was fine with him. This was the current lieutenant's response to heat from the media. Gates was similarly embarrassed by the violent-crime-rate article. He especially hated uncleared murders—still kept desktop pictures of the two women who had disappeared last year from a neighboring town. Gates probably would have responded in a like manner if he was still the lieutenant.

Murray awoke to a sharp noise. A robber? He came to his senses. Right. Someone wanted to steal a used lawn mower. Not very likely. He could hear wind gusting. Probably knocked a branch down onto the roof. Now he could also hear the old lady buried beneath the shed. Fussing. She'd had the prettiest plot in the cemetery until they put this damn storage unit over her. He'd heard it all before and he bet it was true. A hundred years ago this part of the hill must have been beautiful, with hardly any buildings blocking the view to the mountains. A hundred years ago.

Murray found himself wondering if the voices he was hearing beyond the east hedge were actually remnants of an old, old section of the cemetery, a piece that got accidentally separated from the main grounds as time passed. What if they'd been dead for a long time and were just upset because they'd been excluded from their official resting place? He'd have to ask Janochek tomorrow about the cemetery's original boundaries and the way they had changed over time.

He got off the cot, went outside to pee, and watched the wind rattling the oak limbs. Maybe he should get dressed and give Sandray a surprise visit. She might be glad for some company. Sandray. Great girl! And that thought led to Pearl. Another great girl, but way more problematic. Wouldn't it be kind of fun to go tap on Pearl's window? Say hi. Invite her out to see the mini-storm. She'd think that was ridiculous but she might be kind of pleased, too. She'd complained he'd been ignoring her.

What if she asked him about what he'd been doing, what

had been going on lately, and he shined her on. Would she realize he was hiding something? Would she sense that he was hearing new voices? He couldn't take the risk.

Better to go back to bed. Tomorrow he'd find out about the cemetery history, and one more thing. He'd go back to the library and search the newspaper. Had there been other recent kidnappings where they couldn't find the bodies? He couldn't believe it. The Nikki Parker murder had only been two or three months ago. If some high school kid was killed anywhere in the county, everybody at school would be buzzing about it, wouldn't they? But he didn't read papers or check the Internet. Maybe something bad had happened that he didn't know about.

He stopped at the shed door. He was already almost dressed. What if he grabbed a jacket, went back to the east hedge right now and listened? Maybe he'd been wrong before. Maybe it was some kind of echo. Or better yet, maybe it was nothing at all.

The wind whipped at his hair, tugged at his clothes, but it wasn't exactly cold. A small moon gave him enough light to navigate. Before he'd even reached the hedge he was hearing something. Could be cats, or people down the hill drinking in the rodeo grounds parking lot. Those sounds carry. He realized he'd stopped moving and made himself continue. Past the last row of graves, just before the hedge, the sounds were unmistakable. Different voices grumbling, groaning, mixed together, hard to understand. As he homed in he noticed another voice on top of the others. Higher, thinner, but there was so much background noise all he could pick up was "R" and "U."

"Are you." Again and again . . . part of a longer sentence, but the rest was blurred. His stomach rolled remembering the first time he'd listened closely to the murdered cheerleader. He thought she kept repeating "hit me." Later, when they'd actually talked, Murray realized it was "hid me." Right now he thought the reedy voice could feel him, was saying something directed to him. "Who are you?" Or "What are you doing?" Or "Are you going to help?" Too many possibilities to make sense of it. Another girl, kidnapped and killed? That was the last thing in the world Murray wanted to find. The idea practically made him sick.

The voice could connect. Knew Murray was out here. Now what was he supposed to do? He couldn't just walk away.

But he did.

Murray returned to the shed, lay down, couldn't sleep. Sat up. The voice wasn't talking to him. Not really. The voice and Murray weren't connected. It was just talking. Like the other voices, but higher. Murray pictured a wagon train ambush. A long time ago. Several people killed. Women and children, too. That explained it. The burials had been forgotten, lost, in an ancient section that was now slightly outside the cemetery boundary. Nothing Murray could or should do about that.

What a relief! Gave him some energy. Time to do something. Visit someone. Maybe Blessed. Hadn't seen her in a while. No need to mention the other voices. She wouldn't be interested in stuff like that.

The following morning Murray went back to the library and headed for the newspaper section until he remembered the computer lab. Not having one of the things himself, he often forgot how useful they could be.

The library had just opened and three PCs were available. As Murray got to the check-out counter he remembered he'd left his card when he rushed out after his last visit. Asked and the librarian's assistant retrieved it. Murray chose the PC at the end of the table as far as he could get from everyone else, and searched Riverton.com.

Under kidnapping he found several recent articles, but no reported attempt had ended in a missing body or murder. The stories were for the past month, and he couldn't find the paper's archives for earlier crime news. He'd have to check the reference section for those. Under recent murders, he read that a wife killed her abusive husband, one man killed another in a bar fight, a Corning man was shot for no apparent reason while driving his car, but he didn't find any mention of multiple or serial murders.

He accessed a tab called "Database" and examined local crime statistics, found it only had the numbers of crimes, not the locations. He spotted an article on serial killers in Northern California but the cases described didn't have missing bodies in or around Riverton.

Looking at articles on unsolved murders, Murray discovered, to his amazement, that people who were suspected kidnapped and killed weren't listed as murders. They were just called missing. And there was no reliable way to track what happened to them if their body showed up in another state. Only about 12 percent of missing-presumed-murdered cases were even investigated by federal authorities. Of the cases actually labeled homicides, at least a third never got solved. Not good news. The east slope behind the cemetery could be full of bodies, and no one would know they'd been killed.

Murray closed the page and went to the newsprint archives. Found that after a month had passed, the newspapers were stored on some kind of micro-picture cards. He didn't know how to work the viewing machine and gave up. What was the use, if so many people went missing and weren't even looked for? Anyone could be the voices he'd been hearing, and the best way to find out who they were would be to ask them. That realization brought a shudder, like someone holding an ice cube to his back. Could he do that? Would he? Not alone. Not by himself.

Would he tell Pearl what he was hearing?

Janochek was wall-to-wall busy with a sprinkler renovation project. The private owners had bought a new variable-speed on-demand pump with a sophisticated timing apparatus from a company in San Jose. The firm's engineer had been staying in Riverton the past three days teaching Janochek to install, troubleshoot, and repair the system. As a result, he had seen little of Pearl, and Murray only when he glimpsed the boy returning from school in the afternoon or visiting graves in the pump-house section.

Pearl. At least he could keep track of her during quick dinners. He asked questions and received brief answers. He guessed that was par for the course with a fourteen- going on fifteen-year-old. The installation was taking its toll, and lately, while she did her evening homework in the cottage's small living room, he fell asleep in his easy chair nearby. He would wake after midnight to find his book resting in his lap, Pearl already gone to bed.

Janochek was glad Pearl had changed schools this year at Christmas break. Sierra High was closer to the cemetery than her old school, Canyon, and Sierra's sports teams were more competitive, which she loved. Plus, it was the same school Murray attended, which meant they could walk together from time to time.

So far the change was working out. Pearl had made the girls' softball team, played every game so far at second, the result of her clutch hitting and determination to catch every grounder anywhere near her. Pearl was usually happy to talk about the game, the things that went well and what she needed to work on. Some of Janochek's favorite times lately were having her all to himself in the pickup cab, trapped, as it were, for a little conversation.

Driving her home from a loss to powerhouse Colinas High, Janochek saw a skinny boy with wild hair riding a BMX and thought of Murray. "We haven't had ol' Lawnmower Man over to dinner for a month or so. How about I make spaghetti with Alfredo and sausage some night soon?"

"Okay." Pearl studied her glove, adjusted the lacing.

"Just okay?"

"Whatever you want," she said, giving him a brief glance, continuing to work with the leather.

"What happened?" Her tone of voice and lack of affect was troubling. "He was your buddy. Our buddy. You liked him."

"I still like him . . . I mean, I don't dislike him. I don't care very much."

Janochek steered the pickup to the curb at the top of a grassy hill in the shade of a huge pine on Magnolia Street. Turned off the ignition and twisted to face Pearl more directly.

"What happened?"

Pearl exhaled through closed teeth, like this was an unnecessary annoyance. Why did her dad need to know everything? "Nothing in particular happened. In fact nothing happened at all. Murray's just the same as he always is."

"Um, isn't everybody?"

"I mean he's hiding out. That's all he does. Play his dead games. He's not going anywhere and he's not interested in live people . . . in doing something useful or even having fun."

"Did he hurt your feelings?"

"No. He just pisses me off."

"Give me an example."

"He could pay attention to the real world. Watch what's going on. Get involved in something. Come to my games."

"Well, I agree with you. Right now I think we're his contact with that real world, with real people, and if we give up on him—"

"Dad, let's just go on home. I've tried. He's . . . he went to the library and looked up clairvoyance. Says he found out it's phony. He's worse than he was before."

"The last few times I've seen him he's seemed happy enough. Usually smiling."

"Yeah, whistle while you work, right?" Pearl shook her head, disgusted. "He's hanging out with the dead. Wasting his life and loving it."

Janochek thought he saw the ghost of tears in the corner of her eyes.

"Give up on him, Dad. He's given up on himself."

UNCLEAR ENVELOPES

The first envelope on Gates's desk contained a brief investigation log on David Payne, the man Pittman had mentioned. Mission resident missing since mid-January. Disappeared Wednesday, the twenty-second, between noon and evening, didn't claim that night's reserved bed at Mission. Currently earning a stipend training Mission client-volunteers and the bookkeeper on public relations and accounting practices. No mention of plans to leave and no reason to leave.

Random opportunity, or somebody with an ax to grind?

The second envelope had a sheaf of missing person reports under a cover letter signed by Frieda Pittman. She'd obviously gotten the lieutenant's ear. Title: "List of Missing Dispossessed Citizens." Seven names. Disappearance unexplained. Arturo Cespedes, 58 (age and name not verified by ID); Will Duecker, 66; Clarence Holmes, 34; Vaughn Miller, 61; Robert Sederman, 29; Jerel Smith, 15-18 (age and name not verified by ID); Alicia Turner, 44.

Duecker, Holmes, and Miller were listed as client-trainees (greeters/triage); Turner was Mission bookkeeper, Sederman her client-trainee assistant. No additional information was given for Cespedes or Smith.

Gates remembered the name Payne from Pittman's morning report to the deputies. Didn't know any of the others. He'd seen stats for California, in general—50 percent of the homeless were men, 25 percent children, and 25 percent women; in warm urban areas like Los Angeles, sometimes

40 percent women. The number of homeless children had been increasing every week for years.

Gates was surprised by the teenage boy. Jerel "Smith," if that was his real last name. Not many teens showed up alone in shelters. They didn't want to be picked up and returned as runaways. Unusual name, Jerel. Rang a bell but Gates couldn't put his finger on why. It would come to him.

Before he focused on these uncleared cases, he had some leftover business. Bruce and his new medication. "Skag." That word itself was kind of a tip. People selling on the streets of Riverton called it "Lady" or "Tar" or sometimes "China," which was ironic because most of the cheap junk was now made in Afghanistan. The kid didn't invent the name skag. The term was old, older than Bruce, and seriously out-of-date. Made Gates wonder if that's what the seller called it and whether that person was an aging product of the sixties. Time to check out the Sadler.

The Sadler House, downtown near the Cascade Theater, was a four-story tan stucco building with red tile trim, Monterrey-style relocated to the top of the Central Valley. Outside, the sidewalk was swept, the windows clean. Inside the door, the good impression faltered. Poorly lit lobby, dull and broken linoleum tile, moth-eaten furniture sitting on thin area rugs. Perhaps forty years past its heyday.

The first people Gates saw were an older couple on the divan by the plate glass window. If they were drug dealers, their disguise deserved an Academy Award. The lobby held five others. Four were playing Spades or something like it at a card table back by the nonfunctioning elevator. A young woman somewhere between nineteen and thirty in tight black jeans and an Oregon sweatshirt stood at a table corner, watching over the players. Gates thought she could definitely be someone who moved drugs, but he doubted she'd use the term skag.

The front reception counter was unmanned, the mailboxes behind it mostly vacant. The bulletin board advertised "upcoming" events but all seemed far past—a bluegrass concert in a bar that had burned to the ground last year, and so on. The door leading back to an office was open and Gates went around the counter, walked through to find a bald man with a thin goatee sitting, grimacing at a laptop on a scarred walnut desk. The office walls were covered in posters of bright-colored muscle cars and large, tired, framed prints probably acquired at a local thrift store.

"I think this game's fixed," the man said, not looking up. "Help you?"

Gates walked close enough to see the screen the man referred to. Computer poker.

"As I remember," Gates said, flashing on his ruinous gambling, "the house always wins."

The man looked up and quickly closed the laptop cover. "This ain't illegal."

Gates ignored that. "How are your residents doing?" he asked, nodding toward the lobby.

"Sheriff?" the man asked.

Gates nodded.

"Everybody's fine," the man said. His eyes shifted. "You come with that county case worker to deal with Springst— Crap, he's even got me saying it! Uh, Simmons, right?"

Gates nodded.

"Yeah, well, he settled down soon as you brought him back. Gave him an inject probably. He could be woozy a couple a days."

"The others?"

"No problem. We don't have trouble here. This place is a fair deal and we run things right." The man's fingers were tapping lightly on the computer. He stopped when he saw Gates watching, reached to his shirt pocket for a cigarette, but the pocket was empty. The man shrugged. "I get older, I don't never know where I put things." He opened the desk's middle drawer and found a pack of gum. Didn't offer any. Set out two pieces, unwrapped them and jammed them in his mouth. "That all you wanted to know?"

Gates shook his head.

"You being mysterious on me? I don't know nothin'. If I did, I tell that county woman right off so she could nip it in the butt."

"Well, I know for a fact," Gates said, "that you got hired for this position because you're responsible and you have your finger on the pulse of this neighborhood."

"Damn straight," the man said.

"I thought you might set me right on something," Gates said, wiping his forehead with his sleeve like this matter was vexing him.

"If I could," the man said. "You know that."

Gates nodded. "Mental Health Department tells me

there's fewer drugs being sold here downtown. Is that what you're seeing?"

"That's exactly what I'm seeing. Things getting better all the time."

"What do you hear's still available?"

"Well, this medical licenses thing. Everybody and his parrot's got more grass than they can cut."

"What else?"

"Oxy still top dollar."

"Thanks. That confirms the reports we're getting from Glenn County. Anything about the others?"

"Meth's on the downslide. Coke's too expensive. Skag's hit and miss."

Janochek made an effort to locate Murray early the next week. Found him sitting, legs folded, in front of a relatively recent grave in the newer section.

Murray heard him approach and leaned back. As usual, the man was wearing faded brown jeans over laced boots. Red checked shirt under a canvas vest. Janochek was a couple of inches taller than Murray, around six feet. Gray eyes with smile wrinkles, always clean shaven. Slim, strong, big hands.

"Hi, Mr. Janochek. This is Feathers."

"I remember. Accident at the 44–5 on-ramp. What are you guys talking about?"

"Uh, astronomy, I guess."

The surprise left Janochek without a response.

"Feathers is saying there's a big meteor shower supposed to happen this summer. He was finding things like Pleiades, Jupiter's moons, stuff like that with just binoculars."

"Um, how does . . . did he know where to look?"

"He says there's a list. Messier objects. A hundred and ten things. Book he got from the library. Do you have binoculars?"

"I might."

"Let's do it some night. We could come here and Feathers could tell us what to check out."

Janochek considered that. Learn astronomy from a dead boy? Murray would never cease to amaze him. "I was thinking it was about time you came up for some pasta one of these nights. What you been doing lately?"

"You know. School. Meeting new people."

"Here?"

"Yeah. Malik," Murray said, gesturing to the stone in front of him. "And hey, guess what! There's a girl I kind of knew a couple of rows over. A junior like me. Sandray Vance."

Janochek's stomach twitched. "Really?"

"Yeah, she's a dancer. Endeavor High's pep squad. Beautiful. Probably really smart."

Present tense! "Uh, great. You meeting any new people at school?"

"No. Oh, and I'm getting in shape. I've started jogging. I found a web-strap tightener for my pack so it doesn't bounce around so much when I jog home from school."

Janochek didn't ask "for what?" Said instead, "Sounds like you're going to need some spaghetti. Tomorrow or this weekend?"

"May not be such a good idea," Murray said, looking at the ground between them. "I think Pearl's mad at me."

"Why?"

"I don't know. Jealous?"

Janochek kept his jaw from dropping.

"I've found my place, my job, my home, and it's pretty much a perfect fit. And Pearl's so intense, always pushing. She wants me to be more like her."

"Maybe she just wants you to find ways to use your skills like you did for that Parker girl's family."

"Yeah. She doesn't get it. That's exactly what I'm doing. Like Sandray's father would be so glad to know his daughter has a new friend who really likes her."

Janochek cleared his throat. Fiddled with his shirtsleeves.

"Okay, uh, good, so why don't you come up the end of the week, Sunday. We'll eat about six."

"Do you have another minute?" Murray shifted to face the man squarely.

Janochek nodded.

"What do you know about the cemetery's history?" Murray asked. "When was it dedicated? Is it bigger or smaller than it was in the beginning?"

"Well, the place was established in the late 1800s. Licensed by the city around then, I think. As far as I know it's always been the same size. Landscaping's made it seem a little smaller, the hedges . . . and of course the trees have gotten much larger. Main attraction originally was the central oak, huge, even in those days. First graves were just north of that. The crypts and mausoleum were added in the early 1900s. Admin office in the 1950s, about the same time as my cottage and workshop. That what you wanted to know?"

"So nobody was buried outside the fence?"

Strange question. "Not that I know of. Don't see why they would be."

"Oh, no . . . uh, no reason . . . maybe the lawnmower shed's over some old graves or something. I was just wondering."

Janochek was watching the boy closely now. "Yeah, it could be. Are you hearing things again?"

"No. No, not . . . just curious. I clean up . . . pick up papers around the fence line, and I just wondered. You know, the rodeo grounds down the hill, the northeast side going practically all the way to the river? I just wondered. So, Sunday. Right? I'll see you and Pearl at uh—"

"Six."

"Okay," Murray said, turning back to the gravestone. "Thanks."

Disappointed, Janochek stood at the boy's back for another minute before leaving. Always about the dead or the cemetery. Never about school or town. It was worse than Pearl thought. Murray was completely oblivious. Love-struck on a dead girl. Where would that lead? Suicide was the first thing that came to his mind, and he shoved it away.

Good Hope Mission had its usual crowd of families and single individuals waiting on the front sidewalk. A few were sitting wrapped in their jackets, taking a nap while they waited to be processed. Gates spoke with the administrator first. The woman was clearly busy filling out forms but set aside the paperwork. She introduced herself simply as Cathy. Said of course homeless people often came and went without anyone knowing where or why. But not the people she'd reported to Pittman. Several of those weren't really homeless anymore. They'd worked diligently to earn their rent-free motel room or aide's stipend.

Gates sought the day's floor staff but they had no idea why the numbers of missing seemed to increase after David Payne's disappearance. Yes, everyone said, David was a nice man. No, he didn't have any enemies.

Gates found Payne's counselor in the dayroom. The pudgy man had thinning brownish hair and a kind, round face raccooned by black-framed glasses taped in the middle. Gates imagined the professional staff didn't make much money in this line of work. After introducing himself, he said, "I'd like to hear what you can tell me about David Payne."

The counselor, who had brightened when he saw Gates approaching, now deflated, shook his head. "David was a pleasant man. Quiet. Uh . . . competent, professionally trained . . . People like that make up about ten percent of our beds." The man paused. "May I sit?"

Gates nodded and the counselor got two folding metal chairs that had been leaning against a file cabinet.

"Guess I should lose some weight," the man said, with a self-deprecating smile. Gestured Gates to join him. "So, I encouraged David to use his talents; after all, he'd held a very responsible job for a reputable company."

"Were there any people at the mission that David was close to? People he regularly ate or exercised with?"

The counselor was nodding. "They weren't friends or anything."

Gates waited.

"I was trying to get David thinking like a financial officer again. I thought I might jump-start him by suggesting he help our 'client-trainees.'" The man appeared to notice Gates's perplexity and explained, "Our greeters and our bookkeeper and her aide. Ex-homeless that work for us now."

"Would that be the same people who turned up missing shortly after Payne did?" Gates asked.

"Some of them, I suppose, or maybe most of them, yes . . . We get so many, I see so many . . ." The man waved his hand at the dayroom to indicate it was usually crowded. "Uh, at that time, Alicia, Alicia Turner, reviewed our books, confirmed balances. Right up Payne's alley, so I sent him to her. And to our greeters, Duecker and Miller and Holmes. We called them 'clerks.' They pulled shifts in the front lobby, like Walmart greeters, doing triage for those with emergency needs, explaining our system, getting the newcomers clothes or food."

The counselor glanced at Gates to make sure this was the kind of information he wanted. Satisfied, he continued. "I asked David to talk with them about public relations. And . . . who was making sure our records were properly alphabetized at that time? Bobby Sederman, I think. Anything to keep his mind off AIDS. Payne had a session with Bobby."

"Those names were on the missing homeless list you gave Frieda Pittman?"

"Oh, I know Frieda, but I didn't give her any list. That must have come from our director."

"What do you think Payne might have been doing the day he vanished?"

The counselor inhaled and shook his head. "I have no idea. He wasn't working here that day."

Gates nodded.

"Uh, he panhandled." The man held up a finger, went to the nearby file cabinet and pulled out a poster board that had been tucked in behind it.

Three short lines, but "anything you can spare" jumped out at Gates. Made him sad.

"I helped him make that sign," the counselor said, smiling.

Gates wasn't sure how to respond.

"He started like the others, intersections, off-ramps, shopping centers. Just a few days before he . . . uh, he came up with a different strategy. Wild River Casino. I think he stood at their exit, assuming the winners might be generous. Whatever it was, it worked. Right away he bought rain clothes, more alcohol, I think." The man shook his head. "Devastating problem, right?" He looked to Gates for confirmation. "In fact, for the first time, the day or so before he went missing he was chipper. Smiling even. Told me he'd come up with an even better idea but he wouldn't say what it was."

After Janochek talked with Murray, he and Pearl got together for dinner. His rule was to make sure at least once a day he had the opportunity for a few minutes of conversation—schoolwork, sports, films, books, what-have-you. Tonight they sat to corned beef sliders and another variety of his thousand coleslaws, this with zucchini, corn, red cabbage, and hot sweet pickles. Janochek broke the silence. "I think you were right."

"Like I'm ever not."

"About Murray. He's getting more entrenched. Comfortable. Okay short-term, terrible long-term. I think we ought to do something."

"Kick him out."

"That's pretty harsh. Where would he stay?"

"Home. Another cemetery. Where does anyone stay?"

"This isn't like you."

"He just makes me mad. I was so proud of him for finding Nikki Parker, and now I'm ashamed of him for being such a wimp."

"Hey, I'm concerned, too." But Janochek knew it was more than just concern. "Okay, I'm afraid . . . and you may be, too. After the shooting, after all the publicity around the Parker case, he's withdrawn, become almost submerged here. He goes through the motions at school, but everything he looks forward to is here, all his friends . . . including us."

"Dad, all his friends? He's more interested in dead people than you and me. He's made his choice. He's going to sit on graves until he rots, just like they do."

Janochek couldn't let the conversation end there. You can't throw away friends when they disappoint you. We all make too many mistakes in this life. We all need a little mercy.

"Have you ever been ashamed of yourself? Ever let yourself down?"

Pearl frowned. Looked at him. "You know I have."

"What helped?"

"You, I guess."

"Who's Murray got?"

Gates asked the mission counselor if Payne had any acquaintances, men or women, besides those he helped train? Any person that he might have casually talked with once in a while?

The counselor closed his eyes, caught his upper lip between his teeth as if to better search his memory. "Rex, maybe," he said. "He sat with Rex once in a while at meals. I guess they talked."

Where could Gates find Rex? The counselor told him to try the club chairs in the periodicals section of the public library. "He's a character," the counselor said with a small smile. "You can't miss him."

"What about the boy on the 'disappeared' list, Jerel Smith?"

"Never met him," the counselor said.

"Who would have?"

"Well, Eva, probably. Pretty sure she did the intake. She's our . . . I guess you'd say 'intern' now, from Guatemala. Cathy's training her. Eva's been doing almost all the new people when they sign up for services."

"And she is . . ."

"Lobby. Desk to the left of the office."

Eva was not at her desk when Gates walked over but arrived within the minute carrying a bottle of water. Her eyes widened as she saw the badge on his shirt pocket. "Eh, you would like?" she said, gesturing with the water.

"No, thanks," Gates said, "just a couple of questions."

The woman tried a smile, sat, took a deep breath, and waited for Gates to speak.

Gates returned the smile, took the chair at the far side of her desk, and sat, hoping to make her more comfortable. "The questions are not about you. What can you tell me about Jerel Smith?"

The woman's face relaxed and she shook her head. "No . . . I haven't met."

"You did his intake, right?"

"So many," she said, looking up as if there were a list of names on the ceiling. "I don't remember. I will look." She opened the top right drawer and pulled out a scarred ledger, the kind bookkeepers used probably fifty years ago. Numbered rows in green ink, columns in red. "When?" she asked.

"Probably after the start of this year. He was on the 'recently missing' list your administrator provided our liaison, Ms. Pittman."

The woman looked at Gates as if waiting for more information, apparently not comprehending. Gave up and looked at the book, found January with her index finger. "What name do you wish?"

Gates reminded her. She found no such entry in January. Sighed. Looked up at Gates for further instructions.

"Please go on," he said, keeping the impatience out of his voice.

She located the entry two pages later and marked the spot with her fingernail. "Herel Smeet," she said. "He is fron Chico." She turned the ledger so Gates could see.

Jerel Smith, in neat printing. *10 February, Chico CA, age—refus to anser.*

Not much. Gates would call the administrator later to see if she could identify someone who might have actually worked with the boy.

As the mission counselor had suggested, Gates located Rex in the public library, a short, stubby man with wild black hair wearing an orange road-construction vest over faded red sweats. Gates could have found him in a crowd of ten thousand.

Gates took a knee beside the man's chair and introduced himself.

"I ain't in the habit of conversating with pigs," Rex informed him, not bothering to look up from the car mag he was studying.

"Maybe you don't speak oink."

The man continued to ignore Gates.

"Let's try English. We talk here or you visit the lockup for obstructing and I get what I need from somebody else."

"Do your worst, dirtbag." Rex stood and put up his fists.

Gates couldn't help himself, smiled. "Sit down, Rocky, and let's talk about who might have done something with your man David Payne."

Rex looked around to see who all might have witnessed his bravado. Raised both hands in a victory sign and resumed his seat.

"I heard about Payne," Gates told him. "Nice guy. Didn't deserve any more trouble. Think of anybody who'd want to harm him?"

Rex pursed his lips. Almost a smirk, as if he'd known himself to be a key person and had been waiting to be consulted. "Well, yeah, I've given his absentia some considering."

"Do you want to talk about this outside so we don't

disturb anyone?" Gates nodded toward the other readers sitting in the section and casting occasional glances in their direction.

"This'll do fine," the man said, smiling to the room, a king and his court.

Gates took out his pocket notebook. "So, Payne have any enemies?"

"Guy was a wimp. Anything happen, he backed off."

"Get in any arguments that you saw?"

"I told you. By hisself most of the time. Me and that silly-assed counselor only ones he ever rapped to."

"He talk to you about anyone from his prior life?"

The short man scowled. "Don't none of us."

Rex didn't have a shred of information about Payne's other relationships or how the man spent his time during the day. Had no idea why Payne had gone missing or whether there was any relationship between Payne's departure and the several mission residents' disappearances after.

"Did Payne say anything about leaving, moving on?"

"Nope. He was doing good. Good enough to share his hooch."

Gates stood. Put his notepad back in his shirt pocket. Said, "Thanks for your help."

The short man frowned, probably at the idea of losing his audience. Leaned forward. "Tell you what you don't know."

Gates doubted it.

"Dave didn't tell nobody else. Me and him was tight."

Gates waited.

"Payne was onto something. Said he called in a chit. Big bucks. Major bucks. 'Bout the time he split, he told me he was getting his house back."

Gates drove back toward the department on autopilot, ruminating about what he'd learned. Payne was expecting to get his house back? How?

And Smith. At the mission he'd said he was from Chico but wouldn't give his age. Didn't sign anything, no picture, no prints. Gates couldn't think of a way to confirm the boy's identity and appearance. Did the mission have a security camera trained on their lobby? He used his cell and found out: yes, they did, but they'd already erased the first two weeks of February.

Gates wondered what the public thought when they saw him using his cell phone while driving. If he saw them doing the same thing, they got a two-hundred-dollar fine.

At the department, the rosters for Northern California missions and shelters in the cities he'd requested were on his desk. He started with Chico since that's the prior address the Smith kid had given. One hundred seventy-eight names since New Year's. No Jerel Smith, but a Harold Smith, on February 6. Gates was remembering the Guatemalan intern's English. She'd said Herel Smeet but wrote it as Jerel Smith. So the boy probably told her Harold Smith and she unknowingly recorded that as Jerel Smith without any official ID to check it against.

He picked up the Sacramento packet. Eight full sheets of names since New Year's. He found it in less than five minutes. Harold Smith, teen, no age given, arrived January 31. The kid went from Sacramento to Chico to Riverton and then disappeared. The documents didn't have earlier dates for San Francisco so Gates couldn't check if the kid had been there first. He wrote a requisition for the rosters from the Medford and Eugene shelters and perused the ones from Portland and Seattle but found nothing. The kid, if he was still going that direction, hadn't made it into Oregon or Washington . . . if he was still going any direction. So, Jerel Smith, Harold Smith. Same kid?

Gates. Irritated. Why couldn't he remember work things at work instead of during a movie he'd been wanting to see with an attractive woman? Here they were, but he was thinking about a case. A homeless boy. Jerel Smith to be exact. Gates remembered where he'd heard that name, connected to a different last name. The movie disappeared as his memory spooled forward.

Late last year Gates had been driving east on Texas Springs Road, taking what he thought of as a coffee break, hoping to spot wild turkeys that roamed in the area. The males, an other-worldly mix between a pelican and a throw rug, were one of the several species of wildlife that fascinated him. Turtles and jacks, coyote and porcupine, osprey and cranes, he invariably lost track of time watching whichever he saw.

That day he saw nothing because his radio squawked. Domestic dispute. Close by, outside the city limits, just off West Placer Street. Husband, Chuck Barker, was threatening to kill his wife, and according to dispatch, she'd called 911 and locked herself in a first-floor bathroom.

Gates was there in less than two minutes. Manicured driveway. Fancy house. When he skidded to a stop in the white gravel, the front door was standing open. *Uh-oh.* He'd vaulted out of the cruiser, forgetting his phone and nightstick, jumped the stairs to the low porch, and slid inside on a slick tile floor that fooled him and nearly put him on his butt. A man was flailing at an interior door with what looked like a bronze nude, apparently taken from the nearby foyer table. A bent and broken metal lamp possibly from the same table lay at his feet. The top panel of the door had several cracks and one jagged two-inch hole.

The man paused mid-swing. "What do you want?" He saw Gates's hand on his holster and slowly put the statuette down, leaned it against the wall. "The police are here, god-damn it. You can come out now," the man said to the door, but glaring at Gates like if he weren't a cop he'd attack him.

Barker. The name a perfect fit? The man stood before him, red in the face, fists clenched, wearing light brown gabardine slacks and an ivory-colored shirt open at the neck. Expensive clothes for a day around the house. Obviously wealthy . . . retired CEO from the Bay Area, this guy? Top executives didn't often murder their mates with art. White-collar crime boss? Drug money?

"Dolores, I mean it. Get the hell out here." The man had an edge to his voice, suggesting he was seldom disobeyed.

"Step away from the door," Gates told the man, loud enough for whoever was behind it to hear. "Deputy Sheriff Gates," he said for the unseen person's reassurance. "We'll calm down or we'll have this talk at the jail."

The man gave Gates a withering look, said, "I'll be in the living room," and walked away.

Gates heard the door unlocking and was surprised by the woman who walked out. The angry man was near sixty. The woman, disheveled and perspiring but beautiful, could not have been over forty. Her hair, originally in some sort of French roll, had come untucked, and wisps of it hung around her neck and over one eye. She blew on it to clear her vision but it fell again. She glanced at her outfit, made a half gesture with her hands as if she regretted her dirt-stained gardening clothes. "Thank you," she said. "If he'd broken through the door . . ."

Gates appraised her forearms and face. No obvious bruising, but the man might be too clever to leave marks. "Does this happen often?"

The woman shrugged. "Chuck has a temper. We've been having trouble lately, since I came back from Europe."

Her words had a lilt that might indicate a foreign birth. The home and grounds looked like a country estate, complete with circular drive, matching turrets on either side of the two-story house, Greek columns on the front porch. Overseas travel could easily fit their lifestyle.

On the way to join the husband in the living room, Gates had been surprised to see a boy watching everything from atop the stairs to the second floor. Wasn't this a school day? The boy, early teens, delicate-looking, with large dark eyes, narrow face, and long neck, thin arms poking out of a T-shirt touting some band. Gates raised his eyebrows at the woman beside him.

"My stepson, Jerell," she explained. "He doesn't like loud noises."

Gates remembered thinking that was an odd comment. Jerell's eyes had reminded him of his own son's, though his boy was a larger, more muscular, football-player type. When he looked again, the boy was gone. Jerell. Barker.

Once seated in the plush living room Gates's mediation with Chuck Barker and his wife, Dolores Cordova Barker, had taken most of an hour. The man remained brusque but no longer threatening. Apologized for what he called his outburst.

"Do you always look for a weapon when you're angry?" Gates asked.

The man glared. "I wanted to talk things out. She walled herself off. I was getting rid of the wall," he said. "I don't condone violence."

Gates reissued the threat of incarceration should this situation reoccur, and gave the woman the department dispatch number and the contact phone for the local women's shelter. Suggested the possibility of a restraining order. Mrs. Barker declined but agreed to a voluntary follow-up appointment with social services.

Barker seethed but didn't say another word. Collected his wallet and keys from a drawer in the foyer table and strode outside to a solid-looking white Lexus with silvery brushed aluminum sides. Gates expected the man to throw it in gear and spray loose gravel on the parked cruiser, but Barker left in a controlled fashion without a backward glance.

At the department, filing his report, Gates imagined this was a long-standing altercation. LinkedIn told him the man was chief financial officer for Trask Engineering off Air Park Drive in Riverton. Gates checked dispatch records for a complaint history, ran the name Barker through the NCIC database. Found nothing related to either assault or domestic disturbance.

* * *

Mrs. Barker did not attend her social services appointment, but two weeks later she had called the sheriff's office asking how to file a restraining order. Didn't follow through with that either, and the matter was dropped.

Gates straightened his back and rolled his head side to side to relax his neck muscles, which had tightened as he recalled the confrontation with Barker. So now he'd remembered why the missing homeless boy's name, Jerel Smith, rang a bell. Unusual name, and he'd run into it earlier, Barker's son, Jerell.

The boy. At the top of the stairs with the large dark eyes that reminded him of his own son. His dead son. *Could Kiefer talk to him?* Gates shoved the thought from his mind.

Gates remembered where he was and glanced at Duheen. She had taken his arm and was holding it firmly, he supposed in response to the movie's increasing tension. Gates didn't bother looking up at the screen. Maybe he could actually watch this film another time. Closed his eyes. Balanced his weight. Deep breath. A little meditation might clarify the nagging feelings he'd been experiencing, might bring to mind things he sensed he was overlooking.

Gates opened his eyes to Duheen's gentle nudging. When he looked up, the credits were scrolling.

"Doesn't say much for me or the film." Duheen raised her eyebrows as if for confirmation.

"Sorry. Work snuck in and I spaced."

"Like the fog? Came in on little cat's feet?"

"What?" Gates, still a little disoriented.

"Carl Sandburg," Duheen said, reaching down for her

purse, "and I don't think either space or fog snores, but you might be able to make it up to me. I have a taste for some serious food."

"I'm ready," Gates said, wondering if he'd brought a coat, and if he had, where he'd put it. "Um, Jack's is still open. How about a rare steak, a loaf of wine, and thou?"

Duheen lightly punched his shoulder.

As they walked out to the car, Duheen was cheerful, talking about how much she liked Sandra Bullock, but Gates remained distracted. There was definitely something major he had dropped and it unsettled him. Missing pieces were somewhere in those jackets or in his domestic violence report.

Stumbling off a theater step jarred him out of his reverie and he nearly fell, dragging Duheen with him.

"A simple hug would be more effective," she said, pulling her purse strap back on her shoulder and smiling at him.

Maybe Murray was wrong. Maybe he could do it by himself. It would be simpler, and in a way, safer. He wouldn't have to deal with Pearl. Last time she got involved with a strange voice, she wound up uncovering a body. Murray couldn't face that again.

Friday, after school, he walked east on Eureka Way all the way down to Continental, on past the cemetery over to Butte, across the 44 overpass at the top of Parkview where he entered the convention center campus. He circled the western perimeter of the rodeo grounds to the bluff, the steep hill that climbed toward the cemetery. There were six or seven cars and pickups parked fifty yards away, by the stable. Grooms and handlers, he thought. Just to the left of the stable, on the edge of the blacktop close to the hill, sat a big blue Dumpster with rusty metal barrels beside it. He stopped at a barrel, looked in. Just some gunky residue. The Dumpster lid had a lock on it. That surprised him—what were the horse people supposed to do with their garbage? He knew he was avoiding what he came for.

Behind the Dumpster he stopped again, listened, heard nothing, and began climbing. The crow-fly distance to the cemetery fence couldn't have been more than three hundred feet from the foot of the bluff, but the vertical distance at this point on the hill was formidable, at least fifty yards of loose dirt and clods, leaves and twigs. One step forward, slide back, until he started digging each foothold with his shoes and inching up spraddle-legged like a duck. He hadn't climbed more than forty feet when he heard the mumbling. Off to his right, closer to a bushy area above the stables.

He tacked laterally until the high voice came in. This time it sounded sad, moaning or wailing, but not loud. The kind of sound you make when you've quit trying and you're all by yourself, feeling sorry, like when you've peed your bed but your mom won't come help you, won't answer your knock because she's locked in her bedroom with a man you don't like.

Murray didn't want to talk to the voices. Dreaded that. He just wanted to see the grave . . . or would it be graves? See if they were fresh or old. See if they were marked. See if the bodies were just . . . no, he didn't want to see that. Let the bodies be buried. And stay buried.

It had been much easier moving laterally and the area he reached wasn't as steep as where he'd started. Above him Murray saw a patch of earth maybe ten feet square, between a gnarled tree that looked like it had been on this hill forever and a sturdy evergreen that stood straight up even though it was growing on a steep slant. The ground had been disturbed, the dirt broken up and covered with a thin scattering of leaves.

Not what he wanted to see. Not at all. And though they were no louder, the voices seemed to be crowding him, pushing him. He took a little step back, lost his footing, and slid, clawing at the loose earth but not stopping until he bumped against another tree, a small one with strong-enough roots to hold against his weight.

If he hadn't slid, he wouldn't have seen the rope. Maybe half an inch thick, brown and dirty, lying like a dead snake not a foot from his side. It trailed above and below him like a boundary. He reached and tugged it. That pressure tightened it, brought it out of the dirt, but it didn't come down. It was trapped by something or tied to something uphill. He got to his knees and tugged again. This time he saw it looped around the sturdy evergreen at the top of the messed-up patch. He could use it to help him climb back up, and in that moment he got an image. It took his breath, turned his stomach upside down and poured acid. Somebody had used this rope to help him lug a body up the hill. To that patch the voices came from. And maybe it was still happening. The damn rope was in good shape, ready, waiting to be used again.

He slid down the hill on his butt until he was up against the back wall of the stable. Crabbed around, leaned against the rough planks, crossed his arms, and tucked his head. Wished he could yell or cry, something to relieve the poisonous feelings.

He was still there at dusk, like before at the library, robbed of the will to move, until he heard a vehicle drive up and park. Heard the door open and close. Heard footsteps on the blacktop and the brushing, twig-crunching sound of someone beginning to climb the hill. And he was up, flying like a bottle rocket for Continental Street and the cemetery.

By the time Murray got back, he was practically vibrating with adrenaline. The lawnmower shed was a totally stupid room for pacing, six steps in either direction, but Murray had to stay inside; couldn't stand to be seen by anyone right now. It was like he'd not only lost his clothes but lost his skin. He was defenseless, even against something so harmless as a conversation.

He drank from his water bottle and flopped on the cot. Couldn't stay. Stood quickly and started doing jumping jacks like they taught him in gym. Now that *was* crazy, and he laughed in spite of his fear and kept laughing like a damn lunatic. His situation was so dumb, so hopeless, so demented, what could you do but laugh like a maniac and do jumping jacks? Right? He kept on until he was completely out of breath, completely out of energy, until his shoulders ached, his arms burned, and his legs felt like lead posts. He collapsed on his cot, too tired to do anything but get some air back in his lungs.

And just when he knew things couldn't get any worse, he let his arm flop off the cot, his hand down to the floor, where he touched something woolly, and without thinking he lifted it to give it a look.

The homeless man's stocking cap.

Murray was so surprised, shocked really, all he could think was that Pearl must have dropped it the day she got so mad at him and knocked over the bucket. She was so mad she forgot she'd brought it. She— But Murray wasn't thinking about Pearl anymore. Or even the cap. He was at a funeral holding a larger person's hand. It wasn't raining, but it was damp and gloomy. And there were flashes in the sky and he was walking beside a large truck with metal tracks that churned and clanked and the sky kept lighting up and the noise was horrible. Someone was shooting and he began firing shot after shot straight ahead, and he started to run but his rifle was so heavy and then he was in a small store where everything smelled sweet like strawberries or ginger cookies and a woman smiled down and handed him a pink ice cream cone and then he was in a hospital, and people were wearing blue pajamas and shaking their heads. And then he was outside a red brick building watching a beautiful girl walk away, walk down the sidewalk toward the street, and he knew she wasn't coming back, this was really goodbye, and then he was hitchhiking. Murray hadn't done that before but his thumb was up and he was standing near a highway overpass and it was freezing and windy and sand was stinging his cheeks and there were no trees, no houses as far as he could see, and there were no cars, no trucks, nobody to drive by and pick him up and he was terrified he was going to die out there. And then he was in a cave, a small cave, no, a doorway, and it smelled horrible and he smelled just like it, and he reached to wipe his nose and dropped the cap.

He must have slept, because when he opened his eyes it was dusk and he was cold. And exhausted.

Gates awoke feeling heavy, still full from last evening's late dinner. Wondered how Duheen was feeling after downing a sixteen-ounce filet mignon with all the trimmings. That brought a smile. She was quick, fun, quirky, attractive, and had the appetite of a giant squid. Who could ask for more? He found his phone and texted her: "How bout that boeuf? Next week Surfing & Turfing?"

He'd planned house chores for his day off but was too restless to stay home. Something about the names? The kid? He couldn't pin it down. He showered, dressed in jeans and a Pendleton, got a dark-roast at the nearby drive-through, and was sitting at his desk doing paperwork by eight.

Gates's search of county documents turned up his report on the domestic disturbance at the Barker home last year and more. Transcripts from 911 records dated February 13 leading to another case file. That one surprised him. A fairly recent investigation involving the Barker household. Transcripts of calls that reported Jerell Barker missing. Jerell, two l's.

School friends from Sierra High's digital media and drama clubs had made the initial contact. Called both police and sheriff. Each caller used the word "disappeared." To the police, Claudia Clemens, sixteen, added, "No way he'd bail. Jere wasn't like that. He had a part in the one-act and was building a homemade Roku box in lab." To the Sheriff's Department, a boy named Marvin Suh, seventeen, gave a similar statement. "He would have cut us in. Wouldn't just truck it. Him and us, three periods. Every day. We're main. Like family."

Phone calls to the boy's house had not been answered, messages not returned. Because the family's home was outside city limits, a sheriff's investigator was sent to contact the parents. Though Gates's usual beat was that area—west county between Anderson and Mount Shasta City—he had been in Sacramento attending a seminar with SINTF, Sierra County's Narcotics Task Force. Another deputy, the new woman named Faraday, drew the assignment in his stead.

Unlike the boy's worried friends, the father, Chuck Barker, didn't use the word "disappeared." Instead, said Jerell "ran off." Faraday noted Barker's frowning, demeanor more irritated than concerned. Police involvement obviously unwelcome.

"Kid hit the road. He was always threatening to 'jam' when he didn't get his way. I'm not chasing him." The man portrayed his son's flight as an insult, a betrayal of everything Barker had done for him. "He'll learn," Barker said. "Pretty good here, tough as hell out there."

"Is he *your* boy or a stepson?" Faraday had asked.

Barker ignored the question. "He's smart enough to get along for a while." Gestured to his hip pocket. Said, "Took my cash. Wallet and the envelope on the dresser. No way to track it. He'll be back when he runs out."

Barker yelled upstairs for his wife. "Get down here!"

The woman, who according to the female deputy, was significantly younger than her husband, appeared at the top of the stairs wearing a housecoat, holding a small blond lapdog. The woman's eyes looked watery and unfocused, as if she was heavily medicated. She descended, stopped at the bottom step, and held on to the banister. Said, "I wasn't really close to him." Elaborated, "Stepmother," and glanced at her husband as if to make sure he approved of her remark.

When Faraday had asked about the boy's real mother, the woman shook her head and the father answered, "I lost track of Ellen years ago. She never gave a damn about either of us."

Faraday's report included her two follow-up contacts over the next ten days but she had developed no new information. Her conclusion: runaway.

Would the Barker boy have used an alias to hide from his father in the Riverton mission? Jerel Smith/Jerell Barker. Gates had to eliminate the possibility that those were different names for the same kid. He'd review his notes, check the date of "Smith's" arrival in Riverton, and nail down the date of Jerell Barker's "disappearance."

First, he completed newer requisition forms authorizing occupancy lists from shelters in cities along highways 5 and 97. Medford, Klamath Falls, Bend, Portland, and Seattle. Teenage boy, homeless, those were the most likely destinations. Gates needed to know if the mission's Jerel Smith had moved north. Found his notes from his earlier shelter visit. Jerel Smith was logged in February 10, just a few days before Jerell Barker's friends called in to report him missing. Inconclusive.

If Gates had to, he'd guess Barker had injured his son in some squabble. Badly. Badly enough that the boy stole money and ran. Possibly went to a shelter using an alias. Continued going to school until something else happened and he had to flee town. Nonetheless, the name Jerell was very uncommon.

Gates couldn't imagine the boy would use Jerel for a pseudonym. So, was the intern's record of Jerel a misspelling, Smith an alias, or was this a totally different kid? Gates had to keep digging.

After faxing the shelter census requisition forms, Gates turned to the computer. Put in another search, this time adding N-DEx, the national database that kept intel on millions. Asked for anything/everything on two people. Jerell Barker came up empty, except for birth records. Chuck Barker was named in a single federal inquiry. He was the comptroller interviewed during an embezzlement investigation at a Riverton-based company six years earlier. Investigation was terminated for lack of evidence. Nothing strange there. Standard procedure. Comptroller should be the first one debriefed in a financial investigation.

Still, he had a bad feeling about Chuck Barker. Bad enough to run him though the NCIC database after meeting him only once. And Faraday's description indicated the pretty wife's downhill slide. Why? Depression? Intimidation? More domestic abuse?

Gates bought a cold soda and settled in to reread the uncleared case documents. Day off? He didn't care. He wasn't going to log these hours for pay. Just needed to get some balls rolling. Plus, hanging around his empty house always reminded him of his son.

Murray sat up and stared at the cap on the floor like it was a scorpion. Those . . . things he'd seen, the pictures or whatever they were. Like he was there. But he wasn't there, he was here, and he didn't think he forgot that, but the pictures were so real: the gloom, the smoke, the noise, standing out freezing in the middle of nowhere. He hadn't made that up. Couldn't have. They were like scenes in a movie all run together. Maybe he saw things like that on TV when he was still living with his mom.

He leaned over and slowly reached for the cap again, pinched it between thumb and finger and held it in front of him. Dirty, bluish-gray, fake wool. It smelled of sweat and wood fire and— He was nose to nose with a woman, an older woman, and her face was dirty and her breath smelled like vinegar and he couldn't move farther away because their sleeping bag was zipped and the sidewalk was icy but she was warm and he liked her . . . and the explosions made dirt clods fall all around him and hit his helmet. He could feel them but he couldn't hear them and he tried to run but slipped and dropped his rifle and sprawled face-forward in the mud . . . This time Murray threw the cap, hard, toward the front door, and lay back on his cot, breathing like he'd been sprinting.

Pearl had told him earlier. Clairvoyants could find people by touching things. This was something about the gift. That word made him want to scream. Whatever it was, whatever was wrong with Murray, it was no damn gift. It was a tunnel to hell. He couldn't stay in bed. But he remembered the hill and the graves and he didn't feel safe outside. Could he go to

Janochek's workshop or his cabin? Take a book, and if they asked what he was doing there just tell them he needed better light to do homework? He couldn't stay in the shed another minute with that cap. What if it started showing him stuff when he wasn't even holding it? He grabbed his stats book and ran up the road toward the caretaker buildings.

Murray opened the workshop door first. Lights were on, a Dremel plugged in on the workbench, crookneck lamp lit over the computer table, but no Janochek. Another step farther inside showed him Pearl in a nook behind a bookcase, sitting, feet under her, reading. She looked up when she heard him. Said nothing. Continued reading. He backed away, out the door, careful not to let the screen slam, and slipped quietly under the covered walkway to the two-bedroom stucco house Janochek called the "cottage." Opening that door, he found the place lights-off and empty. Janochek still working somewhere out on the grounds.

It would be rude to sit in that cabin when neither Pearl nor Janochek was there, and he was *not* going to roam around the cemetery as upset as he felt, so that left the workshop and Pearl, who was obviously still mad at him. Well, that couldn't be helped.

The moment he reopened the workshop door she stood and let him have it.

"What are you doing? Dad said he asked you up for Sunday."

"I need to . . . I needed, uh, better light . . . to study." Murray hated how difficult it was to think on his feet when Pearl was mad at him.

"Try the library," she said, and turned back to her nook.

"I held the cap," Murray said; he hadn't meant to, or maybe he just hadn't wanted to, but he was afraid to go outside and he was desperate and didn't know what else to do.

Pearl stopped but didn't turn around to face him.

"By accident. I . . . I picked it up and it, or I . . . saw things. Like I was there but I'd never been there and . . . most were sad or scary or just, uh, blue pajamas . . . maybe I saw things like that on television at home but you'd think I'd remember." He ran down. Closed his eyes. Waited for a response.

"The old man's cap," Pearl said. "You saw things."

Now Murray was quiet. He'd said enough.

"Did you ask it anything?"

"Holy hell, Pearl! It was like a horror movie or a . . . I don't know what. I hardly knew what was going on. And then I threw it because . . . it's not right. It's way too . . . like a drug trip or something." He wondered if he should go on. "And there's voices again."

When Murray heard Pearl wheel around, he opened his eyes.

Like the two people in the sleeping bag, neither he nor Pearl seemed able to back away or say anything. Murray thought Pearl could see right into him. Right through his pupils into his mind and down into the ball of fear above his stomach. And he thought maybe she knew him like nobody else in the world knew him. And he thought maybe she liked him like nobody else in the world liked him. And he saw that even though she was disappointed in him, she *still* liked him, and his chest ached and water came to the corners of his eyes and he rubbed his forehead to smear the drops from falling.

Murray stayed frozen while Pearl closed the distance between them, put her arms around him, and held him like his mother might have but never did. And some amount of time passed. And when Janochek barged in the door carrying a bag of fast food, they jumped apart like they'd been electrocuted.

Janochek stopped immediately a foot inside and looked at each of them. "Guess I should have told them to supersize it," he said, and resumed walking through the workshop to the back door and the covered patio that connected to the cottage. "It's better while it's hot," he said, leaving the door open.

Janochek, Pearl, and Murray sat at the dining room table. You could practically hear dust settle. A pin dropping would have shattered glass. No one said a word. And then there was the sound of paper rattling and people eating as if that required absolutely full concentration and left no room for casual glances or chatter.

When every last crumb of food was gone, Janochek gathered the wrappers, stuffed them in the paper bag, and tossed that in the recycling. Returned to the table and rested his hands in front like he was in class waiting for lessons to begin. "So," he said, "what's the latest?"

Pearl started. "Murray . . . you know the homeless man we bought the coat and sleeping bag?" She waited until her dad caught up. "Murray held his cap, I asked him to, and he saw things . . . like they do . . . clairvoyants."

"Some do, apparently," Janochek amended.

"Did you see where he is?" Pearl asked Murray. Noticed the question seemed to make him shudder.

Murray shook his head.

"So what did you see? What did you find out?" Pearl, leaning closer.

Murray looked at the table, felt like he was suddenly out of air, and took a deep breath. He'd brought this on himself. There was no other place to run. Nothing else he could think to do. "I don't know where he is. I just . . . I think I saw things he did or things that happened to him. But . . ." Murray heard himself groan, wanted to turn away from the two of them, didn't think he could make himself say the rest.

"What else?" Pearl said. "What's the matter?"

Like from a great distance, Murray saw Janochek reach over and put his hand on Pearl's arm. He knew why. Janochek was asking her to give him time.

Do it.

"There's more voices," Murray said, "a lot of them. I saw the graves. Someone's killing people."

Murray put his hand over his face wishing he could make it all go away.

When she arrived at the taqueria, Gates already had her carnitas tostada covered in pico and drenched with red sauce. Beside it, a cantaloupe agua fresca.

Her smile showed white teeth. "For a one-horse deputy, you have exquisite taste."

"This isn't exactly a social call, but then again it's not an antisocial call either."

"Flattery will get you nowhere. On the other hand, a tostada . . ."

Gates loved her smile. Looked at her shiny brown hair that she kept pinned up for work, her light touch with cosmetics, her wide shoulders and solid build. Those long legs that could probably outrun him in a sprint. In his forties he had at least five years on her, but anyone who saw the two of them together would probably assume ten or more.

Gates kept himself in pretty good shape, kept his thick sandy hair combed and his steel-toed Wellingtons polished. He knew his face was rough, creased. Not handsome, he thought, but weathered and durable. Hardly seemed like enough for a woman like Duheen; quicker, educated in art and psychology, widely read. And what did he have to offer? A washed and waxed king-cab GMC pickup with new all-weather tires. What woman wouldn't swoon for that?

"You mentioned a while ago that you thought I had an unconscious process that helped during investigations."

Duheen nodded. "Okay," she said, taking a second to stack a jalapeño slice on a chip, "you're fascinated by apparent mysteries, always looking for plausible solutions, actually feel pleasure when you're working a case. You're analyzing situations all the time, but you're not necessarily aware of it. Answers often come when you're not *thinking*."

She stopped for an instant to load another chip with hot carrot and onion. "Your brain works on crimes that puzzle you even when you're doing something else—driving, reading. That's the 'process' I was talking about. Your brain craves explanations, searches automatically, practically incessantly. Neuropsych research has established the mechanisms."

She added more chips to her plate and stirred them into her extra hot sauce while Gates watched. Satisfied with the mix, she went on, "If, hypothetically, you and I were out together sitting around a campfire and there was a sound and I asked you, 'What was that noise?' you wouldn't say, 'Don't worry about it.' You'd do whatever it took to answer the question, including getting up and exploring, to make sure it wasn't dangerous. It's your nature to sort things out, solve puzzles."

While she took a quick break to check her phone that had buzzed a minute before, Gates was shaking his head. Did this woman really know him better than he knew himself? That question was unsettling. He took a deep bite of his taco and put the thought out of his mind, where at least, according to Duheen, it might do some good.

* * *

Duheen waited, looking out the plate-glass window at the leafless trees and the clouds turning from purple to gray while Gates finished eating. When he raised his eyes, she checked her watch. Said, "We have about five minutes. What are you working on now?"

"Missing person. A guy named David Payne. Maybe dead, maybe related to more missing or murdered."

"So what do you know?" she asked, and peered over at his plate as if she was considering spearing the slice of tomato he'd left uneaten.

"Have it." He pushed his plate toward her. "Payne was in his early forties. Laid off last year from a pretty good job. Life collapsed. Now homeless."

The tomato was too slow to avoid capture. "Who might want him dead?"

"Maybe someone in his family? I haven't met any of them yet."

She wiped her mouth on a napkin and waited for him to continue.

"If not his family, then . . . I don't see how robbery could have been a motive."

She put her chin on her hands, thinking along with him. "So, just bad luck? Could it be random, somebody venting or a gang initiation? Hide the body?"

"I think Payne was specifically targeted."

"Who else was Payne close to?"

"I don't know. I don't think he had many friends, or any close friends. Another homeless guy named Rex."

"Payne worked . . ." She glanced at her watch again and reached down for her purse.

"Yeah, a financial planner, auditor, for some local company."

"Anyone there have a grudge against him? Benefit from his death?"

Duheen was looking around the restaurant, Gates thought, trying to locate the restroom. "All the way to the back beside the kitchen," he told her. "Go ahead, I know you're on a time line."

Gates considered the woman's question. A grudge? Payne was fired or downsized or laid off months ago. By reports Payne was "nice," but everyone had enemies. Was somebody from his company still mad enough at Payne to beat him to death? Not plausible. Unless . . . could Payne have been cheating on his own wife, having an affair with a fellow employee's wife and the betrayed husband waited a while to get revenge? Gates would find out where the man had worked, get some answers.

The last thing Rex had told Gates didn't fit any of this. Had Payne's catastrophic losses, job, marriage, home, snapped him, pushed him toward a manic optimism, or did something actually change about his situation? He was expecting big bucks. Going to get his house back. Come into some money or get a new job or find a backer? What could have happened to make Payne think that was possible?

When Duheen returned, she stood behind her chair. "Time to go."

"Hey, I appreciate your, uh . . . diagnosis? Analysis? About my, uh, syndrome."

Duheen rolled her eyes. "Process! God, you're hopeless."

"And thanks for talking shop."

"I enjoyed it. Enjoyed seeing you. Hypothetically."

Gates returned her smile.

Janochek and Pearl left Murray sitting at the table and busied themselves with evening chores, cleaning, straightening. Finished, they settled to read in nearby chairs and waited for Murray to take his next step. Murray slumped, head on hands, rattled and tired from bringing them up-to-date. And now? What was he going to do?

All the options he could imagine scared him. Report the graves to the police and wind up being a murder suspect again? Stay inside here, at the cottage, or down in the lawnmower shed until the voices got worse and he went off the deep end? Take the few dollars he'd kept hidden and buy a bus ticket to . . . well, that was the problem, wasn't it? If not here, where could he go? Alone, broke, he'd wind up homeless, sleeping under bushes or in a barren warehouse with hundreds of other people who had nowhere to go and no one who wanted them.

At least if he decided to report the graves, he'd have Janochek and Pearl in his corner. And he'd still have his friends Dearly and Blessed and Edwin and Sandray. *Sandray wouldn't ever be able to hug him like Pearl had.*

Could the kids at school think he was any weirder? Murray supposed he'd pretty much maxed out socially on the psychotic-goofball scale. How much lower can you go than peculiar and delusional with a prostitute for a mom? In other words, if he told the police what he'd discovered, he wouldn't be much worse off than he was right now—unless they blamed him for everything, and he knew, if they did, Janochek and Pearl would step in to defend him.

"I don't want to climb there tonight." He was surprised to hear his words out loud.

Pearl set her book down, pulled a kitchen chair to his side, and sat near enough to touch.

Janochek stood and searched his desk for a pen and note-paper. Returned to the head of the dining table. "That's sensible," he said. "Where are these graves?"

According to the mission's counselor, Payne's wife was a popular waitress at the local Gold Rush Café. Said the woman moved out right after Payne lost his job, months before the mortgage company took his house.

Gates parked in front of a cedar-shingled, older ranch-style home on Ridge Drive. The woman who answered the door was a bottle-blonde in her late forties. Greeted Gates curtly. Ushered him through an ornately mirrored hall into a living room with bulky leather furniture and dramatic paintings of snowy wilderness scenes. She sat on the edge of the couch facing the picture window and gestured Gates to the overstuffed chair beside the glass-topped coffee table. Didn't offer coffee.

"Thank you for seeing me on such short notice, Mrs. Payne."

"Gibson's my maiden name."

"Okay. An associate of your husband's—"

"Ex-husband," the woman said, glancing at a magazine on the coffee table in front of her.

"—told me that David was expecting to come into some money and get his home back."

The woman sighed. "David was a dreamer. You'd think working with numbers he'd be . . . objective." She used a single finger to turn the magazine ninety degrees so she could better see the writing on the cover. "I suppose I should be embarrassed. I never loved him. Our daughter, Ariel, and I went our own way. David didn't seem to notice. He was more like another child than a husband."

"Were you going to help him get the house back?"

The woman barked a laugh. "Other people have already bought it. I wouldn't have given David another cent and no one else would either."

"What about his work? Would they rehire?"

"They were looking for any excuse to can him."

"Other engineering companies?"

"David never found a job in his life. I did that for him. Asked my customers. Never again, and I wasn't going to take a second job so he could mope around the house. Ariel was ashamed of him."

"Would he have an old friend who'd stake him to a new start?"

She sighed again. "You really don't know anything, do you? David didn't make friends. He was too superficial. He didn't know how to reach out and nobody else bothered."

"He was a financial officer?"

"I suppose so. From the money he brought home every two weeks, more like a bookkeeper."

"Where did he work?"

"Trask Engineering. Up on Air Park."

That name had some meaning but Gates couldn't connect it at the moment. "No one who'd loan David money for another house? No inheritance coming? No parents to bail him out?"

"I suppose it's sad. David was pleasant, too oblivious to be kind but never intentionally hurtful. He was a cypher. Nothing to him. Anyone close is either dead or uninterested. Ariel never asked about him after we moved."

The woman stood. "I wish I could help you . . ."

CARDS ON THE TABLE OR
SHOVEL'S IN THE SHED?

The three of them were sitting together around the wood-stove in the small cabin's living room. Pearl sprawled in the boxy low-armed love seat where she usually read or finished homework after dinner. Janochek leaned forward in his ratty maroon recliner, angled toward Murray, who'd brought in a kitchen chair and straddled it. Murray, fidgeting, embarrassed, didn't want to talk about hearing the voices and, more, didn't want to admit he'd been hiding it from Pearl and Janochek. Thoughts jumbled, he couldn't decide what to say.

Pearl directed. "Tell us when this started."

"I'm not sure. Back at least a couple of weeks or more. First time, they were real weak. Top of the bluff above the rodeo grounds. I didn't think anything. Cats or something. When I cleared trash up by the east hedge, there they were. Each time a little louder. I couldn't keep ignoring it. Decided to look."

"Why didn't you tell me?"

Pearl again, and Murray thought he heard more than irritation in her voice, maybe her feelings were hurt.

"The last time I told you, you wouldn't let it go. You went and got a shovel." Murray wouldn't look at her. "I didn't want to go through that again."

"You won't have to," Janochek said. "This time's different. The three of us are together on whatever it is. None of us will exhume anything. If we think it's right, I'll call the police."

"Not Sergeant Drummond! He hates me." Murray had a

vivid memory of the red-faced man, hardened, like he'd seen too much stupidity or cruelty and could barely contain his anger.

"Okay," Janochek said, "not Drummond or the police. Gates. Sheriffs. He turned out to be reasonable."

"If you don't remember, he accused both of us of killing Nikki Parker." Murray knew he would never forget that particular moment in the hospital when he was recovering from his gunshot wound. Gates, like a giant standing at the foot of his bed, mad and threatening to arrest him.

"I recall," Janochek said, "very well, but he mellowed. He wound up asking for the help we offered. Caught the murderer from information you gave him."

INVESTIGATION TERMINATED

From his interview with Payne's ex, Gates drove straight back
to the department and once again raked through the stack
of reports he'd been given as well as others he'd accumulated
during the course of this investigation. Found what he was
looking for in a handwritten note attached to the sheet re-
cording his Domestic Violence intervention at the Barker
household last year. "Chuck Barker, Chief Financial Officer,
Trask Engineering, Air Park Drive." He would have been
David Payne's boss. It would have been Barker's call to fire
Payne.

Gates knew there was more. Digging through the file
again, he found it in a later addendum, a prior search on the
name Chuck Barker. "Chuck Barker named in federal inquiry,
comptroller interviewed: embezzlement and fraud investigation, Riverton-based company. Investigation terminated for
lack of evidence."

He went to the N-DEx computer that connected local,
state, and federal law enforcement agencies. Entered "David
Payne, Riverton, CA." Within two minutes a single entry
typed itself onto the office printer. "David Payne, accountant/
finance officer, questioned 2008 July. Re: federal inquiry,
embezzlement and tax fraud. Investigation terminated for
lack of evidence."

Gates returned to the N-DEx and entered the FBI inquiry number. Shortly received a one-page synopsis detail-
ing the embezzlement and tax fraud investigation initiated
April 2008 to connect a California engineering firm with a

syndicate-owned Gulf Coast Louisiana/Mississippi gambling operation.

An FBI mole reported an exec from Trask Engineering was regularly investing as much as five million dollars' worth of company assets on "design research and development" for a fictitious casino–amusement park complex in Gulf Coast, Louisiana. On paper, the five mil would appear as an expense, thus substantially reducing Trask's tax liability. The lump-sum investment would be redeemed in a few years. Having been previously written off as a business expense, the money would now be an unreported windfall to put in personal untraceable accounts for the engineering firm's CEO or CFO, whoever was arranging the deal.

September 2008 the investigation was terminated following a catastrophic tropical storm in the Gulf of Mexico that hit the shore, decimating the targeted gambling structures and destroying evidentiary material.

Two employees of Trask coming up in the same case? As a bettor, Gates knew the odds against that were astronomical. Barker and Payne connected? The answer could reveal why these particular homeless were targeted. Gates hoped so, since, as yet, there was no hard evidence linking Barker to either Payne's disappearance or the other missing homeless.

On the surface it made no sense. A wealthy executive whacking street people? Nobody would buy that. And no bodies, no crime. If the homeless were not just missing but dead, it would take phenomenal luck to locate the bodies. Not one had been found during the past month.

Kiefer.

Gates was uncomfortable with his association. Could the kid even do that? Gates shook his head as he realized that somehow, sometime, unbeknownst to himself, he had come to accept the boy's talent even if he didn't understand it, even if he didn't believe in such things. And he also remembered what he really wanted to ask the strange boy.

Speak to my son?

Murray closed his eyes, searching his memory. "The rodeo grounds side of our fence. I couldn't get to where they were from the cemetery. I didn't think so anyway. The moaning scared me. I couldn't make out what they were saying but I couldn't ignore them . . . I imagined they were some people from a long time ago . . . like some massacre and they were buried together and time passed and the cemetery changed."

Janochek was nodding. "When you asked me about boundaries and the history of the place."

"Yeah, but I guess I couldn't convince myself. So this afternoon I climbed the hill over to where the voices were strongest and just as I got there I slipped, slid down a little, and that's when I saw the rope."

Pearl's eyebrows knitted when he said that.

"No, really, just lying there, pretty much covered in dirt so it was hard to see, wouldn't be seen"—Murray knew he was talking faster and faster—"and I knew the guy was using it to pull himself up the hill when he was carrying a body and there were all these people buried between two trees—"

"Easy there," Janochek broke in, "take a breath."

Murray stopped, felt foolish, like a little boy who'd been frightened by a strange man in his living room and run to tell his mother.

"So a rope went up the hill to the grave site," Pearl said, "which looked like what?"

"Messed-up ground, high on the bluff. Dirt clods and stuff. Like somebody'd dug it up and then spread a few leaves back over it. That's where the voices were coming from."

"How many?" This from Janochek.

"I don't know. Four? Eight? I couldn't tell."

Janochek rubbed his forehead. "I don't remember several people being killed. Not in the news." He looked at Pearl. "You?"

"No way. Everybody'd be all over it," she said, absent-mindedly twisting her hair between her fingers. "Could it have happened a long time ago?"

"I looked in the papers, for the past month. I didn't go back further than that but I didn't see anything. So it was probably a slaughter. Maybe a hundred years ago . . . or more. Like people from a homestead or a wagon train." Murray knew that didn't sound very convincing.

"Nope," Janochek said, "the ground wouldn't be freshly disturbed . . . or there'd be more than just a rope. If archae-ologists were uncovering something on the bluff, there'd be equipment. Sifters, frames."

Murray knew the truth. Didn't know how he knew. *Some-one's killing people. Hiding them.* He made himself stay quiet, sit still while his stomach porcupined.

"Can I come when you do it, Dad?"

"Look at the site? I don't think so, honey. One reason, the more people that go up there, the harder it is to investigate for remaining evidence. And . . . until we know more about this, we don't know . . . if somebody's killed several people . . . I don't think I'll even do it alone. Tomorrow I'll call Gates and see what he suggests." Janochek pushed himself up. "You want to stay with us tonight?" he asked.

Murray nodded, surprised as he felt his shoulders loosen,

possibly for the first time in hours. "I could sleep by the fire." He tugged his hoodie collar tighter and crossed his arms.

Pearl rose and left the room. Came back with a blanket. "Warm up, Banshee Boy. We got work tomorrow."

Murray needed to sleep but couldn't find a way. He kept wishing he were different. An ordinary kid. He hadn't felt normal for a long time. Early on, when he was five or six, he realized he could tell how his mother felt, predict what she was going to do next the moment he saw her. This wasn't unusual. Just family. Only two of them. When he met one of her men he immediately knew whether to avoid him at all costs. When he tried to warn his mother about some of these guys, she thanked him. Ignored his concern. Shushed him if he brought it up again. Again, normal.

But he could tell when she was going to go on a crazy speed run before he knew about drugs. Maybe she was extra antsy, or maybe she was suddenly cheerful after she'd been down for days. Or maybe it was just when some new guy left money on the coffee table. She'd leave the house for a while and come back talking a mile a minute, start dancing by herself with the TV and stereo both blaring. She'd pick at her hair and scratch her arms till they bled sometimes. Murray tried to stay out of her way. She was smiling, but she didn't seem happy.

One time, he must have been nine or ten, she went out the door and before it even closed he got this horrible feeling. Scared. Vomity. He ran and caught her on the sidewalk, begged her not to leave. She brushed him off and went anyway. Came home the next day all banged up, black eyes, bruises on her face and arms. She'd said car accident, but she wouldn't talk about it. Maybe that was normal, too. Lots of people got in car accidents . . . except he was sure. Somebody had beat her up.

He'd always felt lonely. Wished for a brother or sister, but it never happened. He read or heard at school about imaginary friends and he tried but couldn't do it. Even when he covered the kitchen table with a blanket and got under it like he was in an old-timey covered wagon and tried to imagine another pioneer boy to talk to, nothing happened. That made him feel stupid and he never did it again.

So how could he explain talking to dead people? It would help to have a story. Maybe he could say he was trapped under the ice, like that boy in Michigan who was frozen but came back to life. He could say that caused it. *I was dead. I got to know how they talk.* Except he didn't remember being dead. He longed to meet just one other person who could hear the dead. Then he wouldn't be so alone, and worse, mental.

A teacher told him.

His third grade class had been on a field trip at Mary Lake and walked near a cemetery. Saint Michael's. And Murray told her he heard people talking in there. When the teacher looked, she didn't see anybody. She leaned and whispered, "Don't say things like that." He had forgotten. Forgotten. How could he? His stomach cramped just thinking about it. Didn't that mean he'd always been nuts? Defective? And he even hid it from himself.

He'd cut off his arm if the voices would just leave him alone. *Oh.* Wait. The dead were his only friends . . . but he just wanted to hear their voices, not the others. And so he went round and round, over and over. It was a twisted loop and there didn't seem to be an alternative. Couldn't have one without risking the other. He knew one thing. If people knew what a freak he really was, they'd put him away or drive a stake through his heart. *This is why people pray, to keep from being eaten by demons.*

He got off the couch and looked for a magazine. Anything to distract.

The following morning at briefing Gates learned Rex had failed to show at the mission. Missed dinner. Didn't appear for breakfast. Extremely unusual. Apparently Rex didn't mind sleeping in a doorway, but never missed a warm meal.

Gates found the lieutenant in his office. Asked to be relieved of Major Crimes duties for a few days to concentrate on the unsolved cases he'd been given. Said he believed he'd made a breakthrough on the Payne disappearance and now had identified a viable suspect that might connect several uncleared cases and possibly a teenage missing person. The lieutenant pulled the duty-rosters clipboard off its hook beside his desk, examined the sheets. Gave Gates a week. Said he'd get more if he needed.

Gates called a judge and got a search warrant for Trask Engineering personnel documents. Made a phone appointment to speak with the firm's CEO later that afternoon. Used his own cloaked cell to ascertain whether Chuck Barker still worked at Trask or whether he'd retired. Found he was in a meeting until noon.

Fine by Gates. He could get the photo he needed when the man went to lunch. Check out a camera with a telephoto lens from the supply room, get a pic of Barker's face without alerting him to the investigation.

At 11:45 Gates was in his pickup at the curb on Benton Drive with an excellent view of the Trask building's entrance and Barker's Lexus in the parking lot. At 12:30, just as Gates was wishing he'd brought coffee and a snack, Barker exited the building and Gates got four close-ups of his face from different angles before the man reached his car.

Couldn't wait. Drove to the mission and showed the pics to the counselor. He'd never seen the man. Cathy, the administrator, came into the dayroom with a stack of orientation flyers. Saw the camera and leaned over. "That looks a little like Mr. Engle," the woman said, turning the small screen to eliminate as much glare as possible.

"If it is, how do you know him?" Gates automatically taking out his notepad.

"He made a sales call about a bookkeeping method his company had developed especially for nonprofits. Asked about our staffing and operations. Asked for our client roster to get an idea of our average census, gender, and age group, to determine if the process might be cost-effective for us."

The woman looked up. "He's going to send us a price quote sometime this month," she said, searching Gates's face. "Shouldn't I have done that? Why are you asking?"

"Broad inquiry. If you see him again, please give me a call." Gates handed her a card and was out the door before she or the counselor could ask more.

Gates had felt his phone buzz while he'd been in the dayroom. Back in his truck he got his voice mail. Roth Trask, the engineering company's CEO, had declined meeting with Gates on the advice of his attorney. If Gates insisted, the man would only speak, if at all, with his lawyer present. Cited prior negative experience with law enforcement officials.

Gates had suspected the man might equivocate regarding knowledge of Payne and Barker and the earlier federal investigation. At this point, it didn't matter. Gates had everything he needed to proceed with his main suspect. Now it was only a question of tactics. Should he bring Barker in for questioning and present the pile of circumstantial evidence? Or should he meet the man at his house after work and inquire about his son's disappearance? Catch him off guard with a follow-up question about the federal investigation and the man's relationship with David Payne?

Saturday morning Janochek didn't call Gates and he didn't go to the burial site alone. Murray took Janochek and Pearl to the top of the hill, to the hedge separating the cemetery from the bluff overlooking the rodeo grounds. The voices hit him like a burst of wind but he ignored them as best he could. "This is where I hear them," he said, pointing at the hedge. "On the other side, almost to the top? That's the evergreen the rope's tied to."

Janochek did his best to part the hedge's thick branches and see through. Gave up. Said, "Let's go to the other side."

When they'd walked back as far as the cottage, Janochek stopped and faced Pearl. "You stay here, honey. If someone's keeping an eye on the hill . . . I can't imagine anyone is, but I don't want them to see you. Don't want you to be a target."

Murray had overlooked that possibility—if someone saw him nosing around the graves, they'd kill him, too. Obvious, now that Janochek said it. Maybe he could just draw Janochek a map. Not go back there again.

"You want me to go with the two of you or you want me to go by myself later?" Pearl asked her father, eyes blazing.

Pearl was so brave. Once again made Murray feel guilty. He noticed Janochek stiffen, his face flushing.

"You would willfully disobey me when I'm trying to protect you?"

Pearl didn't answer.

"Damn it, we're just going around to the bottom of the hill. There'll be nothing to see. We're not going to get close or disturb anything."

Pearl remained silent, keeping her eyes on her father.

Murray thought he knew how this would turn out. Victory often went to the most stubborn.

Janochek stopped at the corner of the old skating rink on Sundial Drive, the three of them staying near the building, watching the stable and the hill behind. Murray was patient. He didn't care if he never got any closer.

"It looks like it did yesterday," Murray said. "Parked cars, nobody outside."

"Where are the graves from here?" Janochek asked, raising his bird-watching binocs and zeroing in.

"Right near the top, pretty much straight line from the stables. Not easy to get to. Nobody'd ever find them. Can you see the real straight dark green tree? Maybe twenty feet tall?"

"I need to get closer," Janochek said, checking Pearl. He stepped close. "I hope you understand this," he said. "I couldn't bear it if anything happened to you. Your mother dead. You're all I have. Everything."

Murray was spellbound. No one, ever, had said anything like that to him.

"I would rather stop right now and call Gates than risk anything happening to you. If you won't stay with Murray, let's leave right now."

Stalemate.

Pearl nodded.

Murray was relieved. He hadn't wanted to get any closer.

"I go to the near edge of the stable and it's straight up from there?"

It was Murray's turn to nod.

He watched Janochek carefully walk the perimeter of the parking area, looking side to side every few feet to see if he was being observed. The man went behind the Dumpster and the rusty barrels, made the rear wall of the stable, and leaned against it. Murray saw him raise the binocs.

"He's looking in the right place?" Pearl asked.

"Pretty much," Murray said, scanning Pearl's face, wondering what prompted her question.

Janochek returned from the stable area with a dark frown. "I looked hard," he said. "No rope. Doesn't seem like anyone's been climbing up there."

"I slid straight down the hill yesterday. Practically right to the near corner where you were," Murray said, swallowing a fear that he had somehow imagined the whole thing.

Janochek glanced at the stable. Scratched his jaw. "I don't see how we can call Gates without evidence. Not sure how he'd respond. Maybe put us back in the crazy-citizen category."

"Let's wait a day and see if anything happens," Pearl said.

Murray didn't know what to say. He couldn't believe the whole thing would just go away. What he really wanted to do was watch the hill, all afternoon if he could, to see if anyone was going to climb it again like he'd heard yesterday. Had he told Janochek that part? "Uh, yesterday afternoon while I was sitting behind the stable I heard someone drive up and park. It sounded like they got out and starting climbing."

"They?" Pearl asked.

"One person, I think. I didn't see who."

"So you're thinking they might have cleaned the place up? Taken the rope?" Janochek scanned the parking area. "That makes me wonder if someone is watching. If somebody knows you went up there?"

Murray's sense was yes. He'd been uncomfortable since they'd arrived but he'd put it down to the nearness of the graves. While Janochek focused on the area from the front of the stables to the river, Murray began examining the vehicles and grounds between them and the convention center. As his gaze reached the shade of the concrete building's covered entranceway, he began to have a bad feeling, like someone was there with his own set of binoculars, but Murray couldn't picture the person. He was afraid to tell Pearl and her father. What if Janochek went over and got hurt . . . or killed?

"I don't see anyone," Janochek said. "Let's do what Pearl said and go home. I don't see how a few more hours could make much difference."

Murray was relieved, though all the way back to the cemetery he kept looking over his shoulder, wondering if they were being followed. If they were, he was afraid he wouldn't be able to sense it.

The same day the three cemetarians were exploring the bluff behind the stables, Gates was arriving at Barker's home out in the Montgomery Ranch subdivision. He'd gone back to headquarters to switch from his truck to his patrol car. He wanted to arrive in an official capacity. The big Chevy patrol car made a racket on the gravel entry drive. Something was different about the entrance from the time he'd been here before.

Earlier, he remembered, the two-story white house with Greek columns was the centerpiece of the drive. This time a visitor's attention was drawn instead to huge rust- and charcoal-colored boulders intermittently placed along the driveway. Stark contrast to the white gravel lane. The rocks matched colors often seen in rivers and fields throughout the Riverton area. The two nearest the house were massive, irregular slabs perhaps four or five feet high and at least six feet long, suggestive of natural gates to a kingdom. How much did it cost to have such enormous stones trucked in to accent a driveway? Trask Engineering. Guess their chief financial officer would get a pretty good deal on that kind of landscaping.

Exiting the cruiser, he expected someone to come to the front door and open it. Listened for barking from the little dog that Faraday had mentioned in her report. All the way to the brick porch the only sound was his footsteps.

He rang the doorbell. Waited. A minute passed with no response. Gates left the porch and walked around the garage side of the house. No cars evident. He peered in a window.

Saw the white Lexus and a dark-colored Mercedes sedan, so both people should be home. At the locked side gate in the tall white fence that surrounded the backyard, he pushed inward until he could see a good slice of the patio: empty hot tub, lawn, and landscaped pool.

Back at the door, he knocked this time. Loudly.

"Sheriff's Department. Open the door." After another minute, tried again. *"Sheriff's Department. Open up."*

After his shout he heard footsteps. In a few seconds the door opened and the beautiful wife stood behind it. Once beautiful. Today her hair was uncombed, her face puffy as if she'd been sleeping. She held the side of the door with one hand, held her terrycloth robe together with the other. Her feet were bare.

"I apologize," Gates said. "I didn't mean to wake you."

The woman looked at the floor. Said nothing.

"Actually I'm here to see your husband but I could ask you, too. Have you heard from your son?" Gates took his hat off in case the woman had bad news.

She shook her head.

"Not a word?" Gates asked. "No idea where he is?"

That last question jerked the woman's head up involuntarily, just for a second, and then her eyes returned to the floor. She shook her head again.

"Has your husband heard anything?" Gates persisted.

The woman didn't respond.

Gates was searching his memory for the woman's first name but couldn't come up with it. "Jerell seemed like a good kid," he said. "Quiet."

No response.

"How's your dog?" Gates asked, anything to get more of a response. It worked but not in the way he expected. A tear slid down her cheek.

"Did you know your husband was questioned a while ago as part of a federal embezzlement and tax-fraud investigation?"

The woman's eyebrows lifted slightly but again she said nothing.

"Is Chuck out buying new table lamps?"

That brought a frown. The woman didn't understand his reference to the prior altercation when they'd met, when her husband had been trying to beat in the bathroom door with a bronze statue to get at her. In fact, there was no sign she recognized Gates at all.

"Do you know when he'll be back?" Gates asked. "Should I wait?"

The woman shook her head a final time and closed the door.

Puzzled by Mrs. Barker, Gates immediately thought of Duheen. Maybe she'd like to get a milk shake. When he phoned she was going hiking with women friends, but said she had time for a short chat. "The homeless case?"

"I've made some progress," he said. "Payne was named in an FBI investigation a while ago along with a top exec from the firm that later fired him."

"And you're thinking they could have been coconspirators?"

"Maybe. Or maybe Payne got fired because he knew what went down even though he wasn't directly involved."

"Either way . . ."

"Right. It's a strong fit with the rumor that Payne said he was going to get his house back. His wife said that was just his usual pie-in-the-sky thinking."

"Weren't there other ways Payne might come into money—relatives, rich childhood friends, retirement annuity, that sort of thing?"

"His wife said no. Zero, zilch, nada. Basically painted him as hapless, friendless, with no chance of improving his lot."

"Are you thinking what I'm thinking?" Duheen asked.

"I hope so," Gates said.

"Not that," she said. "If I were you, I might conclude blackmail. One way a penniless person could get a fund injection."

Gates drove the length of the Barker driveway and parked near the porch. No cars visible. Before he went to the door, he checked the garage again. Lexus and Mercedes both there. If Mrs. Barker had been telling the truth yesterday and Barker really hadn't been home, he must have another vehicle. In this county Gates always bet on a four-wheel-drive pickup or SUV. In the garage: white Lexus and black Mercedes. A residue from his years of gambling addiction, Gates bet himself five hundred dollars Barker's other vehicle was a white Cadillac Esplanade with custom wheels.

When it showed an hour later it was white. Not a Cadillac. A Land Cruiser. The SUV stopped about a hundred feet from the porch. The backup lights went on as if Barker was considering turning around and leaving. Determined to have this conversation, Gates put his hand on the ignition in case he needed to start the cruiser and pursue the man.

Barker's lights winked off. The man killed the engine and got out, as did Gates.

"What are you doing on my property? My wife call you?"

"Why would she?" Gates asked.

Barker ignored that. "What do you want?"

"Heard from your son?"

"What's that got to do with you?" Barker said, striding toward Gates like a linebacker, ready to tackle. Ground to a halt twenty feet away, as if reconsidering his impulse.

Gates wished he'd thought to unbutton his holster. "The missing person report you didn't file," he said. Knew he was goading the man but he wanted him riled for the surprise question.

"I told your girl, Jerell left. Stole money and ran. He's not missing."

Gates wondered how Deputy Faraday might respond to being called his girl. "If he's not missing, where is he?"

"How should I know?"

"You're his father."

"He quit that when he robbed me."

"You've disowned him?"

"Why bother? Is that all?" Barker turned to go toward his porch.

"Why did you fire Payne?"

That halted Barker. "Payne?"

Gates waited.

"David Payne?" Barker gave Gates time to clarify but continued after several seconds. "Because he was a worthless piece of shit, but that's none of your business."

"Was he a worthless piece of shit when he spoke to the FBI during the embezzlement and fraud investigation?"

That question lifted Barker's brow. He blinked and tried to cover it. "I don't know. I wasn't present," he said, turning again toward his front door.

"What was your role in that scam?" Gates said to his back as the man continued walking toward his front door.

"Why did you kill Payne?" Gates asked, and that froze Barker just short of the porch.

"For god's sake, he's a mope but he's not dead." Barker spoke to his front door rather than turn around.

"How do you know?" Gates asked, even voice.

"I talked to him a few days ago. What? Did somebody shoot him?"

"Why would they?"

Barker wheeled. "That the best you got? *CSI Riverton?* Get off my property."

"Did Payne ask you for money?"

That drove Barker up his steps into his house. Gates wondered, if it hadn't been unlocked, would he have broken through the door? Sixty, but the man looked like he could still go twelve rounds.

The afternoon sun had warmed the lawnmower shed. It would stay cozy for a few more hours. Murray was lying on his cot, reading his world history text. Earlier he'd picked the old man's cap up with the point of a stick and put it in a plastic grocery bag to take to Pearl when they met for dinner tonight. As long as they were kind of working together would Janochek go ahead and make the "Sunday" spaghetti? Janochek and his food. Probably put something unusual in the sauce, too. Bacon or artichoke or something, but Murray loved it. His mom had rarely cooked anything unless she was trying to impress the latest man.

A knock and the shed door opening surprised him.

"Ready?" Pearl in a dark pullover, dark sweatpants, and black running shoes.

Murray couldn't contain a laugh. "Ninja?" he asked.

Pearl swept in and plopped down on his middle before he could get up.

Murray's air went out in a whoosh.

"Samurai." She cut her hand through the air like it was a sword. "We're going looking, so get up before I cleave you in twain."

Murray didn't have the air to respond and was grateful when Pearl stood and went to the tool shelf in the back of the shed.

"Think we should bring a weapon?" she asked.

"Your dad will kill me if I go over there with you."

"And I'll kill you if you don't, so make a choice, Grave Rapper, dead now or dead later."

"If you tell we did this he'll make me leave." Murray's greatest fear.

"No way." She lifted a big screwdriver. "What about this?" she asked. "Or is a hammer better?"

Murray made Pearl take the long route to the rodeo grounds so they could walk through the convention center portico, make sure nobody was parked beneath it, watching the stable. About fifty yards off, a big gray van started and drove away before Murray got close enough to see who was inside. Saw it looked dirty. Saw the doors on the back but was too far away for the license plate.

Pearl sensed his interest. "What?"

"Nothing," he said, "but if you see something like that again anywhere near us, tell me."

"That truck? There must be a jillion of those in Riverton."

"Kind of rounded in back? Most vans are pretty square."

"You think that person might have been watching Dad?"

Murray shrugged. "Let's go the long way to the boat ramp and over behind the sheds to get to the hill."

"More cover?"

Murray nodded, already on the move.

At the back corner, where her dad had been earlier, Pearl started climbing.

"Hold up." Murray scrunched against the corrugated wall. "Your dad said not to disturb the evidence."

"You slid down here, right?"

"Right about where you are."

"There's no sign of it so somebody already disturbed it." She continued moving.

When she was forty or fifty feet up, Murray couldn't stand it anymore. "Stop before you get to that thick tree. The rope's there in the dirt." Started after her.

"No, it's not." Pearl kept climbing.

"Wait a minute, damn it!"

A woman's voice was getting louder as he climbed.

Pearl slowed, let him catch up.

Murray scraped the leaves on either side, brushed, dug a little. She was right. No sign of a rope. "See that evergreen, straight up?"

Pearl nodded.

"The rope's tied to that."

"Not now," Pearl said. She crawled around the thick tree and started higher.

"Wait!" Murray croaked, fighting to hear himself over the noise of a woman yelling. "The graves are just above you."

Pearl stopped crawling and raised herself on her knees. The uphill ground was covered with leaves and pine needles and twigs like everywhere else on the hill. There was a plastic grocery bag caught on a low branch, and, lying around, a moldy cardboard box that said CAL-SUN PRODUCE and a corroded beer can half-buried at an angle.

"This couldn't be the place," Pearl said, annoyed.

"Damn it!?" Murray, irritated by her hasty conclusion. "The graves are right below that tree and I'm hearing a voice so loud I can hardly stand it."

"What are they saying?" Pearl, ever the practical one.

Murray hadn't considered actually listening. He'd been doing everything he could to blot out the sound. When he focused, it wasn't a crowd like before with everyone talking at once, angry and begging. Only the familiar voice he'd been hearing as he climbed.

". . . are you . . . Don't . . . are you . . . DON'T!" Over and over. A woman. Terrified. Was she talking to him? He wasn't sure.

Murray gave up. To really communicate he'd probably have to sit above her and touch the ground, and he definitely wasn't going to crawl up there.

"What did you get?" Pearl at his elbow. "Do you know who they are—"

"Freeze!" A voice below them, like a megaphone. "Come down here! Now!"

Pearl gripped Murray's arm so tight, pain shot up to his shoulder.

"Now, I said!"

They backed down the hill, slipping from time to time, but one anchored the other and they didn't slide far. Stood at the bottom.

"Turn around."

Murray wondered if he was going to die in the next minute. Stepped in front of Pearl to see a tall fat man in a uniform, long black flashlight in one hand, small bullhorn tucked under his arm. Not a cop. A security guy?

"You're trespassing."

"This is public property." Pearl. Over Murray's shoulder.

"It's public during the day. Closed after five."

"No, it doesn't. They have rodeos and events at the center that last till midnight." Pearl didn't seem nearly as nervous as Murray.

"Not this part. Stable's only for event stock, a couple a renters. Kids messing around disturbs the horses. I got a call."

"Does the person who called you own a big gray truck?"

Murray wished Pearl would just shut up but he knew telling her would be useless.

"You're too young to be mouthing off to a cop. Does your ol' man know you're here with this boy?"

That shut Pearl up.

In the momentary silence Murray was aware of voices . . . the ones from before. He shot a quick look at the stable. No. Was a van parked nearby? He didn't see one. He put the voices out of his mind.

"Are you a policeman?" Murray asked. He didn't think so. RPD wore dark blue uniforms, and even in the poor light Murray could see the man wore a gray shirt with dark pocket flaps, gray pants with a dark stripe down the leg.

"Let's just call this girl's parents and see how much of a policeman I am," the man said, pulling his phone out of a belt holster.

"We're leaving." This from Pearl, and she was already walking toward the trees south of the Dumpster.

Murray sensed her plan. If the man tried to stop her she'd run for cover, probably the thick patch of trees beyond the old skating rink. If the guy followed she had several options including jumping in the canal if she got desperate. When Pearl was mad, she was fearless. Murray's thoughts were interrupted by a hand on his shoulder.

"I'm watching you, son. Don't do this again. Next time, you're arrested, sure as shit."

Murray wondered if the guy could hear his heartbeat, wondered if the guy had any idea how scared he was. Too scared to speak, for one. He twisted out of the man's grasp and ran.

Gates drove away from the Barker house with an uneasy feeling. All these years in law enforcement, had he learned anything? At this moment he wasn't sure whether he'd advanced his investigation or destroyed it. He knew for certain that the anger he'd felt confronting Barker was dangerous. He'd learned it second day of training: "When you're angry blood leaves the brain and goes to arms and legs, fight or flight." Questioning a suspect was best done dispassionately.

Gates turned west on Placer up to Texas Springs Road and parked in a favorite turnout with a view of Montgomery Ranch Lake. Went over the exchange to the best of his memory.

He wasn't sorry he'd confronted the man at his home. That, if anything, could lead to more careless remarks than an official setting. Gates believed if he'd brought Barker to the department for questioning the man probably would have lawyered up. Immediately. The prior experience of being interrogated by FBI officers in a federal investigation will do that to a person. Gates had hoped he'd get a better read on Barker's responses to the questions about Payne. Unfortunately, he came away wondering whether the man was growing increasingly anxious in response to the closeness of Gates's guesses, or simply agitated that he couldn't throw a punch. Every time Gates had seen him, the man's immediate response to something he didn't like was aggression. And Barker challenged Gates: "Did my wife call you?" So something was still wrong at home, deteriorating by the look of his wife. More bothersome, the man continued to show no concern for his son. Gates couldn't imagine. Then he could.

Barker had been momentarily rocked by the question about the FBI investigation. Admitted he'd talked to Payne recently but may have been surprised by hearing Payne was dead. The question had stopped Barker short of his front door, but he didn't turn around, and Gates had no way to discern the man's expression or the emotions behind it.

What was next? Gates needed to speak to Mrs. Barker again. See if he could learn what was sapping her vitality. See if she knew what Barker did on his evenings and weekends. It takes substantial time to kill people and hide their bodies. He'd have to drive them out in the wilderness and bury them well enough to dissuade animals. Even then, some would eventually be found.

Now that Homeland Security had guards and cameras watching the dam at Sierra Lake, the most convenient corpse disposal method had been eliminated. Barker didn't own a junkyard with a car-crusher or a cement manufacturing company, but didn't his company help create office buildings and shopping centers? Was Trask involved in any project that would accommodate several bodies in foundation work?

The following morning Gates pored over the engineering company's description. Designing and building commercial sites: office buildings, apartment buildings, shopping centers, hospitals. Founded by Charles R. Trask. In 2007 the man split his ownership, retaining 70 percent, and giving the remaining 30 percent to his son, Roth, who'd joined the company earlier that year. January 2008, C. R. Trask died, leaving everything to Roth. In 2009, Chuck Barker purchased 10 percent.

Add a partner? A comptroller who'd been questioned in an FBI investigation the year before? Why? Extortion? Did Barker know something Roth wanted to keep hidden? Or did he just need to raise cash to offset company losses? And yes, Barker had been Payne's supervisor; his signature appeared on Payne's termination papers.

Roth had declined to meet with Gates on advice of his lawyer? Seemed ultra-cautious for an everyday Riverton businessman. Gates turned to his personal investigator, Mr. Google.

Roth Trask: Born 1973, graduated Chico State University 1995. Air Force after college. Gulf War fighter pilot, honorable discharge 2004. Joined firm in 2007. One thing Gates hadn't known. The years between discharge and company employment? Roth Trask became the teaching pro at the local Ponderosas Golf Club. A scratch amateur golfer, playing and placing in several western state pro-am tournaments, he gave up the game after failing to qualify for the Professional Golf Association tour '05 through '07.

Murray barely caught the whisper as he bolted past the old skating rink running for home. He made sure he was out of the fat guy's sight before he stopped.

"Over here. Don't let him see you."

Pearl didn't need to worry. That was Murray's first priority. He wanted to keep running, but he couldn't leave Pearl. She'd hurried south, and when the rink blocked the guy's view she slid behind the trees to see what was going to happen. He knew without a doubt she'd have run back and attacked the man if he'd gotten aggressive.

"Let's get out of here." Murray was puffing more from fear than sprinting.

"Just watch."

"We can't do anything."

"Who called him? Where'd this guy come from? Bother horses, my butt! Let's see if anybody meets him."

"If nobody does?" Murray was desperately searching for any argument that would get her out of here.

"See how long he stays around. Like he's guarding that hill? That can't be his job. Security stays on the move, patrols; supermarkets, hospitals, the museum—places with valuables."

"Horses are valuable."

"Did you hear any? Do people store an expensive horse in an empty public stable?"

"We didn't look in the stalls." Murray knew he was wasting his breath.

"Hang on. One of us may have to run for Dad."

When Murray zeroed in, the guy had a cell phone to his ear and was slowly walking back and forth scanning the hill as he talked. He stopped, held the phone away, and looked in the direction Murray and Pearl had run. Made a slow three-sixty before resuming his conversation.

"See?"

Pearl had whispered right in his ear, so close he had briefly felt her lips.

"Somebody asked him about *us*. Not about horses."

Murray had to admit it looked that way.

The man holstered his phone, adjusted his pants higher on his waist, and went back to lean on his car hood. Stayed that way, looking at the hill another fifteen minutes before driving away.

By that time it was cold and Pearl and Murray had a different problem. Night. It was past time for dinner.

When they opened the cottage door the whole place smelled like tomato sauce and spices and garlic bread. Janochek was sitting in his comfortable chair shuffling a deck of cards. Murray had never seen him do that before.

"Thought I'd try my hand at fortune-telling," he said to neither in particular. "I asked the deck when my daughter and her friend might be home for dinner but it didn't know."

Murray wanted to say something, break in, but absolutely nothing came to mind.

Pearl started, "Dad—"

Janochek spoke right through her. "So I asked what my daughter and her friend were doing, and it answered right back. 'They've gone to look at the graves.' And then I threw my genie. And while I was picking up his pieces, I was thinking, good thing it wasn't a crystal ball."

"Dad—" Pearl tried again but her father held up his hand.

"While I was down on my hands and knees I wondered what I would have done at your age. You never met him, but I loved my father, and even respected him. He was what they called a common man, a laborer, a sawmill worker. I was proud of him and tried to please him when I could."

Peripherally, Murray could see tears. See them make a line down Pearl's face toward her chin.

"Dad, please—" The hand again cut her off.

"Before I got all fifty-two I knew I would have promised one thing and done another, even though I loved him. I knew that some things made me so curious I had to see for myself and no reason or promise in the world would keep me from it. And I knew that willfulness did not mean I loved my dad any less. It just meant that sometimes I had to live my own damn life and suffer whatever consequences."

Murray found his tongue. "It was my fault. I asked her," he said. Blackness filled the air in front of him, like he'd entered a tunnel.

Janochek shook his head and the motion brought Murray back to the room.

"Son, you don't have it in you," he said.

A sob escaped Pearl, but she caught it and shut it off.

"In a minute or so, we're going to sit down and have some spaghetti," he said.

His voice was so even Murray couldn't begin to guess

what was coming next. This might be his last meal, his last night in the cemetery.

"Before we eat we're going to have an understanding."

He rose and got two straight-backed chairs from the table, faced them a couple of feet in front of his easy chair and sat again, motioned the pair to join him.

Murray snuck a glance at Pearl, at her face, now flushed and a little swollen.

"Disobedience is unwanted, mostly unwarranted, usually unpardonable between a father and fourteen-year-old . . . No, forget that, it's not what I wanted to say." He rubbed his face and started again. "Lying now and in the foreseeable future is unacceptable. Unacceptable . . . Do you hear me?"

The man hadn't raised his voice but his words were crystal clear. Murray nodded, as did Pearl.

"We'll not further discuss the disobedience. We will discuss what you saw and what you learned and what you're going to do in the next days and you will tell the truth, the whole truth, and nothing but the goddamned truth. And keep telling it whenever we're together . . . Because I'm afraid." He paused, pursed his lips just for a second. "I'm afraid if you don't, something infinitely precious will be lost between a father and a daughter. Something that we may never be able to retrieve." He let that stand for a few seconds before adding, "And, Murray, if I can't trust you, you can't live here. You understand that, don't you?"

Murray did. He really did. He did so fully, he didn't think answering the question with words did the question justice. He'd answer in blood if he could.

Janochek once again rose, but this time he went to the stove and began filling plates from a large skillet.

Later, Murray awoke on the small couch in the cottage. He'd slept over, still reluctant to stay so far away in the shed. He remembered the dream that woke him. The dead were walking. Groaning as they moved. He was pretty sure what brought that on. Why was there only one voice when he and Pearl climbed the hill a few hours ago? Where were the rest of them? But at the bottom, he'd heard them when he and Pearl were with the cop. How could that happen?

He thought about waking Pearl or Janochek but was more afraid of doing that than walking to the hedge by himself. He pulled on Janochek's canvas jacket and quietly opened and closed the doors. Picked his path cautiously, trying to stay on the grass and avoid sticks that would break under his weight. Ten feet from the hedge he could hear her. Her. Not the others. That sent a chill through him, sent him back to the cottage.

He sat in Janochek's easy chair . . . *Wear his coat. Sit in his chair. Ought to drink his porridge.* But the chair and coat were comforting. That's as close as he could come to a justification.

What about the voices? Had someone moved the bodies? Was that the parking and climbing he'd heard the evening he first climbed the bluff? Somebody going up to take the bodies and untie the rope? Why leave the woman? Didn't have time to get them all? Hard to believe. What if somebody was planning to finish the job yesterday, but held back when he saw them messing around the stable? Murray shivered. That could be why he'd called the cop. To get them out of there so he could move the last body. But he hadn't. The woman's voice was still up where Murray had first heard it. Didn't make any sense.

When Janochek shook his shoulder, Murray yelped and then got embarrassed when he remembered he was still sitting in the man's chair and wearing the man's coat. "I, uh, I—"

"Didn't mean to startle you. How about flapjacks and burger patties?"

Murray composed himself, watching Janochek take down the big mixing bowl and gather the ingredients. He stirred the pancake mix together with eggs and milk and shook in some spices, finally adding a spoonful of what Murray recognized as vanilla. That done, he shaped the burgers and started them frying in one skillet, put butter in another and added three dollops of batter.

"Smells good," Murray said, rising. "I'm really grat—"

"Pearl always razzes me about burgers for breakfast, but I notice there's never anything left on her plate. I think she likes the meat-syrup combination."

Murray heard Pearl in the bathroom and postponed his own needs till she finished.

After the dishes and pans were set to dry, the three returned to the table. "Got to figure the next step," Janochek said, putting his clipboard in front of him and taking the ballpoint out of the old coffee cup that held assorted pencils and pens. "I believe we had our understanding last night." He looked at each of them in turn.

Each nodded.

"Okay, what did you see?"

"You were right," Pearl said. "No rope. Um . . ."

"A man called us off the hill," Murray said, watching Janochek's eyes widen. "He said he was a policeman and he had a cop-type car, but his uniform was gray with black trim. I think he was a rent-a-cop."

"There? By the stable?"

Murray nodded.

"Can't remember seeing security around the rodeo grounds when there wasn't an event." Janochek looked away, thinking.

"He said he was going to arrest us and then he said he was going to call you," Pearl said, eyes on the table.

"Well, we couldn't have that, could we?" Janochek asked, scowling. "So you . . . ran?"

"Yeah, but we hid by the skating rink, behind the trees at the canal, and watched," she said.

"He was on his cell to somebody," Murray said.

"Right after you left?"

They both nodded.

"And then he took the phone away from his ear and

looked around the whole area like he was seeing if we were for sure gone before he talked again. I think he called somebody about us."

"Could be. Or some citizen walking by the stable could have heard you and phoned security and he was just calling back to report that the situation was handled."

"Dad, we were whispering. Way up the hill. Nobody could have heard us."

"Yesterday I felt like somebody was watching us while you were looking around the hill," Murray said. "I think somebody followed us when we left. And last night, a light-colored truck, a van, pulled away from the front doors of the auditorium just as we walked up."

Janochek's face darkened. "Lord loves a duck! That's just why I didn't want you messing around there anymore!" He leaned away from the table, rubbed his eyes. "There's probably a normal explanation. Cars and trucks stop under that portico all the time to load and unload. It's a quick way into the auditorium's kitchen." He sat forward and made himself a note. "Kind of truck?"

"Like a business truck. Boxy. Dirty. The back looked kind of rounded at the top."

"A Chevy or GMC? A lot of those are white."

Murray was at a loss. He didn't know much about cars or trucks, didn't drive, his mom didn't have a car anymore.

Janochek looked at Pearl.

She avoided his stare. "Sorry. No idea. But I thought there was just one person inside. Didn't it look like one of those?" She pointed to the newspaper, to a dealership ad Janochek had been skimming during breakfast.

Murray nodded. "Maybe," he said, "but that's a side view."

Janochek shook his head. When he was a boy he knew the make of every car in town. "Rounded on top of the back doors," he said, "probably one of those GM commercial vans." Was going to add more but knew it would just confuse them. "Writing on the side or rear doors?"

Pearl shook her head.

"Don't think so," Murray said.

"Okay, the cop guy. See the name of the security company?"

Murray considered. It was a little too dark to see the emblem on the guy's shirt and his car was facing them, no way to catch an emblem on the door.

Janochek rose and strode to his work desk, fumbled through the drawers until he found the phone book. Sat back down with it and took out his own cell and dialed.

"Who's in charge of security at the rodeo grounds, the stable and everything?" He had his pen ready but he didn't need it. "The police. Thanks, that's what I thought."

Pearl looked at Murray as if to say "see."

"I'm thinking it's time to call Gates," Janochek said, thumbing through the government section of the phone book for the sheriff's number.

"Uh . . . there might be one more thing," Murray said. He hated that once words left your mouth they were out in the world with no way to get them back or control them. "The voices?"

Pearl and Janochek waited.

"Last night, up the hill? It was just a woman's voice. The

others were gone. They, uh . . . I heard them at the bottom of the hill when we were talking with the guy. I wasn't trying to hear them. They were just there. Not in the stable I don't think, and probably not in the guy's car—" A horrible image flashed to his mind of tangled bodies jammed into an automobile trunk. "They weren't louder in that direction."

Murray could see Pearl and Janochek didn't know what to make of that information, so he kept going. "Early this, well, in the middle of the night, I got up and walked up to the cemetery hedge to check. Uh, that's when I put on your coat. Sorry."

Janochek waved it off.

"So it was still just the woman. The others . . . I'm not sure where they are."

Janochek was up getting his keys off the desktop. "Let's go see," he said, going out the door.

It was chilly but neither Pearl nor Murray bothered with jackets. Two minutes later, having driven through the now empty portico, they were parked by the stable.

When they got out Pearl and her father scanned the area, while Murray walked to the base of the hill and walked it all the way to the edge of the stable and then to the far end. He came around the stable on the other side and looked in the stalls. He walked around a parked car and a nearby truck. Walked out around Janochek's pickup and back and forth over the ground where they'd been talking to the cop. Nothing. Nothing at all. Gone.

He came to stand with his friends, shook his head.

Janochek took out his phone and dialed information for the sheriff's. The operator made the connection. "This is Paul Janochek. I have some important information for Deputy Investigator Roman Gates. Is he available? Can you patch me through?" He waited, looking at the portico, frowning.

Gates met them at the rodeo grounds in twenty minutes. Murray purely dreaded seeing the man again. He reminded Murray of some big TV cowboy, tall, rangy, not fat but heavy, face lined, weathered. Gates had finally acted a little more friendly after they gave him the name of the killer. New Year's night, after Pearl uncovered the body and they all met at the police station, he had actually smiled. Still, Murray had hoped he'd never see the man again.

No such luck. The black-and-white cruiser with gold lettering and flasher bars rolled slowly into the parking area and set up next to Janochek's truck, where Pearl and Janochek were waiting. Murray himself had stayed inside the pickup.

Gates unfolded from the cruiser and shook Janochek's hand, did the same to Pearl. Bent to peer in at Murray.

Crap. Murray didn't want to seem like a scaredy-cat so he got out and shook the man's hand without meeting his eyes.

Gates left it at that. "So?" he said, withdrawing his ballpoint from his shirt pocket.

Janochek started. "Murray's been hearing voices on this ridge behind us. They were outside the cemetery fence so he came around here to confirm it. He told me and I came to look it over." Janochek paused.

"And?" Gates was scanning the whole stable area, like he was getting a feel for it.

"He had told me there was a rope tied to a tree, like a tow rope leading up the hill. Near the top, voices of several . . .

dead people, and a roughed-up place where bodies could have been buried."

Murray couldn't help noticing that Gates was actually leaning a little closer to Janochek as he spoke. He didn't think Gates realized it.

"Yesterday morning I went over by the corner of the stable and glassed it. Didn't see anything. Then, late afternoon, Murray and Pearl came back—"

"Without you?"

"Yes, and saw a light-colored gray or dirty white van, like the GM commercial series. In the convention center portico, facing our way."

Gates looked toward the center. "Why was that unusual?"

"The person drove away as soon as they saw him. Might have been a coincidence."

"Him?"

"A guess. Anyway, when they climbed the hill again, the rope was gone and he heard *only* a woman's voice up top."

Gates looked at Janochek, irritated. "Again! Climbed where bodies might be buried?"

"For a closer look."

Those words brought a grimace to the big man's face. Gates looked at Murray. "You knew you were disturbing a crime scene!"

Murray was stuck. Yes, he knew that, but Pearl . . . He didn't reply.

Janochek waded in, hoping to deflect Gates's anger. "When they were back at the bottom, Murray heard the original voices again. They'd moved."

"They'd . . ."

"Like someone had moved the bodies that were making the sounds. And today, they're gone, except for the woman, who's still up there," Janochek finished.

Gates, still clearly annoyed, summarized. "So, it's possible several bodies were buried up the hill and all were recently moved except a woman."

"She just kept saying the same thing," Murray added, hoping to move on from the mistake. "'Are you?' like who are you, and 'Don't.' She screamed that last one."

Gates squinted, suddenly suspicious. "Has anyone talked with you? Suggested that people are turning up missing?" He stopped to register their reaction to the question. Walked closer to the three of them. "You know after the tremendous help you've given me on the Nikki Parker case, I'd hate to think you kids are trying to cash in on that goodwill for a little more publicity."

Murray felt a charge in the air, a difference in the way Janochek was standing. Looked to see the man's face red and jaw knotted.

Janochek bristled. Said, "If you're too pigheaded to accept our information, and I mean that in *every* sense of the word, then we'll leave right now and you won't hear from us again."

Pearl reached for her father's arm.

Murray was afraid the men were going to fight. Here in the parking lot there'd be no one to stop them.

"Answer the goddamn question!"

"Go to hell!"

Murray could hear Janochek's breathing. Gates was focused, watching them very closely, but didn't seem so riled.

"Easy," Gates said. "Several homeless may have disappeared recently. It's not been in the papers. I thought maybe friends or acquaintances said something about the missing people and you thought you could make a suggestion, maybe get a little public recognition again."

Murray saw Janochek's hands become fists.

"You're a jackass!" Janochek said, eyes blazing. "Murray and Pearl deserve gratitude, not suspicion. I called you because I thought you'd want to know. I didn't guess you'd be looking to blame someone for your own ineptitude."

The words echoed. Nobody moved. Nearby sparrows flew off in a clatter.

After a moment, Gates broke the stalemate. "I'm not going to apologize for doing my job the best way I know how, but I agree you three probably didn't deserve that accusation. Tell me what you've heard lately about the town and what's going on."

"Absolutely nothing!" Janochek, still steaming.

Pearl shrugged. "Um, some kids from our school are going to fight some kids from Colinas at the Bella Vista School Saturday."

Murray looked at Janochek again. The man was too angry to react to Pearl's comment.

Everyone's eyes went to Murray, but he wasn't sure if he should say anything. Would it get him in worse trouble? He had no idea. "I tried to find out." When no one spoke, he went on more quietly. "I went to the library. Searched newspapers and the Internet for murders and kidnappings in this area. There weren't any with missing bodies the past month . . . Is that illegal?"

Janochek softened, moved closer to put his arm around the boy.

"No," Gates said, "that's not. It's smart." He took his time, once again looking around at the hill and the stable before turning to face them. "I asked because I had to eliminate that possibility. This is a complicated investigation. I can't afford to jump at a false lead. I couldn't move, especially involving you three again, until I had more information."

Gates rubbed his nose like the tip of it itched, but Murray thought the man was just gathering his thoughts.

"People are missing," he said, "and it hasn't been broadcast. For no obvious reason several homeless people have vanished without a trace. It's possible they were murdered, their bodies hidden."

Murray could feel Janochek's muscles relaxing and took a deep breath of his own. Pearl let go of her father's arm and shook her head like she could dispel some of the fear that had gathered there.

"In the past few minutes I've been extremely careful because your story fits a plausible scenario. At least four men have dropped off the grid, and one woman. If they were killed, the planning has been careful and complex. Though you may still be angry at me, would you be willing to meet at the department in a couple of hours—no, say one o'clock—to give some detailed statements?"

Pearl and Murray nodded as Gates walked past them to his radio. Called in a forensic team. When he finished, he turned to find Janochek standing in front of him.

"I have never given you the slightest reason to doubt—" Janochek bit the words off.

"You have not, sir," Gates said, meeting his eyes. "Can you tell me these kids have never fooled you?"

Janochek thought that over. And over some more. Said, "I cannot." Walked to his truck with Pearl and Murray right behind, not looking toward each other at all.

Before Gates brought them to a medium-size room with a small brown veneer conference table, he asked if anyone wanted water or coffee. No takers. He closed the door, pushed two more dark chairs with padded seats to the table, and the four people sat.

He arranged his notepad and the digital tape recorder on the table and spoke the date, time, and those present. "If you were suspects," he said, "we'd be in a different room and I'd never interview you together. I say this to clear a little more air. I believed this would be the most effective method in this situation because I hope you've tried to keep each other fully informed." He stopped, having noticed the energy that remark brought to the table.

When no one said anything, he went on. "Listen to each other very carefully. Add anything you think the other has forgotten. We'll build a comprehensive picture."

It took almost an hour to cover Murray's story, a few more minutes to go over the reconnaissance trip the three of them took where Janochek used his binoculars, where they might have been seen investigating. They went over Murray and Pearl's return trip, and when they got to the part about the cop calling them off the hill, Gates said, "Let's go extra-slow through this part."

They said the man called himself a policeman but the uniform was wrong, and Murray described it. Gates stopped the interview long enough to go into the other room, saying he needed to have someone run the private security firms in Sierra County, color and style of their uniforms.

When they resumed, Gates wanted the man's words verbatim. He also paid close attention to the description of the guy's phone conversation.

"Can you give me an exact time on that?" he asked Murray and Pearl.

Murray looked at his bare wrist. Pearl scrunched her face, thinking.

"We didn't leave till he did. What time did we get home, Daddy?"

Murray had never heard her call him that.

"Happens I know," Janochek said. "Six forty-three p.m. give or take a nanosecond."

Pearl hurried on. "Okay, so he left about fifteen minutes before that. And we'd been watching him while he made his call and walked around the stable and waited by his car to see if we were coming back. That probably all took about a half hour. Forty-three minus fifteen is twenty-eight, and minus thirty is negative two, so he was making his call or somebody called him around six o'clock, plus or minus five minutes."

Murray was so proud of her right then. Jeez, she was so sharp, so take-care-of-business! Noticed Janochek looking at him and turned away to hide a blush.

"When we find this guy, and we should, unless this is an incredibly elaborate masquerade, we'll find who did what. Both parties." He looked around the table. "Is that it?"

"What can you tell us?" Janochek asked.

"Jackpot," Gates said. Frowned. "Old habit," he explained. "We found the body of a woman that seems to fit the profile of the person we were hunting for. Early forensics say it looks like other bodies might have been up there originally. We should know by tomorrow." He turned to Murray. "Quite a day," he said.

Murray nodded.

"Would you mind if we visited back at the stable late this afternoon? Say five o'clock. I could pick you up at the cemetery and we could drive. You could go over hearing the voices when you and Pearl were down the hill, talking to the cop."

"I don't think there's anything left to tell," Murray said. "I listened. I couldn't figure where they were."

"Would you give it a shot anyway?"

Murray nodded again.

Gates turned to Janochek. "Want to ride along?"

They parked beside the stable around dusk, having driven all over the convention center area without seeing either a suspicious truck or a security cop.

"Is this where he was?"

"About ten feet back and ten feet over," Murray answered.

Gates adjusted the cruiser's position. "Here?"

Murray checked with Pearl in the seat beside him. He'd known she wouldn't miss this for a million. "Yes," he said.

The deputy shut off the engine and they got out. Gates said, "Show me where you two were standing. Facing him, right, and he was facing the hill?"

"Yeah," Murray said, "but it was just me. Pearl had already run."

Pearl pointed. "I hid over in that tree line."

Gates smiled. Janochek, too.

"Okay, so where were you?" Gates addressed Murray.

Murray got in position about eight feet in front of the three of them.

"And you heard the multiple voices again, and then what?"

"I looked at the stable, but I don't believe they were there. I looked for a van or even a truck where someone might have stashed them, even just for a while, but there wasn't any. I looked at the guy's car, but I couldn't see how he could have them."

"We'll check his trunk for that very thing as soon as we find him," Gates said. "What else?"

"That's it. I couldn't figure it out and I stopped listening."

"But at that time, around five-thirty or six, you heard them at the bottom of the hill in this parking lot?"

Murray nodded. "Somewhere around here."

"But they were gone this morning?"

"Yes. I mean, I think so. I couldn't hear them anymore."

"So they're not under this asphalt?"

"I don't hear anything."

"So what's missing?"

"What do you mean?"

"What was here then that isn't here now?"

"Nothing," Murray said, and wished he were better at this stuff.

Department's morning briefing centered on the hillside body. Forensics had made a positive identification: the mission bookkeeper, Alicia Turner, beaten, raped with evidence of semen, strangled, clothes removed and tucked beside her. The team reported thinly covered depressions that could indicate more bodies were stored in that location and later removed. The only specific evidence: the torn edge of a 3-mil black garbage bag that was sent to the state crime lab in Sacramento for more detailed analysis. Team also reported that deep, foot-size depressions below the burial area suggested someone had climbed up and down the hill twice or more, perhaps carrying extra weight. They found fiber remnants and rub marks confirming that a rope had been secured to the trunk of a sturdy fir at the top of the site. As far as Gates could tell, everything pointed to a scenario that matched what the Kiefer kid had been saying.

"Got time for a quick check-in?" Gates, for once, got Duheen a few seconds after he'd requested her.

"Not much. I have two admissions from outpatient and I'm going to stay and finish the paperwork. Five minutes tops. What you got?"

"The Kiefer boy, remember from the missing Parker girl? New Year's?"

"The clairvoyant kid."

"Well, at the rodeo grounds on that hill that abuts the cemetery, he's found another body. Woman that probably ties into the missing person cases I've been working. Probably something Payne's disappearance kicked off."

"Wow."

"I've interviewed the boy, Kiefer, the cemetery caretaker, and his daughter. Kiefer senses there were other dead bodies involved but can't come up with any useful specifics. He has this . . . what? Feeling? And he says the dead people are 'gone' now. But he hates doing this stuff, talking about it, thinking about it. I'm wondering if he could be forgetting something or repressing something about the other bodies that he's not in touch with."

"Do you think his clairvoyance is only useful or pleasurable to him as a hedge against loneliness? Has no real friends so he believes he can talk to the dead?"

Gates broke in. "Do you believe it?"

"I don't know," Duheen said. "Don't know how to know. Anyway I'm running out of time. Uh, to the extent that working with you, using ESP, leaves him vulnerable to accusations of mental illness, then it's in his self-interest, conscious or unconscious, to say as little as possible. So yes, he could be withholding or repressing some information."

"What do you do about that? How can I make him break through that resistance?"

"My work is different. In psych we usually follow the patient's lead. We tend not to dig for memories; we wait until the person is ready to retrieve them."

"I may not have that luxury. More people may be in harm's way if I can't figure this out."

"Okay, well, visualization sometimes prompts or opens memory."

"What?"

"Like guided imagining. You help someone relax. You ask them to close their eyes and look with their mind. Maybe you set the scene a little. Maybe say, 'You're looking at the hill. You're comfortable, laid-back, enjoying the warm sunshine, and you notice the trees and buildings and people around you. Look at them. What are you seeing . . . impressions, colors, movements?' . . . That sort of thing."

"I don't know if I could pull that off."

"Your own tone of voice is really important. And you have to be at ease. Convey safety, no pressure. Just gentle curiosity and confidence that of course the person can see what they saw before, perhaps even better this time because they're tranquil and focused without any agenda other than seeing and describing."

"Would you do it?"

"I told you. I'm full-up and will be for the next several hours."

"If I arrange it for after work and pick you up, will you do it?"

"I'll be off after five," she said, and the line went dead.

Was that a yes? He thought so.

Later today he'd pick up Duheen and Kiefer. Go back to the stable one more time to picture what happened to the other bodies. If Kiefer could detect the dead, the least Gates could do was follow a hunch.

He looked up to find Deputy Faraday standing in front of his desk. Gates barely knew her. Came from Alameda County Sheriff's in the Bay Area. Joined Sierra's department a month or so ago. She was late twenties, short brown hair in a mannish cut, a few inches under six feet, stocky. Gates thought her face looked Slavic but couldn't put that together with the name Faraday.

"You're full-court press on this uncleared with the homeless, right?"

Gates nodded. "Get anything on the security company uniforms, any matching?"

"Two. My notes there, under your cup."

"Oh, right. I'm getting up to speed . . ." Gates gestured to a chair. "Sit a minute?"

She ignored the invitation. "Elite out of Anderson has the same uniforms, no Riverton contracts, drives white SUVs. More likely, CarterGuard from here, same uniforms, mixed cruisers. A couple gray with black doors."

"Did you—"

"Heavyset young man, Gary Slazak, had one out two nights ago. The hospital and community clinic on Butte Street, primary client. Secondary, office buildings along Park View."

"Same area." Gates fumbled in his middle drawer for a working ballpoint. "You get a company client list?"

"Women can't do policework?"

"Hey, cut me some slack." Gates gestured again to the chair and Faraday again ignored it.

"Second page," she said, pointing to the notes.

"Look. I read your reports on the missing Barker kid. Good details, good work. You've got a better memory. More recent course work. I got a couple of years' experience." He held up his hands like surrender. "What do you want me to say? I needed your help yesterday."

"I was busy myself. Thanks would have covered it." She took a few steps to her desk, checked her iPhone for messages, and sat to her work. "I read your investigation logs," she said, without looking at him. "Adequate."

Once she left, Gates set her notes down and picked up his desk phone. He knew a local reporter, Doni Davis, who was relentlessly, marvelously nosy.

"Got time to help local constabulary?" He arranged a clipboard where he could write and talk at the same time.

"Not unless you're off traffic and onto the serious crime wave around here," Davis answered without missing a beat.

Gates held the phone away from his ear for a second. That was uncanny. "You got bugs in our dayroom?"

"You got bats in your belfry?"

"What crime?"

"That's most of the problem. Everybody ignores stuff that just keeps building. Another woman raped on the river trail, just last weekend. Anyway, if I have to tell you, we need to switch jobs."

Gates could hear noise in the background, the reporter was probably cooking something as she talked.

"I need some intel."

"Fire when ready."

"Chuck Barker?"

"Zilch, sorry."

"Uh, Roth Trask?"

"Met him. Don't know him. But you might be in luck. His mom's a sweet old purple-hair who just loves an opportunity to talk. Her travels, her volunteer work, her son, she can go for hours. She's usually at the country club around cocktail time."

"Which one?"

"Old money. The Riverdale on Bechelli."

"So when's cocktail time?"

"Now, if you're buying."

Gates waited.

"For her, I'm betting eleven-thirty until she sleeps in her dinner plate and they call a cab."

"A lush?"

"I'm not sure . . . Lonely."

"Hear anything about the homeless situation?"

"I hear they're a target."

"Hear from who?"

"The woman who heads the Progressive People Thrift Store was complaining to the mayor at the last council meeting I covered."

"Good source. Got any others?"

"I'll see what I can do."

Gates had changed out of his uniform into an old but respectable charcoal suit with a tie his wife had bought him before she left a hundred years ago.

No one stopped him when he waltzed into the the Riverdale Country Club like a longtime member. With the help of a bartender, he found Mrs. Trask where the reporter had suggested, sitting at a second-floor window table overlooking a practice green, enjoying a late-morning drink. She wore a light gray cashmere outfit with an A-line skirt and three-button jacket. A white satiny blouse peeked from underneath the coat and a fat string of costume pearls accented the line of her collar. There was nothing costume about her rings, at least two carats each in white gold settings. Her silver hair was softly curled and her face had a pleasant but slightly unfocused expression, like she'd been waiting quite a while for something to happen and nothing had materialized. She brightened as he slowed and stopped beside her table.

"Aren't you Mrs. Trask?" he said. "Didn't we meet at one of Roth's parties a while ago?"

The woman looked away from her glass of white wine, her eyes searching Gates's face for recognition. "Why, we very well might have, Mr. . . . uh . . ."

"Gates. Roman Gates. I'm an associate of your son in another business field."

"Oh, Roth. He certainly gets around. He met a million people through our business and he just keeps on."

"He's an amazing guy," Gates agreed. "May I sit for a few minutes before my twelve o'clock?"

She smiled and gestured to the chair.

"Wasn't he a fighter pilot?" Gates asked, and sat as she began talking.

"Oh my goodness, those nasty things. Their name escapes me but he flew jets."

"Warthogs?"

"Why, yes. Isn't that the most awful word?" She took a sip and waited for his confirmation. "Roth always said the men who flew them deserved the name. Cowboys, he called them."

"He and I went to the same high school but were a few years apart."

She nodded while she took one more careful sip. "He is so versatile. Good grades, debate, sports, and you know he went on to finish a double major at Chico University."

"You must be very proud." Gates clasped his hands on the table in front of him and gave her his undivided attention.

"My lord! Such a student. And of course he was on the golf team, but even then, I think his true love was flying. His first true love before Lillian."

"Lillian?"

She didn't seem to hear him.

"After college of course the Air Force was a dream come true. Fighter pilot. His snapshots looked like . . . Errol Flynn! Or is that too old for you? Everybody said he was so handsome, dignified . . . But that war. They say nobody gets out alive. I saw changes in him when he got home . . . Of course, he overcame those . . . things. Almost immediately, and threw himself into golf."

"Does he golf with Chuck? Officers in the same company . . ."

"You know Chuck? Of course he's Roth's half brother. His father's son by that earlier marriage. Took his mother's name after the divorce."

Gates hid his surprise, nodded as if this was old news.

"I think Chuck joined that club after Roth did. But Roth worked there. He taught, you know. My games are bridge and canasta," she said, touching her hair. "Exercise is so . . . uh . . ." She looked out at a foursome practicing putting and shook her head as if she could hardly believe the folly of it all.

Watching her drink was making Gates thirsty. "Wasn't Roth going pro?"

"Well now, wasn't that just the biggest disappointment? And him home from fighting that silly war. He was so good, and he tried and tried, and he simply didn't get any breaks." She took a last sip. "Would you like something?" she said, gesturing with her nearly empty goblet to a nearby waiter.

"No, thank you. I only have another minute or so."

"And when they wouldn't let him join that major . . . that tour I guess it was, he got so angry. I've never seen such a thing, more than disappointed. Furious. Enraged, I guess you'd say. It wasn't fair. A couple of silly scores, a couple of silly tournaments, and they barred the gates. I haven't watched a match since. Won't."

"It can be hard to recover from something like that."

"We didn't see him for a while. I guess he traveled. I was traveling. But maybe my Rothie just needed that setback in order to move forward. The next time I recall seeing him he knocked my hat off. Arm in arm with my husband. And no more polo shirts! Three-piece suit, four-hundred-dollar shoes. He was an executive! He told me he'd joined our company with the promise he'd be a partner in a few short years. I can tell you. He already looked the part. My husband, Charles . . . did you meet him?"

Gates shook his head.

"Charles had already hired Chuck . . . something about finances."

"Comptroller?" Gates asked.

"I don't know. I didn't pay much attention to the company." She broke off for a swallow from her newly arrived wine.

"Anyway, Charles made no such promise to Chuck. The company would eventually be Roth's and Roth's alone. Those two are so competitive—like any brothers, I suppose."

"Isn't Roth married?"

"Was. Was married." She shook her head sadly and took another sip. "While he was still in the service, Rothie married a local girl who'd gone away to university and returned. They had a daughter, Lillian. She's going to be eleven this year. I can hardly keep up. She's such a beautiful girl, and I suppose in my own way, I've helped raise her. Well, I certainly see her more since the divorce, but you know how silly young girls can be. We hardly have anything in common. It became final when she was seven. Of course, Roth fought for custody and won. The wife, god help me, I can't remember her name right now, just bowed out. I don't know whether she still lives in town." She paused for a decent swallow, dabbed her lips with the cocktail napkin.

"Roth still goes seventy hours a week at the office, but,

really, he lives for Lillian. Buys her everything, takes her everywhere. Vacations? My lord! Weren't they just in Venice? You'd know better than I."

She turned her head to look out beyond the putting green toward tall trees, placid in the afternoon sun, and recommenced her soft musings as Gates said a quiet goodbye and left without her seeming to notice.

Driving away, Gates thought Mrs. Trask drank the way he used to gamble. Too much was never enough. Must have a liver the size of a septic tank.

Back in the squad room, he made several phone calls gathering more info on Trask. Caught Faraday at her desk. "Got a minute for some late-breaking?"

She set the report she'd been reading on her blotter. "More homeless?"

"Looking at a different suspect."

"You were thinking Barker? Worked with Payne at Trask?"

Gates tried not to let his surprise show. Young and savvy. "Like that," he said, "same company, different guy."

Faraday uncovered a lined tablet from a stack of files. Poised to write. "Ready."

"Roth Trask, company's CEO?"

She nodded.

"Just met with his mother. Delighted to speak about her son. A couple of liters of wine didn't hurt."

Faraday tapped her pen on the tablet.

Gates got it. Impatient. "Hang on," he said. "A quick summary with a little research thrown in."

Faraday nodded but didn't smile.

"Roth probably came as a surprise," Gates began. "Both parents in their forties. Probably special from day one. Big expectations. In high school good grades, good at several sports, maybe too pompous to be well-liked. Father probably always expected perfection, criticized anything less. Mother thought he could have been a politician." Gates raised his eyebrows. "She said he surprised her with his 'thrill-seeking.' True love flying, later golf."

Faraday looked up at Gates. "I have a lot of work here."

"Duly noted. Think personality profile. Could a man like this kill David Payne?"

Faraday sighed, shrugged.

"After college, Air Force pilot. Action during the early Iraq War. Despised his peers." Gates watched Faraday make a note.

He continued. "Mother said the war changed him. Made him bitter and mean. Had terrible nightmares. Eventually snapped out of it and threw himself into golf."

"Train them to kill anything that moves and then put them back in town," Faraday said, shaking her head.

"Turns out Chuck Barker is Roth's half brother. Chuck is Charles Trask's first son by an earlier marriage, nearly twenty years older. Chuck had a serious falling-out with his father during the divorce, took his stepfather's last name when mother remarried. Barker also plays golf but not in Roth's league. Mom said no love lost between the two men. Competitive. Working relationship at best."

"Barker's a one-trick pony. Intimidation," Faraday said.

Gates nodded. "Mother said Roth was livid when he

failed to make the pro tour. Left home and disappeared. According to a golf buddy, Roth wound up spending time in New Orleans, Gulf Coast Louisiana and Mississippi. Tried his hand at professional gambling. Didn't work out."

Gates wanted to add, it *never* does, but didn't want to teach Faraday his own history if she didn't already know it.

"Came back, went into father's business with a partnership and the promise he'd inherit the company. Father Charlie Trask had previously mended fences with Chuck. Hired him as financial officer but never promised him anything. Roth kept Barker on in that position after Charlie died, until Chuck finally bought stock. Looks like buying in for ten percent elevated Barker from comptroller to chief financial officer."

Faraday was again drumming with the pen.

"Last bit," Gates said. "While he was in the Air Force, Roth married a local girl who had his child. The daughter may be eleven or twelve now. The couple divorced a few years ago. He fought for custody and won."

Gates noticed Faraday doodling a circle with a star inside.

"One more thing?"

The woman deputy groaned.

"Mother said he still goes seventy-hour weeks, but sounded like he's lost his passion for the company. Thinks he only cares about his daughter."

"Maybe the brush with the FBI shook him?"

"Could be."

Faraday looked at Gates. "So Roth's PTSD from the air wars, maybe even misses the hunt-and-kill. People say all that firepower at your fingertips is awesome. Hard to put aside. Residual anger flares up when he's thwarted. A workaholic narcissist, skilled with a golf club, competitive with his brother, implicated at least by association in the tax fraud. Daughter probably the only one in his life that passes muster."

Gates blinked. Good summation.

"Payne's barely in the same universe," she said, "until maybe he threatens to cash in with his insider info."

"That's what I've come to," Gates said. "Think we can prove it?"

Murray couldn't get comfortable on the short couch. He was too cramped, then too hot, then too cold. Didn't seem like he'd slept at all when another nightmare, dirt clods falling like hail, left him shaken. After that, there was no getting back to sleep. He grabbed Janochek's coat off its hook and left to visit Dearly.

"Hi, hon, how you doing? How's your girlfriend?" Dearly was perky as usual.

Did the dead ever sleep? Was that a stupid question? Murray had no idea. "Uh, haven't seen her lately. I don't know if she's my girlfriend. I'm not sure how to . . . or what I . . ."

"Guess it's complicated, huh?"

"I'm . . . not so good. Hearing more voices. I think they're from people who've been killed."

"Like that other girl? Murdered?"

"Yeah. Close to here. You don't hear anything like that, right?"

"How would I?"

"I've never asked. I thought there might be a difference between people who were killed and hidden, versus people who officially died and got buried."

"Officially died? Murr, you never fail to surprise me."

If a person could hear a smile, Murray did. "You know what I mean, right?"

"Like I told you before, I only know what my life was and what you tell me. I don't get any news."

"What do you think about?" Once the question was out, Murray realized it might be very rude. Very personal.

When Dearly finally spoke she was quieter.

"I'm . . . I don't really remember. Unless you're here."

"Oh, sure. You're . . . Sorry, I didn't mean to— Sorry." Murray knew he'd hurt her feelings. *Stupid!* "Could I ask you something else? Why would a person bury bodies on a steep hill?"

There was a minute or so of silence while Dearly considered the question. "Only reason, 'cause that would be a lot of work, only thing I can think of is so nobody would stumble on them."

"Yeah, nobody'd climb that hill. Nothing up there. A fence, cemetery on the other side, and it's simpler to get to that by walking around."

"Kids wouldn't go up there to drink?"

"Probably wouldn't think of it," Murray said. Starting to get a little sleepy, he rested his head on Dearly's stone, eyes level with the writing.

DEARLY BELOVED
BORN 1944   DIED 1969
IN BEAUTY REPOSE

"Why would somebody move the bodies he'd buried up there?"

"That's easy," Dearly said. "Found an even better place."

"Like where?"

"Deep lake, empty well, furnace . . . guess you have to ask the mafia."

That sounded right. There were lots of lakes and probably hundreds of abandoned mines or wells close to Riverton. Murray didn't want to picture a furnace. "Why would you leave one body behind?"

"That's a tough one."

Murray pictured Dearly scratching her head.

"Forgot?" She was thinking aloud. "No. Hard to imagine after he'd gone to all that trouble . . . Huh. Give me a day. Let me think about it."

Murray said good night, returned to the cottage, fell asleep as soon as his head touched his pillow.

Pearl padding to the bathroom and closing the door roused him. Two or three hours. Better than no sleep at all. He had to look as normal as possible for school. Nobody could get a whiff that he was back on the murder trail.

He folded his blanket and put it on top of his pillow, put both on the arm of the couch nearest the wall, began searching the living room for his homework. Pearl came out of the bathroom dressed with a towel rolled around her head like a turban. Murray didn't mean to, but he laughed. Pearl reddened and tore the towel off as she wheeled back to her room. *That went well.*

Murray found his school things and was standing in the cooking nook, trying to decide if he should make toast for everybody, when he heard Pearl yelling to her father about her softball mitt.

Janochek opened the door to his bedroom and headed toward the front door, flannel pajamas, leather moccasins,

197

and hair like a haystack. He banged out without a word and came back a minute later holding a baseball glove under his arm. Noticed Murray in the kitchen. "Toaster only works if you put the bread in it," he said, and tossed the mitt on the dining table before going into the bathroom. Immediately stuck his head back out. "Word to the wise. Tomorrow afternoon at three? Sierra's conference schedule begins. Pearl's first actual league game. Sierra Field. A smart man would be there. Cheering. Loud." He closed the door and in a couple of seconds the shower was running.

Murray stuck in four slices of bread and found peach preserves in the cupboard. Found the butter in the fridge. Noticed that the programmed coffeemaker had already brewed a pot and wondered if a cup would energize him. He and Pearl had missed school yesterday. He couldn't afford to miss again today and fall behind. He was still going to be the first Kiefer ever to graduate from high school!

It didn't motivate him, but the bitter brew did make him feel a little crisper, and he tried not to think about missing bodies while he buttered the first round of toast and set the pieces on small plates around the dining table. Did Pearl want milk? Probably. He filled her glass, then one for himself, and set a coffee cup by Janochek's plate. Was this what it was like to have a family? If it was, it felt great. Doing something for people you . . . loved? Could he use that word?

Pearl broke his reverie. "Hey," she said, spreading jam on her toast and sorting through the fridge before coming out with a hunk of cheddar. "What you doing after school tomorrow?"

Thanks to Janochek, Murray had the right answer. "I'll be there," he said, and wondered if he would.

Gates called him out of trig. Knocked on the classroom door, poked his head in, and then stood in the hall waiting. You could see him right through the dang window. This was not the low profile Murray had been trying to cultivate. Before he even stood, his classmates were buzzing. Murray caught the words "dead" and "creepy," and he couldn't get out of class fast enough. Wouldn't the teacher shut them up? Old man Fender was probably lost in a quadratic equation and hadn't heard Gates in the first place.

"I'd appreciate a little more help and I have someone I want you to meet." Gates, hat in hand in the hallway.

Great. Not *How are you* or *I'm not here to scare you* or *I'm sorry I reminded everybody in your class that you're delusional.* Murray kept his eyes on the floor and waited for this to pass. Maybe the man would just go away.

"I asked at the office. Your principal said I could borrow you for the rest of the afternoon."

Murray glanced at his wrist. Years ago one of his mother's guys had given him a plastic watch. He'd only had it for a few weeks before it froze up, so how did he form this stupid habit? He put his left arm behind him.

"You don't have to talk for a while," Gates said, leaning a little closer as if to make sure he wasn't overheard. "I have some things to tell you and I want to get out of here to do it. Do you like donuts?"

That brought Murray's head up. What the hell was

the matter with this guy? Murray never thought about donuts.

"I mean we could get a snack or we could just drive over to Mary Lake and sit at one of those picnic tables. It's actually kind of sunny. Anyway, I'll talk for a bit and then I want you to meet someone. Do you need anything before you leave?"

Murray nodded. Went back into class for his books and papers, no eye contact, humming to himself to keep from hearing comments. Stopped down the hall at his locker for his history and English notebook. Looked up at Gates. The man nodded and led the way out the front door to the cruiser.

Mary Lake was always a surprise—sometimes an algae-covered pit that looked solid enough you could drive a truck across it. Other times clean, green, and mysterious with glimpses of wispy ferns swaying along the bottom, small fish moving among them. Murray sat at a concrete one-piece picnic table. Within a minute the thick cement bench had numbed his butt and threatened to vacuum away every degree of warmth he possessed. To distract himself from the chill, he scanned for turtles basking on mostly submerged limbs close to the shore.

Gates stood beside the table, facing the lake, tracking small, fast-moving birds darting from bush to deadfall to bush again. He shaded his eyes to better see a blue heron poised in shallow water by the reeds. "I'm never sure," Gates said, "are there kingfisher here, too?"

Murray knew he wasn't asking, just talking.

"That's a cormorant." Gates pointed across the lake to a large black bird perched on a stump, studying the surface. "Great fisherman." The man half turned away from the water to watch a family of quail scurry out of the brush, run along the paved path for a few feet, and dart back in.

"You've had bad experiences with people like me."

Murray knew the talking had started even though Gates was still standing beside the table not even looking at him. "I visited your home along with a county social worker a few years ago to see if we needed to remove you."

Murray winced. He didn't remember Gates, but he remembered that visit. Remembered being terrified. Not that he'd have to leave his mom but that they might put him in a crazy hospital. For a long time he'd felt strange and different and didn't know what might happen if doctors got ahold of him.

"Last winter, I accused you of killing the Parker girl. Not because I knew you or thought you could do it, but because you seemed to know a lot about her and that made me suspicious. You wouldn't tell me what was really going on and that also made me suspicious. And you were right. I didn't believe it, but I finally used what you told me to arrest the killer."

Gates sat now, and continued to watch the lake as he talked. "And just yesterday I couldn't believe you knew something about the case I was currently working on. Too big a coincidence. You had to have heard it from somebody and decided to get a little more press. But you hadn't. It was a different coincidence—somebody buried those people close enough to your cemetery that you could hear their voices.

The killer's going to kick himself for that." Gates zipped his jacket higher.

"So our . . . rocky relationship is mostly my fault," he said, glancing at Murray. "I couldn't believe that you actually hated publicity. That you weren't proud of your . . . ability. I thought you were shucking and I was wrong. This isn't fun for you. Just the opposite. Right?"

Murray didn't respond.

"Your ability is worrisome and strange and kids at school tease you about it and you don't exactly understand it yourself, right? That's my guess. Well, more than a guess—I've been trying to pay better attention."

Gates shifted his weight as if the bench were cold for him, too.

"If I were you, I'd be very wary. I'd think this cop is just trying to manipulate me." He took a deep breath. "And that would be true. I'm trying to work together because I need your talents." Now he caught Murray's eye.

"Several times when I'm on a case . . ." He trailed off and shifted his gaze back out to the shoreline. Absentmindedly rubbed above his ear.

Murray felt the man's discomfort and wondered what he was trying to say.

"I'm embarrassed to admit," Gates continued, "I've been wishing for your, uh, expertise. Wishing I could get you to ask a dead person a couple of questions that would help me solve some . . ." He shook his head. "Sorry. I'm out of line. Forget about it."

Murray raised a hand as if he could push Gates's words away. The man who'd once called him a liar and a killer had somehow come to believe in his talking with the dead? Didn't seem possible. More, it was a scary idea. And yet . . . what if he could actually help catch other murderers?

Gates broke into his thoughts. "Anyway, you don't have to make a decision right now, about me or working with me. You have every right to examine my words, my actions, as closely as I examined you. Decide if you'll trust me. I'm hoping I can gradually earn that from you and the girl."

"Pearl," Murray said.

"She's a pistol, huh?"

If you only knew!

"We're done for now," Gates said, looking like he was ready to get up. "Anything you want to ask?"

If I tell you something impossible, will you believe me or will you start accusing? Murray decided to wait and see.

Gates stood. "Let's get a couple of burgers and go meet a woman named Duheen. She might teach us something."

Murray thought Duheen pretty. Taller than he was, shiny brown hair, nice smile. She walked down the steps of the sprawling building, opened the back door of the cruiser, and introduced herself. Murray said his name and they were off.

"In a few minutes we're going to do some memory work," Duheen said. "It's an exercise you may not have tried before but it's pretty common. Artists do it, writers do it. I often use it with people to help them think about things they enjoy. When we get to the . . ."

"Rodeo grounds," Gates supplied.

"We'll do this together. I'll ask some questions and you'll

see if there's anything you remember. There's no right or wrong answers. It's all good either way."

Murray felt his chest ease, glad this wasn't going to be a test.

The three of them stood in front of the cruiser, facing the hill maybe thirty feet away. Duheen began. "Take a couple of deep breaths, see if you can get your stomach to pooch out when you inhale so you get a lot of air. That helps some people relax, and then you'll close your eyes and tell me some things about being here before. Okay?"

Murray nodded, and when he started it was nothing special.

"Can you picture the hill in front of you?"

Nod.

"What's a couple of things you see?"

"Bushes and trees."

"Higher up?"

"More trees. There was a rope tied to a tall one near the top."

"What else?"

"A couple of times the ground was all messed up like somebody'd raked it."

"Anything more?"

"There's a hedge way up at the top."

"More?"

He shook his head.

"Okay move back down, and in your mind's eye, what

do you see to your right?" Duheen's voice was so soft and smooth.

"The stable . . . the wall, actually, and the posts that keep the front roof up." Murray was surprised how easy it was to see with his eyes closed.

"Anything else?"

"A few cars and trucks . . . parked."

"Anything more?"

"Some buildings . . . sheds way farther down."

"Anything in them?"

"I don't know. I never went close."

"Okay, in your mind's eye, what's behind you?"

"This blacktop and white parking stripes . . . a big lawn in front of the center . . . the center driveway, uh, street, by the front doors."

"Can you see a truck in that portico?" This from Gates.

Murray was jarred by the different voice but kept his eyes closed.

"For the rest of the time I'll be the only one that speaks," Duheen said.

Murray heard an edge in her voice and imagined her frowning at Gates.

"It may be shady under the portico . . . can you see anything in there?"

"A truck . . . one time . . . I think somebody watching."

"What do you notice about it?"

"A . . . I don't . . . whitish. A van shape." Though his eyes were closed, Murray squinted. "Maybe blue license plates. I'm not sure."

"Can you see what's on the plate?"

Murray shook his head.

"Okay, anything else?"

Murray turned his head to the right, radar. "No people. Other cars, way over on the far road along the river."

"All right, look to your left. What do you see?"

"A bit of the freeway, the rink, the start of the trees where Pearl hid, the blue Dumpster—" Murray forgot what he was doing and opened his eyes. "Right there by those barrels," but even as he said it he could see the waste container was no longer there. "It was locked. I couldn't understand. How's anybody supposed to—" *Oh.* He knew where the bodies had been when he heard them at the bottom of the hill while he was talking to the cop. And he knew why he didn't hear them later. The Dumpster was gone.

"I forgot," he said, looking at the barrel area. "I think . . ." but Gates was on his cell phone and Duheen had passed behind him heading for a faded dirt outline beside the barrels.

Gates stopped for drive-through donuts on his way to drop Duheen back at the hospital. Three glazed old-fashioned. Murray took his gingerly, remembering he'd had donuts before but never one that looked like this. He watched Duheen eat hers and half of the one Gates held. Got busy eating his own.

When she left for her own car, Gates turned to Murray. "That was really good work."

Murray colored. "I should have remembered before."

"Nobody remembers everything. Thanks for being willing to try this."

At the department Gates immediately checked Faraday's notes. No mention of CarterGuard's or Trask's waste disposal contracts. No reason there should have been. Now there was. He couldn't reach anyone at Trask after five. Got a Carter-Guard dispatcher. The security company shredded unnecessary documents and emptied their green city container once a week.

The following morning at eight Gates was on his cell with the operations manager at the engineering company.

"Since we have such big projects, it's been cheaper for us to obtain our own waste disposal permit on land adjacent to the industrial park," the woman told him. "We rent Decker's Dumpsters for the same reason. Cost-effective. They place and pick up wherever we're building."

Gates thanked her and called Decker.

A secretary answered the phone and then his question. "Color? Blue. That sets us apart from the green city containers."

Next call, Roth Trask's office. The CEO's secretary said he'd been called out of town and wouldn't be available until the following week.

Gates didn't know whether Trask and Barker were involved in the homeless crimes separately or together, or for that matter, at all. All his evidence was circumstantial. Not nearly enough for a home search warrant.

He got Trask's residential address, Harvard Heights subdivision. Drove across town and up Quartz Hill Road to a five-thousand-square-foot McMansion. No one answered the front bell, and the attached garage had no windows. Gates checked the street, the surrounding neighborhood. Didn't see anyone. Put on a glove and forced the roll-up door. One car, a racing green Corvette with convertible top. No light gray van.

In the backyard, a pool surrounded by wide tile paving,

a pump shed peeking from behind huge, terraced boulders. Centerpiece, a waterfall. No one there.

He spent the next two hours trying to eliminate one of the two men as a suspect.

Couldn't.

Gates pulled Kiefer out of afternoon class for the second day in a row. Watched the students while the boy gathered his things. Some derision, but maybe some envy? Not everybody was important enough to an investigation to be called out of school two days running. And Gates bet at least some of the kids knew Murray was helping. Kids found out everything whether you wanted them to or not. Probably a few rumors had Kiefer being interrogated like a criminal, but others probably had him solving another crime. At least that was how it seemed from the expressions he saw following the boy to his locker and out the front door.

Murray watched Gates adjust the blue tarp to make it thicker. Smoothed it on the bench at his side of the concrete table. Took the army blanket and folded it into a two-foot square pad. Laid it on Murray's bench.

"Takes the chill off," he explained. "You ready for another story?"

Murray wasn't sure.

Gates put his hands on the picnic table and looked at them as if words might be printed on their backs.

"I've been with the Sheriff's Department most of twenty-five years. Early on I got married and about twenty years ago my wife and I had a son. For most of those years I loved my work. I loved my family . . . and I enjoyed my hobby. Gambling." Gates looked into the distance for a moment, at nothing in particular.

Murray could sense the man's increasing discomfort and wondered why he was talking about his family. What difference did it make?

"Something happened to me ten or eleven years ago, and I began to lose track of my work and my loved ones. Gambling became nearly all I thought about—winning, of course . . . the unpredictability . . . I wouldn't have said it ruled my life. I'm not sure I even realized it, but gradually, it took me over . . . or I gave myself to it. A hundred percent.

"I was restless. Could hardly wait for the next casino, the next game . . . some seemed to be luckier than others and they shifted back and forth . . . and like any gambler who gets obsessed, I began losing more than I could afford. It was obvious the only way to get out of the hole was to gamble harder. Bigger bets, bigger payoffs . . . but not many paid off." He caught Murray's eye. "You understand this so far?"

Murray didn't trust his voice right then. Nodded.

"I wagered and lost my savings, my wife's savings, spent my son's college fund, and then I refinanced our house and went through that and defaulted, couldn't make the mortgage. I sold my truck and drove a junker . . . I lost everything. Every last thing. And one evening I got in a fight trying to borrow money to pay a debt . . . a bad fight . . . I was desperate, crazy by that time, and I wound up in my own jail. I usually tell people I resigned because I'm still ashamed. Truth is, I lost my job. Fired. And within weeks my wife left me. And my son came to hate the sight of me."

Gates bit his lip for a second, continued. "I had to go to rehab south of here, down in St. Helena, had to start attending twelve-step groups . . . but my son . . . who'd once loved me and been proud of me . . . got sick at heart . . . lost his way . . . I don't . . . my son wound up overdosing on a 'speedball.' Cocaine and heroin. And the coroner said it . . ."

Murray had put his own hands on the table. Pushing. Ready to get up and run. *Don't tell me!*

But Gates finished. "Said it was intentional. Suicide. My son meant to kill himself."

It was quiet except for a dog barking behind them and the occasional rattle of branches as the breeze rifled through.

No! Too many feelings. Murray was up, away from the table, heading toward the paved path that circled the lake among trees and heavy foliage. Gates would still be there when he returned.

Murray knew way more than he wanted to know. That's the thing about living people. They have terrible secrets or terrible sadness. Pearl's mom didn't really love her. Ran off with some man and only returned home when she was dying from cancer. And then Pearl and Janochek had to take care of her and watch her die.

Sandray had a really sad story, but at least hers was over. It wouldn't keep getting worse. Awful things wouldn't keep happening.

He knew he would never see Gates the same. The man was big and tough but he hurt. Murray knew what that was like. To be hurting, helpless in the face of it. Can't find a way to make the hurting stop, can't find a way to make anything better. Murray's mom and her men and the way some of her men treated him and the way his mom took their side . . .

Gates wasn't a superhero. He was a father with an ache. Deep. Painful. Murray was familiar with an ache you could drown in.

Ten minutes later, on the far shore, he was too busy with these thoughts to pay any attention to the foliage or the wildlife, or the water. Too absorbed to notice a van parked where the path left the lake and became a sidewalk. Too distracted to hear doors open. Too stunned to yell when the bag went over his head.

By the bottom of the third, Pearl already had two unassisted put-outs and had batted once—a grounder to third—out on a good throw. Resting on the dugout bench, she calculated if the next two girls got on base she would bat again this inning. Her team was behind by a single run, but she was pretty sure they could come back on the Lake Central squad. Especially in front of home fans. She had waved to her dad a couple of times and noticed he was alone in the bleachers. Murray must have been held up.

By the seventh inning, she didn't have such generous thoughts. *He's not coming!* At the plate she struck out on three straight pitches, swinging for the fence every time, and threw her bat all the way to the backstop. Earned her a lecture from the coach. At the top of the eighth, another girl took Pearl's place at second base.

That was fine with her. She couldn't focus on the game anyway. That creep! If dead people were playing he'd be here in a flash. Come on, Cadavers! You can do it! He was hopeless. Such an idiot. She hated herself for caring about him. She'd told her dad that. But she kept getting sucked in. Murray had touched the cap. That started it this time. And the body thing. He got in such interesting predicaments it was hard not to join him. He was so different. But when it really counted, he disappointed you.

Was that true? She had to dig up Nikki Parker by herself. Murray hung back and watched. Just a day ago she'd had to threaten him to make him go back to the hillside and discover the bodies had been moved. *Oh god!* Here she was, pissed and fuming, but what if something had happened? What if somebody had been watching and followed him . . . and . . .

She couldn't think of anything to say to the coach that would make sense. He was mad at her anyway. She scooped up her glove and snuck out the side gate to the astonished looks of her peers. Coaches were on the field managing the game. They didn't see her leave or hustle behind the bleachers, forgetting her gym bag in the dugout. Didn't hear her yell her dad's name.

When Janochek joined her behind the concession stand he was sputtering. "What the heck do you think you're doing? They'll throw you off the team. You'll get a reputation you might not be able to erase."

Pearl held up her hand, like he did to her sometimes, to stop his tirade. "Murray's not here, right?"

Her father's face fell. "No," he said, shaking his head. "Something must have come up." He looked at the sky for a minute, thinking. Rubbed his cheek. "Maybe he forgot again. I know he didn't mean to." Janochek wondered what he was accomplishing by making up these excuses.

"I'm worried." Pearl's voice shook.

"Worried . . . ?" The possibility that Murray might be in trouble had never occurred to Janochek. Maybe if Pearl had no-showed it would have, but Murray was just missing a softball game. As usual. Janochek automatically reached for his cell, and stopped when he remembered Murray didn't have one. It was still in his hand when it rang.

The number was cloaked and he didn't recognize the voice. A man asking about Murray.

"Say again?" he asked as he and Pearl looked at each other. "No. No, he's not with us. We're at a softball game. Why?"

Within seconds Janochek closed his eyes as he listened. "We're going right now." He grabbed Pearl's hand, pulling her toward his truck as he tucked the phone back in his shirt pocket.

Pearl dug her feet in and pulled him to a stop. "What?"

"Gates. Murray was with him at Mary Lake and left for a walk. He might be missing." Janochek cursing himself for not anticipating this.

They jogged for the vehicle.

Janochek and Pearl were unable to identify Gates's cruiser when they got to the lake so they looked for Murray. Took the three-quarter-mile drive around the shoreline, followed each street that led out into the Mary Lake neighborhood. After no success, they drove back to the picnic tables at the eastside shoreline and waited for Gates to appear. Janochek attempted to reach the deputy by phone but didn't have Gates's "unknown" number.

When they saw him, he was walking beside a female deputy and speaking into a handheld radio. He put the radio away but continued a conversation with the woman. Caught Janochek's wave and headed in their direction.

"We've got units all over this neighborhood, down Placer, down Eureka Way. Why don't you all go on home and wait for him there? He's probably just wandering back." Gates noticed the deputy at his side staring at him. "This is his, uh, family," he explained. "Mr. Janochek and his daughter, Pearl. They're involved in the homeless investigation . . . found the woman's body."

The female officer's look softened.

"Pearl, Mr. Janochek, this is Deputy Faraday. I'm her right-hand man."

Faraday scowled at him.

"Mr. Janochek's the cemetery caretaker, the place where Nikki Parker was found?"

Faraday looked at Janochek, who nodded.

"Anyway," Gates said, "Faraday and I have to coordinate the neighborhood search, maybe somebody saw . . . I'll get back to you as soon as we know anything." He handed Janochek his card with a phone number ballpointed at the top. "This'll reach me anytime."

"Find a guy with a van," Pearl said. She could see it.

That reminded Gates he hadn't finished examining the CarterGuard security firm's client list, nor had he done the necessary DMV vehicle registration searches. In spite of his late start, Gates had actually thought himself a little ahead of the curve. He had two major suspects for the bookkeeper's murder and he believed he had the motive. Mistake. Now things were breaking too fast. The Kiefer kid might be in grave danger and Gates had lost the trail of the other bodies. He was suddenly embarrassed to bring Faraday up to speed. *Men can't do policework?*

When he did, she was all business. "You call the interview team," she told him. "I'll call DMV."

"Ask for both," he told her. "Roth Trask and the vehicle list for Trask engineering. We might be looking for a white or gray GMC van." He paused for a second. "Check Barker's wife's name. See if he registered a van to her."

She scowled again and he got it. She'd read his log and case reports, had anticipated his request. It had been a while since he'd partnered with another investigator so quick on the uptake. "When you can, get a line on Trask construction sites." Gates felt like adding "worst case scenario" but didn't want to jinx the boy.

Faraday drew her phone and spoke as she dialed. "CarterGuard e-mailed. I remember their clients. You're looking for Trask about the rodeo grounds? The answer's yes. And Carter patrols Trask construction sites."

Gates, nodded, impressed again, but now on the phone to deputies and community liaison workers that were canvassing Lakeside Drive and the nearby subdivision. He faintly heard Faraday ask a DMV clerk to e-mail the vehicle information "priority one, missing juvenile." Looking around him, he saw Janochek and Pearl were gone, their truck no longer on the street. Had the girl been wearing a baseball uniform?

Janochek was chewing his lip, furious at himself for overlooking this possibility. Pearl, restless beside him, crossing and uncrossing her legs, window up, window down, made it even harder to focus on driving.

"I forgot my goddamn bag!" she said, out of nowhere.

He knew what she meant. "I'll call the coach. Somebody'll have it."

"He could already be dead," she blurted, and hid her face.

Nothing Janochek could say to that. It might be true. Or maybe they were upset for nothing. Gates always made Murray nervous. Maybe the boy couldn't stand any more contact and walked away. Murray wouldn't try to explain his feelings. He'd just go.

Janochek took every shortcut to the cemetery, but before they turned in he drove the length of Continental, then swung by the rodeo grounds just in case Murray'd taken a detour.

Gates gave instructions to call him immediately if anyone in the neighborhood had seen something useful. Took his car down back streets on the chance he might see Kiefer walking. By the time he reached the department he felt sure the boy had been taken.

He needed more information in order to guess which man to target. He'd learned a good deal about Roth from his Google search, his phone calls, and his conversation with the mother. He'd been focused on Chuck Barker, early on. Wife beater. He had his personal impressions, but really, he didn't know much about Barker's history. Company CFO, half brother to Roth, apparently not the father's favorite. Gates sat at his desk, clicked search on the computer.

Chuck Barker graduated from Sierra High in 1972. Lettered in football and track. Went to Sac State on a football scholarship but never played. Why? Argument with the coaches? Played no college sports of record. No activities other than ROTC. Graduated with business degree in 1976. Joined Army Infantry that same summer but was not offered a commission. Got a General Discharge 1979, suggesting punishment for unacceptable military behavior.

Got an MBA from a Bay Area diploma mill, 1983. Held a variety of jobs in Northern California businesses until 2003 when he was hired as a financial officer in his father's engineering firm. Promoted to comptroller March 2008, shortly after father's death. In 2009 became Trask's chief financial officer after purchasing 10 percent of the stock.

Gates's search on LinkedIn revealed several memberships

in business organizations. Only hobby listed, target shooting. Gates shook his head. He'd hoped for more.

He called Duheen, left a message that the boy had disappeared on his watch. Phoned the Barker home. No answer. The woman was probably too depressed or sedated to respond. He drove by the Trask building, saw Barker's Lexus in the lot, and drove on to speak with Mrs. Barker again in person.

No one answered his knock. Side door to the garage was unlocked. Gates decided he could use a personal welfare check on the wife as justification for entering the premises. He gloved and walked in past the dusty Mercedes to the Land Cruiser. Opened the doors, looked for any evidence that Murray had recently been a passenger. Nothing.

Back on the front porch he knocked again, courtesy, but didn't expect a response. He remembered Barker charging through the door the evening Gates confronted him. When Gates tried the handle, it turned easily and the door glided inward.

No response when he stood in the foyer and called her name. The guest bathroom door was open, the living room empty. Ditto the kitchen, dining room, and vast glassed-in porch across the back. Gates stood at the foot of the stairs and called. Called from the top of the stairs. Started all the way down the hall to his left. Jerell's room. Everything tidy. Books and papers in neat stacks on the large computer desk.

Gates took a moment to open the big laptop and turn it on but it wouldn't light, wouldn't boot. When he turned it over he saw loose screws, as if the battery, maybe even the hard drive, had been removed.

Rock band posters and American city scenes—San Diego, Seattle, New York—plastered the walls. Did the boy dream of running away to another city? Had he been planning to "disappear" for a long time? Gates picked through the stacks of notebooks and loose papers hoping for a journal, but found nothing useful and returned to the hall.

The next door revealed a bathroom, the next a guest room, and at the far end, a huge master bedroom with French doors to a balcony. Those let in the available light; the rest of the windows were close-curtained. First, a dressing and reading area. In the middle, two leather recliners and floor lamps. On Gates's left, padded benches flanking two walk-in closets. An equally generous bathroom to his right with granite counters, double sinks, double toilets, and a tiled doorless walk-in shower. An archway led to the rest of the suite, more sitting areas and a mirrored makeup table with a carved wooden chair near more curtained windows.

Mrs. Barker lay on the king-size bed, hair tangled and dull. She wore a frilly gown, a thick comforter pulled to her waist. Her snore was regular but light, and a ribbon of drool slipped from the corner of her mouth down her chin. She roused when Gates shook her, but not enough to speak coherently. Her eyelids opened to half-mast, she didn't appear to comprehend, if indeed she saw anything in particular.

The side table had a small lamp, digital clock-radio, glass of water, and eight or nine half-full orangish prescription containers, several with their lids off. Gates picked three of the lidless. Zoloft, Klonopin, Ambien. Common meds he recognized from street busts: antidepressant, anti-anxiety, and sleeping pill. He returned to the bathroom and wet a washcloth. Sat the woman upright, held her with arm around her shoulder, and gently bathed her face. She faded, head lolling on his chest, and he called for an ambulance. There'd be no interview this afternoon.

When the paramedics left, Gates put a note on the kitchen table telling Barker the name of the hospital. After following the ambulance and making his report to the admissions nurse, he headed back toward the department. Since he had no messages, he phoned Faraday for a report. She sounded weary.

No witnesses. No sign of the boy.

He stopped at a local taqueria for a burrito. Had no taste for it, ate to keep going. No sense staying at his home tonight. He'd sleep at the office and wait for something to break. In the office he changed his mind. No place in the squad room or the locker area that was comfortable. He'd take his radio and cell to his truck, recline the seat all the way, at least get a long nap.

Murray blacked out after he was slammed on the floor. Some-one hit him really hard in the stomach and he couldn't get any air and he'd hit his head when he was dropped . . . but now he realized he was riding, being driven somewhere. *Uh-oh.* The fear hit him, brought him wide-awake. *Kidnapped.* His thoughts raced too fast to organize. *Yell! No, don't let them know you're awake. Run! Stay still! You're going to die! Get a grip!* . . . He struggled to quiet his gasping, struggled to think, but the vehicle stopped and fear again overwhelmed him.

He was jerked backward and pulled to his feet. Banged his ear on something and it blazed while he was being steered forward, stumbling, having to walk faster to stay on his feet. In seconds he was smashed against a wall. Chill metal, not wood, and then the sound of a door opening, and he was pulled away from the wall and shoved forward. His shins and knees cracked on unseen steps and he was skidding on a cold slick floor, concrete or linoleum, and a person's steps were coming in with him but a phone began ringing and a man began cursing and a door slammed and the room vibrated briefly and became still.

Murray had no idea where he was or who had taken him, but he knew this was lethal. He thought he was alone—hoped he was alone, probably not for very long, and he had an idea from the feel of the outside wall and the vibration of the room that he was in a trailer and he knew he had to do something. *Right now!*

When he tried to pull the sack off his head he found he was handcuffed; he'd been so scared he hadn't felt it, hadn't even noticed. What do you do about that? He pulled his hands apart. Too tight. Tried to shrug like you'd take off a coat. Still too tight. He bent his knees and tucked his feet and slid the cuffs over his shoes so his hands were in front and he could pull off the sack.

He was in a trailer. Directly in front of him, a wooden chair with a roll of duct tape resting on the seat. Murray knew that was for him, knew he had to run. Thank god his feet were free! He wheeled and saw the door he'd been pushed through, but the man was probably too close. Another door? Desks at one end, booth on the other, upholstered benches on either side of a built-in table. Closet-looking door at the back middle, just past a small sink . . . He tore it open—tiny toilet, no window. Window! He jumped on the built-in table and kicked at the window above it. Nothing. *Kick the goddamn thing!* The blow, loud as hell, shook the whole trailer and the window cracked across. He jumped down, grabbed and swung the wooden chair through it and it broke out still cased in its corroded metal frame and he dived, in the air, picturing landing on glass, shards in his chest, but no, he hit dirt and gravel and he was running. A twenty-foot shipping container . . . around the side . . . no ladder, can't fit under. A fence! . . . too tall . . . a big yellow whatdoyoucallit? Loader? No doors, cracked leather seat, steering wheel—big yellow arms holding a huge scoop high in front of it. Murray gained the floor in a leap, was up on the seat and jumped for the bucket—hit it halfway and lost his breath again but no time. He scrambled over the lip and down, scrunched in the gravelly bottom. He heard a yell, but he was still wheezing too hard to make out the words. Not far off. Running steps, running past, now cursing, now more running and then silence.

Murray tried to imagine what the person looked like but couldn't—had to be strong, at least a little taller. Nothing useful. Nothing but pure red fear. He started to close his eyes so he wouldn't focus on his wrists and the damn handcuffs. Hesitated. His right wrist was bloody, ripped by the metal band during his scrambles. His left wrist . . . the cuff wasn't exactly on his wrist. It was a couple of inches up his arm, pretty tight around the fabric of his hoodie. *Jeez!* It took several minutes to work the cloth above the cuff and slide the thing down to the meat of his hand.

Was it possible? He had to do it even if it was impossible. He kneaded and tugged the skin under, pushed the cuff farther and farther toward his fingers and now that hand was bleeding and he was sure he was breaking his thumb. He tried to use his feet but his shoes kept slipping. He trapped the cuff on the back lip of the bucket and used his weight to hang and pull. When the joint of his thumb gave way, the thing popped off. Murray fell to the bottom cradling his damaged hand, squirming, trying to stifle his damn moaning.

When his breathing quieted and his heart stopped ramming his chest, he lay as still as he could, as if still equaled invisible. He hurt. The steel bucket was cold, little things were poking him, his back itched, wrists burned, thumb throbbed, but he didn't move. At all. For hours. Even after it got dark, because during that time he was listening. At first, one voice yelling, and thirty minutes or an hour later two or three more. And the sound of cars. Brakes. Starting, stopping. Doors opening and closing. And he pretended he was dead, still as death. And there was more . . . he couldn't believe it. He was hearing other voices not far away. Voices he'd heard before. On a hill.

Came a time when he hadn't heard anything except the dead voices for quite a while. Like a snake, like an oil slick, he oozed to the lip of the bucket, to the front corner, and hair by hair, raised his head till he could see. It wasn't that dark. Five or six bright lights on tall poles shone down on a . . . junkyard? An equipment lot? A construction site?

Way off, maybe a half mile away, some new buildings were joined together with metal scaffolds around them. He could see past the container where he'd wanted to hide, could see part of a light-colored trailer.

Surrounding everything a tall chain-link fence with barbed wire staked at the top. Forty or fifty feet in front of him, two patrol cars. White with gray doors. Trunk to trunk. Beside them, two men standing, facing opposite directions, scanning the lot, shining their flashlights toward any noise. Watching. Waiting for Murray to give himself away.

He was trembling. Fear? Cold? Or maybe it was his thumb. It was killing him. Small blessing. At least he was right-handed. He knew he had to make a run for it. Couldn't stay in the bucket till daylight and somebody needed to use it. And daylight would screw him anyway. Darkness was the only thing he had going. And surprise. That reminded him. He shoved the empty cuff over the first three fingers of his right hand and twisted to tighten the short cuff chain—a big clumsy ring but he couldn't afford to have it rattling loose or clanking against the bucket. When it felt tight enough to stay, he slipped down and sorted through the gravel for a stone big enough to throw. Big enough to make some noise. Found two, a little over an inch in diameter. He'd throw them both. At the same time. Opposite from where he'd run. So which way would he go and what could he do about that fence?

He slithered to the lip at the back of the bucket where the men couldn't see him and surveyed the yard. If he hung down and dropped from that side, he'd land on dirt. The fence was maybe twenty feet away. He could climb it. *Had* to climb it. The barbed wire? He'd take off his hoodie right now and carry it with him. Lay it over the points and hope for the best, because he had to get all the way to the top and jump. Out beyond in that direction he saw only darkness, no houses or lighted farm buildings. The field by the fence might be plowed. That would make his landing softer but it would be harder to run. And the sweatshirt would be stuck up on the fence, telling the men where he'd escaped.

Maybe that was the answer. He risked rising even higher to look in the opposite direction. Dark. Tiny light on a hill miles away. Okay, he'd jump and brush his footprints for thirty or forty feet so they wouldn't know which direction he was heading. He'd run around to the opposite side of the compound, to where he'd first thrown the rocks because the guys would have heard the damn fence jangle and come toward the loader. A stab of doubt hit him like a spear. Was this even possible? But he couldn't stay. He was pretty sure they were going to kill him and put him with the others.

He kept scanning till he found the entry gate. Good, he'd run for the other side.

GO!

He tore off the hoodie and flung the rocks. Watched the men react. Shine their flashlights, jog toward the sound. And he was off, leg over, hanging by his fingers, dropping, running for the fence, jamming his fingers and shoes in the chain-link holes and scrambling. At the stakes he flipped his hoodie over the three wires and it caught and he tugged it until it was wide enough to crawl on . . . *Ow!* It poked him anyway but he was at the top and got his feet under him and jumped praying not to break anything and hit and lurched face-forward getting dirt in his mouth and jamming his bad thumb when he tried to break his fall. But he could stand! He ripped off his T-shirt to wipe his footprints and hustled, a count of thirty, brushing as he went. He didn't have long. And then he lay flat in the dirt to see what the men were going to do before he ran any farther.

Their flashlight beams jabbed this way and that until they spotted the hoodie and then he could see them at the fence focusing straight out and yelling. One left within seconds while the other continued to shine his flashlight back and forth in a short arc the way they thought he'd run.

And now Murray ran again, low to the ground. Had to get to the end of this fence and turn the corner so if the one guy who'd left raced out the front gate and drove the perimeter to the hoodie, he wouldn't see Murray up ahead. It felt like a mile, couldn't have been that far, when Murray made the corner and stopped, hands on knees to get a good breath. Saw dirt mashed in his bloody wrists. Nothing to be done about that.

Headlights? *NO!* Murray barely had time to register that

the guy'd gone the other direction. *WHY?* But no time! Murray low-crawled back around the corner he'd just passed, gathering weeds as he moved. He dug in as best he could, used the weeds to cover himself. The car couldn't make a real sharp turn and maybe the guy'd be looking out toward the fields.

Drive, you bastard! Murray heard the car, steadily closer, too close, and then even with him . . . and then the crunch of a turn. Murray didn't take time to look. Crawled back around the corner and ran down the fence line, staying in the packed wheel marks hoping they couldn't track him. Ran till his legs gave and he fell, keeping his head up this time but tearing more skin off his knuckles.

Now what? He stood and surveyed the land away from the compound, glad his eyes were adjusted to the dark. He saw no lights at all. Open field ending . . . was that a fence? A regular fence? Would there be a road by it? He looked down to find his T-shirt still in his hand. Began brushing his steps as he walked. Thirty yards from the tire tracks he shook the dirt out, pulled his shirt on, and took off again.

The fence. No road beside. But another field, and somewhere ahead probably another fence and maybe a road. He'd been stumbling the last couple of minutes; legs too tired now to run and keep his balance. Kept moving forward, looking for a stick to lean on, finding none. In minutes he reached a third fence and a dirt road that bordered a shallow ditch. Good. Couldn't risk meeting a car without cover.

Long after dark, Pearl was in the bathroom sick to her stomach. Janochek was in the living room in his easy chair, turning his deceased father's World War II .45 over and over in his hands, wondering if he should shuck the clip and oil it, wondering if he could find the box of extra ammunition, wondering if the gun still fired.

Janochek hated feeling paranoid but he couldn't shake it. He put the gun out of Pearl's reach, out of sight on top of a kitchen cabinet, and picked up his house phone to see if it was still operating. Got a dial tone. Turned off the lights in the kitchen and living room and went to his front window to spot anyone watching the cottage. Side window, back door, the same thing. Didn't see anybody.

He crept outside, stayed in the trees and darker areas as he paralleled the small road down toward the street. Maybe Murray was hiding in the lawnmower shed. He wasn't. Maybe he was across the street at the side of that commercial building, watching to see if it was safe to come in.

Near the front border at Continental Street, Janochek snuck along the thick hedge until he could crouch behind a stucco gate pillar and examine the pavement in each direction. If it were him, he'd come in from the north and sneak along the bushy shrubs all the way to the entrance. Janochek didn't hear anything, didn't see Murray or anything unusual. He was turning away when he heard the engine.

A squad car was rolling slowly down the street from the 44 freeway underpass toward the cemetery. Yes! Gates or someone from law enforcement was patrolling, perhaps going to station someone here so they'd know as soon as Murray returned. He watched the spotlight rake the fence and parked cars on both sides of the street, stood to hail the cruiser, saw it more clearly and ducked. Light-colored chassis with black doors—the security company the kids had described. After Murray or Pearl? He stayed low and speed-crawled back to the dark, ran for the house. Should have carried his cell. He needed Gates.

No luck. Couldn't reach him. Left a message with dispatch who agreed to contact Gates at home.

Pearl had gone to her room. Good. Janochek didn't want her to see him checking and oiling the pistol.

Murray tried to mentally backtrack and establish which direction the sun had set several hours ago. He pictured the loader bucket; the sun had gone down on the right side. The chain-link was on the right side. He'd climbed it and run halfway around, so that should be east. He'd struck out the same direction through fences to the road, and had turned right. South.

He should eventually hit east-west roads. Maybe hear the 5 freeway. It worried him that he hadn't encountered more houses. Wished he hadn't been unconscious during much of the ride. He had no idea how far he'd been driven, how far he was from Riverton, and whether he would be able to find anything he recognized before he gave out or they found him. And more bad news. He was exhausted. He found a small depression deep enough to lie in, twenty or thirty feet beyond the shallow ditch, where no one could see him unless they were within a few feet. He was asleep the minute his head touched the pillow of his forearm.

When he woke it was still dark, but his eyes were totally used to it and the sky seemed a little lighter. The land on either side of him looked like it had been graded. Almost no plants left standing. His path ran straight through a flat plain, a basin surrounded by low hills. He stopped. Needed a better plan. It was still somewhere around the middle of the night, no moon. What if he could see a brighter area? Wouldn't that mean town? After studying every direction he decided there was a very faint glow ahead, angled to his right.

Cresting a rise a few minutes later he saw the source. A

brightly lit service station with eighteen-wheelers parked toward the back. He made the entrance in a few minutes, could see the freeway, could see hills beyond, thought the cluster of lights he could see some miles away might be town.

He needed a ride. A person in a car might be afraid of him. He imagined how he looked: filthy T-shirt, muddy face, handcuffs. So, one of the trucks. Maybe a smaller one. He picked a white cab with a bin on the back that carried dirt or gravel, stuck his cuffed hand in his jeans pocket, and approached the driver at the pump.

"Are you going to Riverton?"

"Who wants to know?" The person kept filling the tank, didn't turn around.

"I need a ride. To get home . . . just as far as the convention center." Murray had never hitchhiked before. Hadn't planned his request.

When the person replaced the hose in the fuel bay and turned, Murray saw it was a woman, hair chopped short under a ball cap, rough face with deep lines around the eyes and mouth. Canvas jacket, Levi's, and ankle boots.

The woman smiled. Crooked teeth. "I'm heading to Yreka, don't mind pulling off on 44."

"Uh . . ." If she was put off by his condition, she gave no sign. Murray wondered if she was high.

"Hell, get in. It's unlocked."

The woman let him out at the convention center overpass, and he sprinted west along the roadside until he crossed the canal and threaded his way down the berm into the southeast corner of the cemetery. Stopped at the narrow paved road above the cottage. He needed breath and he needed to think. Could the people who took him have gotten to Janochek? Taken Pearl?

He stayed to the shadows at the edge of the road until he could see the front area. The workshop was dark. Light on in the cottage living room. Janochek's truck parked beside. No other vehicles. He snuck to the front door and was poised to knock when it flung open and all he could see was the barrel of a pistol.

"Cheese and rice! I almost shot you!" Janochek set the gun on the door-side table and threw his arms around Murray.

Murray hadn't regained speech.

"We were worried sick. Actually sick. Where were you? What . . ." He, too, ran out of steam.

Murray could feel the man's body shake a time or two as he crushed him and rocked side to side.

"I'm sorry," Murray said.

Janochek released him and stood back. "Come in. Let me rouse Pearl and you tell us what's been going on."

Murray watched the man shaking his head as he walked back toward Pearl's bedroom. He'd been so scared for the past several hours he hadn't imagined how they might be feeling.

Before Janochek reached her room, Pearl flew out and tackled Murray, knocking him against the front door as Janochek watched, his hand uselessly poised to knock and wake her.

Murray held her and let her cry. Noticed he'd never held a girl this tightly. Noticed a tingling. A different kind of tingling. But he didn't let go.

When she'd pulled herself together she went back to her room for a robe and returned to the kitchen table.

Janochek noticed the handcuffs. Began searching for tools. It took a while but hacksaw and vise-grips did it. He washed the dirt and gravel out of the boy's wounds at the sink. Pushed Murray's thumb back into joint, or as close as he could get it anyway. Bandaged it tightly to his hand and first finger.

Janochek made hot chocolate and instant coffee. "Hate this stuff," he said, gesturing to his cup. He'd no sooner joined them at the table than he stood and found his cell phone. "Need to reach Gates," he said. This time, instead of the department, he called the cell number on the card Gates had given him.

Wound up leaving another message.

Gates awoke, neck aching, steering wheel crowding him. Clicked the overhead light to check his watch, almost three a.m. Quiet. He twinged when he remembered Kiefer. Out there somewhere. Maybe already dead. What could he do? Decided to revisit Barker's wife in the hospital.

He had hoped she'd come around but found her still unconscious. Nurse said Barker had been in briefly, left hours ago. Gates sat at the sleeping woman's side, holding her hand, whispering simple reassurances, stopping as he himself began to fall asleep. Gave up. He'd come back in the morning.

At the department he let himself in the side door, saw no one, sat at his desk and sorted the reports from the Mary Lake canvassing. No eyewitness. Cars and pickups were always parking and leaving around the lake's perimeter. People in and out of cars so ordinary as to be invisible. Biking, strolling, walking pets. Strangers were business as usual.

Restless, he nevertheless decided against finishing the dregs of the squad room coffee. No sense adding an ulcer to insomnia. He would go back to his truck just in case he might be able to nap once more before daybreak.

Gates woke this time to a gray dawn, sun not yet coloring the eastern horizon. Inside, he washed his face in the locker room sink, finger-brushed his teeth, pitched the black syrup of yesterday's coffee, and started a new pot. When he reached his desk he saw he'd left his cell phone on top of the reports he'd read earlier. *Idiot!* Checked it and found five messages from Janochek. Called immediately. Got no answer. Checked voice mail. Janochek's last message said Murray was there. Gates felt the muscles in his neck relax . . . hadn't been aware how tightly he'd been carrying himself. He'd grown certain the boy had been taken and probably killed. Both Kiefer and the girl had told how, after they explored the hillside grave site, they were observed and maybe followed by a van . . . a van, the preferred vehicle for kidnappings. Gates had acted on that assumption, acted immediately to intercept the kidnapper, but it didn't work because the boy hadn't been taken.

He collapsed to his chair, put head in hands, gritted his teeth at the thought of telling Faraday when she came in. Kiefer had plenty of reason to disappear for a while. Gates had overwhelmed him by telling his horrible family story, addiction and suicide. What had he been thinking? He had no business sharing, he knew, and it shamed him further. He had hoped in telling Kiefer the boy would see him as human first, law officer second. See him as just another person with troubles of his own and therefore trust him. Work with him. But he was guilty of a hidden agenda, also wanting a personal favor. Kiefer talking to his son. Gates shuddered in a long exhale of grief. He hadn't cried in a long time and the sheriff's office wasn't the place to start again. A few deep breaths helped him collect himself.

He could understand. The kid had needed space to shake off Gates's painful story. Of course. The boy hadn't expected it and didn't know what to do with that information. Gates imagined Kiefer walking halfway around the lake and then following Kilkee Drive to the West Side trail. Hiking up in the scrub hills where trails wandered for miles, no houses, very few people. The kid had walked till he felt better, maybe taken a nap, and then late last night had gone back to the cemetery. That made sense. That's why the canvassing and the Be-on-the-Lookout hadn't picked him up.

Besides. Why kidnap Kiefer? The horse was already out of the barn, the damage done, the body on the hill found. Someone observing would probably think the boy had been messing around the rodeo grounds and stumbled onto it. How many people knew Kiefer could locate dead people? Janochek and his daughter, and Duheen. Someone watching would have no idea, wouldn't suspect that Kiefer knew other people had been buried there and were now moved and missing.

The van driver, possibly the killer . . . what could he know? Probably only that the site had been discovered. Kiefer had been bringing other people to the grave. And if the killer had been watching he'd already seen the forensic team at the woman's burial ground. No reason to keep pursuing Kiefer.

Janocheck and the kids were probably sleeping after a difficult night. In a couple of hours he'd drive over and get Kiefer's story.

It was quarter till seven and Mrs. Barker might be awake. He called to find she had begun to respond. Good. He'd go over in a couple of minutes. With a cup of fresh coffee, he brought himself up-to-date on the homeless investigation, the missing Dumpster, and its possible relationship to Trask Engineering.

He needed a list of all Trask construction sites and all of their staging compounds where they might store equipment. Any warehouses. But maybe that was too obvious. He also needed a list of Trask properties. Lately he'd been focused on Roth Trask, but both he and his half brother, Chuck, might be implicated in the tax fraud and therefore in the missing homeless. Better get a list of the Barker properties, too. And that reminded him to send another info request to West Coast homeless missions to see whether Jerel Smith or Harold Smith or even Jerell Barker had turned up.

He finished writing and posting the inquiries: property list requests to the county clerk and recorder, census info to the Homeless Children's Network and the shelter directories in California, Oregon, and Washington. Noticed a shadow on his desk. Faraday. Holding a sheaf of file cards.

"Any news on Kiefer?"

"Home. Safe. It's a long story," Gates said, reluctant to meet her eyes.

"Glad to hear it. Made for a miserable night. How long have you known?"

"Got the voice mail a few minutes ago. Haven't spoken to Janochek or the kids. What are you carrying?"

She set the cards in front of him faced so he could read them. "Yesterday afternoon I asked for this month's 911 call cards related to missing teens. Wondered if Kiefer had disappeared before or if there were any reports of a vehicle attempting to lure a boy, that sort of thing."

"Good thinking. We assumed his disappearance was related to the homeless but it might have been something else altogether." This would be the time to tell her about running the boy off with his inappropriately personal and gruesome story, but he didn't.

"I found something else," she said, pointing at the stack of cards. "Look at the top five."

Gates picked them up and fanned them to see the dates. Roughly one per week. Four weeks ago a boy named Marvin Suh complaining that police still hadn't found his friend Jerell Barker. Three weeks ago, Claudia Clemens, same complaint. Suh again same week. Two weeks ago, Clemens. Yesterday Suh again. Gates looked up to see Faraday biting her lip and frowning.

"These kids aren't giving up." Faraday shook her head. "They're certain he wouldn't run away. They know something we don't. Something I didn't bother to ask. I looked back at my mis-per report on the Barker kid. I think I got it wrong. I think something happened to him and the dad's stonewalling."

Janochek swept up the phone on the first ring. "Gates, finally! Murray's here."

"I know."

"Where have you been? I've been trying to reach you."

"This isn't Gates. Do not hang up. *Do not hang up.* Your children's lives depend on it."

Silence. Janochek struggled to assess what he was hearing.

"If I have your attention, say 'good.'"

"Uh . . . good."

"Listen very carefully. Give the children no cause for alarm or I will kill all of you immediately. Do you understand?"

Janochek was frozen. Disbelieving, then afraid. "Yes," he said. He kept his face blank as he stood and walked a few feet away from where they'd been sitting at the table. He could feel Pearl and Murray's stare at his back. "I understand," he said. "Gates can't come to the phone right now."

"We have very little time," the voice said. "If any of you run out the front, I will shoot you dead. If you go out the back, my man will kill you. All of you. Immediately. Do you understand?"

"Yes."

"If you disobey I will detonate the package I've taped to your gas line. The explosion will destroy everything within twenty yards, leave a ten-foot crater. Do you understand?"

"Yes."

"Without worrying the children go to your kitchen

window. Your screen has been removed. Look where the gas pipe enters your foundation."

Janochek lowered the phone. "The Sheriff's Department is going to secure our grounds but for the next couple of minutes you all need to stay seated and wait for specifics. Can you do that?"

Pearl and Murray nodded.

This must be serious, because Murray could see the strain on Janochek's face, perspiration beading on his forehead.

Pearl, sensing her father's discomfort, pushed against the table to stand and go to him. Murray put his hands over hers, shook his head, held her there.

Janochek nodded in approval of Murray's effort and walked around the butcher block to the kitchen window above the sink. "They want to know if I can see the patrol car yet," he explained, opening the window, leaning out, and looking down the hill. He saw no one. When he checked along the wall below him, he saw a four-inch box taped to the metal gas pipe where it entered the wall. A small green light blinking. He eased the window shut and made himself walk calmly toward the fridge in the corner, so his face would remain hidden to his daughter.

"The green light shows it's armed for my signal. Do you understand?"

"Uh, yes, I see it." Janochek's palms were sweaty and the phone was slipping. He changed hands for a moment while he wiped his right on his pants leg, walked two more steps to the fridge door, and quietly tore a single sheet off the notepad magneted there.

"In a moment I will hang up. You will put your cell by

the sink and leave it. You and your children will walk out the front door and get in your truck. There will be a phone on your seat. Start the engine, drive to the bottom of the hill, take a left, and put the phone to your ear. Do you understand?"

"Yes," Janochek said, "we can temporarily evacuate." He turned his back to the window, tugged a pen from his shirt pocket, and set the paper beside the sink. Scribbled "taken at gunpoint." Left the pen and writing on the counter.

"We negotiate or you're all dead. No middle ground, no alternative. My own life depends on it. We're going someplace to talk. Do you understand?"

"Srrh . . . sure," Janochek said, clearing his throat.

"I have killed several. Do you believe me?" The man's voice, measured, stern.

"Yes," Janochek said, glancing at Pearl and Murray, seeing their eyes wide with concern. He put his finger to his lips, reminding them.

"I'm serious. Don't force me to kill three more."

Janochek wanted to say something reassuring but nothing came to mind.

"Do you remember what I have told you?"

"Yes."

"You have fifteen seconds. Leave the house."

The phone went dead.

Janochek made himself casually set the cell on the counter. "We've got to go, but we'll be right back," he told them, lifting his keys off the top of the refrigerator and returning to Pearl and Murray. "The sheriffs need us to leave while they search. I'll answer your questions when we get rolling." He pulled Pearl from her chair, shot her a fierce look as she started to protest about the fact that she was only wearing her pajamas and robe. "Not now!"

Murray was up, tugging her along with them.

Janochek paused for a second at the front door, hesitated, looking at the door-side table. His back to the kids, he swept the weapon into his pocket, praying he wasn't making a fatal mistake. First to the truck, he threw open the door, picked the phone off the bench, and keyed the ignition.

Pearl clambered into the passenger side with Murray right behind. "Are we in—"

"Hush!" Janochek cut Pearl off.

Murray, hiccuping now, held tight to the armrest as Janochek bumped the truck down the narrow road to the street. He'd never seen the man like this. He thought he knew what was happening. They were going to be shot. He grabbed Pearl and pushed her toward the floor, held her as she fought. Didn't notice the phone until Janochek slewed a left on Continental and put it to his ear as he raced down the street toward the 44 freeway.

The phone buzzed and Janochek answered.

"Slow down! Don't attract attention. Look below the steering wheel."

Janochek did. Another box with a blinking light. "Yes," he said.

"I am in range. One button, instantaneous. Do you understand?"

"Yes." Janochek needed to clear his throat again but was afraid to.

"Stay on Continental to Florence Street, one block before South."

"I know it."

"Take a left and drive up the ramp into the cargo truck near the corner."

"My pickup may not make something steep."

"Do it."

"Tighten your seat belt," Janochek said, setting the phone beside him and locking the doors. "Pearl, stay down, and Murray, hold on, protect your head."

Murray bent over his lap, arms shielding face and neck.

Janochek turned a corner and Murray risked a quick glance to see a large delivery truck, taillights shining, its dark cab fronting an aluminum container. Its rear door was fully opened and a metal ramp angled from the street into the interior, orange traffic cone on either side. Janochek goosed the accelerator just as he reached the ramp. Murray saw sparks as the bumper scraped before he ducked his head and felt the pickup bounce into the cargo bay.

Janochek had a millisecond to jam the brakes before hitting the back wall.

Murray banged his head on the pickup roof, his forearms and elbows on the dash, but didn't directly hit his face. In his haze he heard the rear door rattling shut. He felt Pearl struggling on the floor beneath his legs and scrunched to the side to give her room.

Pearl was swearing, yelling "Dad!" Fighting to climb up on the seat. It took several seconds to push through the tangle of Murray's legs, his high tops caught in her robe. When she wedged herself onto the bench it was nearly too dark to see. She could feel Murray sitting up on one side, her dad slumped on the other. What was that green glow? She bent to see a small light blinking under the dash on her dad's side. Strange. She'd never seen it before and didn't like the looks of it.

There was always a flashlight in the glove compartment. She leaned across Murray's legs, pressed the release button, pawed in the glove box, and found it. Gasped when she shone it on her father. Janochek was bleeding from a swollen gash on his forehead, but his chest was moving. "Dad?"

No response.

She was afraid to touch him, knew first aid from sports. If he had a head or neck injury, touching him had to be done carefully if at all. But he was jiggling! Whatever they were riding in had started moving. Tucked on the pickup floor, she had no idea what had happened. Were they on a train? Who was taking them? Where? Beyond the cracked pickup windshield and the truck's hood there was only a dented silvery metal wall. No windows.

Murray was little help when she asked.

"In back of a truck." He was rubbing his head, face scrunched in pain.

"Why?"

"The sheriffs? . . . I don't know."

"We're inside a . . . trailer?" That didn't make any sense.

"It's like a delivery truck."

"That's crazy. Why didn't we just drive wherever we're going?"

"I don't get it either. He was on the phone with someone, turned a corner and saw this big truck and headed right for the back of it. Your dad was really scared," Murray told her. "I've never seen him like that."

"Right now, he needs help." Pearl got on her knees beside her father and reached to wipe the blood that dripped toward his eyes.

Gates arrived on the trauma unit shortly after seven, just after the patients' breakfast. Asked the charge nurse at the counter for a report.

"No intake," she said. "We're holding her on IV fluids. She was responsive"—the large woman looked to the chart on the counter in front of her—"from six-fifteen to six-twenty or so. Reflexes, blinked eyes, nodded to name, tracked stimuli, but didn't speak. As soon as we told her she was doing well and starting to clear, she folded. Eyes closed, unresponsive, but it was volitional. She jumped at a pinprick."

"Uh, she wants to be unconscious?"

"Seems like it," the nurse said.

"Guess that's why she took all those pills," Gates said. "Can I talk with her?"

"The resident has upgraded her to stable. Be my guest."

"Can you see that we're not disturbed for five minutes, even if it's her husband?"

The nurse nodded.

Gates measured the woman. Probably early sixties, overweight, soft arms, but there was a ramrod in her carriage and her light blue eyes never wavered. He believed her. Barker was a hard man, but this charge nurse ruled her territory.

He stopped at the door to Mrs. Barker's room and watched her for a moment. Her eyes were closed and she was still, breathing evenly. He saw her very slowly reach over with her left hand and scratch her other wrist where the IV rubbed against the plastic hospital bracelet. Saw the hand slowly retrace its path to her side.

"I can ask them to put your identification bracelet on your left wrist if that would be more comfortable," he said, walking to her bed.

Her eyes made a tiny flinch of surprise, but they didn't open and she said nothing.

"I know you're awake and so do the doc and the nursing staff. Sometime this morning when he comes in, they may give your husband that information. I don't imagine he'll be so patient with your possum act."

No response.

"I think something you know or something you've witnessed is killing you. Would you like police protection?"

Gates thought he noticed the slightest lift at one corner of her mouth. "Don't think it'll do any good?" he asked. "Too late for that?"

He watched closely, noticed her breathing was becoming slightly more rapid. His words were making her uncomfortable.

"What happened to your pretty little dog?" he asked. Cruel, he thought, but he needed her to speak.

Her bottom lip trembled. Stopped. She turned away from him, toward the side of the bed with the hydration unit and the monitors.

"I think that's probably an ugly story," Gates said, "but there's something worse than that, isn't there?" He watched her shoulders rise and fall as she worked to steady her breathing.

"You know what happened to Jerell and you know it's just

a matter of time till it happens to you." Gates was guessing but he didn't need to be right. He just needed a response so they could begin a conversation before Barker got to her.

She grew very still, seemed to be holding her breath for a few seconds before she tore out the IV and blood went shooting onto the sheet. Monitors sounded alarms. Gates was hip-butted from the room by the heavyset nurse as aides and medical personnel surrounded the bed.

Gates sat on an uncomfortable orange plastic chair in the nearby waiting room while the IV was replaced and order restored. He overheard a consultation in the hall where a sedative was proposed and decided against. When the charge nurse returned to the station, Gate approached her.

"She's awake," he said.

"We knew that," the woman said, face pointed toward the chart she was updating while she looked at him above her glasses. "ODs like hers irritate the brain. She's going to be hair-trigger for a day or so. Come back day after tomorrow."

"Don't know if I can wait that long," Gates said. "If she talks to any staff, find out what she says. Don't let her husband take her out against . . . what is it?"

"A.M.A. Against medical advice."

"Need a deputy 24/7 to help enforce that?"

"Wouldn't hurt. Is she on a hold?"

"Material witness, possible accessory."

"Paperwork?"

"Before noon," Gates said, wishing his own department operated so concisely and efficiently.

On his way to the parking lot Gates phoned the lieutenant, left a message to request the extra hospital guard duty, and, that done, phoned Roland Oats, an ex–pro footballer now on disability for his knees. Asked Roland to come to the hospital and keep an eye on Mrs. Barker for the rest of the day. Roland was a pal from Gambler's Anonymous and Gates could trust him. Never a bad idea to have a little extra backup with a guy like Barker, especially since Gates didn't know what all the man needed to protect.

When he returned to the office, Faraday got out of her chair as soon as she saw him. "I called those kids, caught them before they'd left for school," she said, handing him what looked like transcript copies. "Mistake. I should have done it before. They keep calling because Jerell loved school, was totally involved in his studies and collaborative projects. The three of them were tighter than most families, nerds with common interests, scads of smarts."

This time she did pull up a nearby chair. Sat. Shook her head. "Jerell hated home. Hated his dad. Terrified of him. Told them Barker was a maniac. Screaming at him. Hitting. Threw him against the wall, down the stairs. According to Jerell, Barker was 'trying to make a man of him.' Like pitching a kid over Niagara Falls to teach him to swim."

"I'm thinking this war on Jerell is a major contributor to his wife's deterioration. I said that to her an hour ago and she snapped. Ripped out her IV."

"I think Jerell's gone for good. Barker crossed the line," Faraday said.

"You run the kid though NCIC and N-DEx. I'll see if the Trask and Barker property inquiries have come in." Gates got up to check the docs-requested tray.

Faraday left without another word, pulling her chair with her, stationed it in front of the office's main desktop, and went to work.

Whatever they were riding inside was noisy and stuffy, going slow, vibrating with every bump, jostling them, making it hard to help Janochek.

"I'm scared."

Murray didn't think he'd ever heard Pearl say that before, but he knew what she meant. A truck inside a truck was very strange and he couldn't think of a good explanation. A bad one? He was kidnapped again, trapped, and this time he wouldn't get away.

"Are you okay?" Pearl asked Murray without looking at him, keeping her attention on her father.

Murray hurt, but nothing seemed broken and the head-ache behind his eyes was subsiding. "I cracked my head. Hit my elbows . . . left arm's numb, thumb's bad, but yeah. You?"

"Worried about Dad. He started acting weird with that call and . . . did the sheriffs put us in here to protect us?"

"Your dad was freaked. I don't think this is the sheriffs. I didn't see a shield or lights or uniforms. Just this big truck with a ramp out the back. Your dad headed right in."

"You think . . ."

"Yeah, I'm . . . I think we're in trouble."

"Where's the phone?"

Good question. Murray started to scoot toward Pearl and couldn't. *I'm paralyzed!* After he yelled he realized his seat belt was still fastened. It took him another moment to calm his breathing before he made it to her side. As best she could, Pearl had braced her father's head with one hand, put pressure on his wound with the other to stop the bleeding. Didn't seem like Janochek had opened his eyes.

Murray took the flash. Looked in Janochek's lap, felt his shirt pockets, felt the seat beside Pearl. Scooted down to look on the floor. Carefully moved Janochek's feet to look under the brake and accelerator. "What's this green light?"

"Don't touch it."

Murray crawled back to the seat and tried to remember the final moment before hitting the ramp. Rose to his knees and looked on the dash. The phone rested up against the windshield.

"Okay," he said. "911?"

"Hurry."

Murray pushed the call button but nothing lit. Found the on button and held it down. Nothing happened. Nor when he released it.

"Damn it!" This from Pearl, watching over his shoulder. "Let me do it."

He handed her the cell and she fussed with it for another minute before giving up. "I have to keep holding Dad's head. Take the battery out and put it back. Maybe it hit pretty hard. Needs to reboot."

Murray did as he was told but the phone stayed dead.

Pearl swore. "Come help me a minute."

Murray set the phone back on the dash. Maybe it would recover if they gave it more time.

"Take the flashlight and shine it in Dad's eyes, first one and then the other when I tell you."

Murray knew. This had something to do with checking for a concussion, but he didn't remember if it was dilated eyes or pinpoints. He hoped Pearl knew. Even so, what could they do about it?

"Now," Pearl said.

Murray shone it in the eye Pearl held open, then the other. "What are you looking for?"

"His pupils constricted and he followed the light a little," she said.

Murray guessed that was okay. She didn't sound any more worried. "So what do we do?"

"Tuck the flash back under my chin. I'll keep pressure till the bleeding stops. You look for something we can fight with."

Whack somebody with a road map? Murray hadn't ridden in Janochek's truck very often, but he'd never noticed a weapon. Glove compartment? He realized he could see a little. Both the light spill from the flashlight and the green glow from the floor area.

He found the maps he'd predicted, gum, and a tape measure. Under those, a tire gauge and a screwdriver. He stuck the screwdriver in his jeans pocket and slid to the floor to search under his seat. Oil rags. A four-headed tire iron, useless . . . unless you threw it. He brought it with him.

Gun rack? No such luck. Behind the seat? He couldn't reach anything from the top. Realized he could open his door almost a foot. Got out. On his knees he reached into the narrow space between the seat and the cab's back. Something metal. Ax? It was stuck, head facing toward him. He closed the truck door.

"Roll your window so we can talk." This from Pearl. Taking charge.

Murray cranked the glass down, reshut the door, and worked his way along the side.

"Check the bed." Pearl, somehow monitoring him.

It took Murray a moment to remember that was what you called the pickup carry space. Wait a minute. Why was it so dark? Why weren't the pickup lights still on? Didn't they stay on when the truck stopped running? Oh. He remembered. Barely daybreak but Janochek had been driving fast without headlights! He probably wouldn't be doing that at the sheriff's instructions. So Murray had been right. Probably whoever'd grabbed him before had him again. With Janochek and Pearl in the same net. His fear vanished in a wave of disgust. Murray had told his friends about the voices and put them in danger. This was his fault. So he needed to do something. Something . . . but he couldn't see well enough. "Can you turn on the lights?" He heard Pearl grunt with effort.

"Can't reach 'em. I could press the brake, I think."

A red glow filled the box. Better. A roped bundle at the back of the cab. When Murray untied it he found a new sleeping bag, a new coat, and some cans of Vienna sausage. "Found the stuff you were going to give the homeless guy with the bump on his head."

"Check the coat pockets," Pearl yelled. "I stuck my old Swiss army knife in there, too."

Murray got it, put it in his pocket. Continued. Felt around to make sure he didn't miss anything. Found a coiled rope, a plastic bucket, a rake. Might be useful. He set the tire iron next to the rake and edged farther around the back, banging his shin on the trailer hitch. Edged on to Janochek's door.

Knocked on the frame. Pearl looked up at him, accidentally shining the light in his eyes, momentarily blinding him.

"Hold him!" Murray yelled at her.

She tried to get a stronger grip.

Murray slowly opened the door, had even less room on this side. He reached behind the seat and fumbled around till he got ahold of the tool handle. Pulled as hard as he could while still keeping his balance. The tool inched, inched, and then slid free as Murray fell backward onto the floor, jammed between the truck and the wall. He struggled to his feet, put the ax in the bed with the other tools.

"How do you turn on the lights?" he asked. The dashboard had too many knobs and switches.

Pearl had wheedled her dad into letting her drive the truck a couple of times, but she was far from familiar with it. "You pull one of those round knobs on the dash between the blinker lever and the door."

Murray wedged his way beside Janochek to pull on the lights and saw the blinking green one again. "This doesn't have any round things."

Pearl glanced down. "What doesn't?"

"The blinker?"

"Describe it."

"It's a small box taped to this pole that goes into the floor."

"The steering column."

"Okay. It's got wires on it."

"I don't think that's part of the truck."

The small box was disturbing. Murray was afraid to guess what it might be.

As Murray withdrew he heard Janochek groan. "He's waking up?"

"Getting there," Pearl said. "Try the knobs between you and the steering wheel."

The second one Murray pulled brought the headlights. When his eyes adjusted he could see the pickup was a very close fit. Maybe two feet from the cab top to the ceiling. Three feet or so from the rear to the box door. In front there was a dent, a couple-inch push-out where the pickup had struck. Amazing! Janochek had threaded the needle. Murray remembered the sparks when they hit the ramp.

Janochek groaned again, and Murray shuffled back around to his own side and got in.

"Ax, a screwdriver, Swiss army, a rake, tire iron, a rope, and a bucket," he said, expecting some praise for his sleuthing.

"You forgot one," Pearl said.

"No, I . . . What?"

"The pickup," she said. "We start it, put it in reverse, and it's a battering ram."

Faraday was back at Gates's desk with more papers. "Databases have nothing on Jerell but your shelter census printouts came in."

"Yeah, well it's still early. Barely eight." Gates took the pages, started with the Seattle Shelter Census. Nothing. Portland? No. In Eugene, a Harold Smith, seventeen. Medford? Same name, two days earlier. The boy was gradually moving north. Gates searched the Oregon mission rosters plus Chico, Sacramento, and San Francisco. No mention of a Jerell Barker.

"You read these?" he asked.

Faraday nodded.

"We missed it. Harold Smith's accounted for. A kid traveling north on the shelter circuit. Jerell Barker's in the wind."

The woman took a deep breath. Nodded again. "Big mistake," she agreed. "His crew had it right."

"He could be nearly impossible to find," Gates said. "A, he ran away so cleverly there's no trail to follow so he really could escape from his dad, or B . . ."

"Barker has the resources to hide the boy anywhere," Faraday said, thinking along with him.

"Around the home?" Gates pictured the palatial house and grounds. "Convenient but risky. We'd never get a warrant based on what we have."

Once again, the name surfaced. Kiefer. God! The boy, if he could really do what he seemed to be able to do . . . invaluable.

Faraday left and returned in less than a minute. "Thought I heard these printing," she said. "The properties?" She pulled a chair next to Gates and they reviewed the new information simultaneously.

Roth Trask—Riverton home and condo in Tahoe. Engineering company's in-town property. Trask's current shopping center complex under construction southeast of town near the new industrial park. Located on adjacent acreage, the company's staging and storage lot, materials and equipment.

"Blue Dumpster?" Faraday asked.

"Get dispatch to send a patrol, to Industrial Park first." Gates stood. "We need some luck."

In a few minutes the patrol deputy called in. There were four Dumpsters at the construction site and one at the staging compound, all blue, but they held nothing significant.

Faraday made a phone call to Decker's Dumpsters. "Can you tell me how many Dumpsters Trask Engineering is currently renting?" She waited. Turned to Gates. "Six," she said.

"Have patrol swing by Trask's office building. The other one could be there."

Patrol reported a green city container at the corner of the parking lot. No blue.

Faraday broke the silence. "Where is it?"

"The bodies . . . plastic bags like the bit we found at the woman's grave? Not much odor."

"Aerial reconnaissance? That's a bright blue."

"Might miss it under trees or a roof."

"Barker's property?"

"I'll check his home but I doubt it."

Faraday had her eyes shut, brainstorming. "Investment property, either of them?"

"None that I read about other than company building projects. Several out of state and the new shopping complex south of town. Nothing else under Trask's or Barker's name." Gates thinking, absentmindedly looking out at the wall clock. "They have to put it somewhere they know . . . someplace they're pretty familiar with," he said. "Otherwise they couldn't be sure it would stay undiscovered."

"There's something we're not seeing," Faraday said, practically stomping back to her desk.

Gates sighed. Embarrassed. Knew she was right. Decided to call Duheen. Bring her up-to-date. Mine for ideas.

Duheen said she was glad Murray was back safe, but was too busy to talk about missing Dumpsters. When the call ended, Gates left once again and drove west to Barker's home. Parked and quickly walked the grounds. No Dumpster. Thought about Jerell. Could he be imprisoned? Gates would have probably seen or heard him when he searched the house and found Mrs. Barker. A basement? Didn't look like it. A shack on the edge of the property? No.

So was he buried here? Twice in the past few years, men had killed their wives and buried them in the foundation of a new gazebo. Ironic, since a new gazebo might have been part of the marital discord in the first place. Gates walked the perimeter again looking for new construction. Saw nothing.

Did the boy take the cash and run? Far enough away that

nobody from this area would ever find him? Couldn't afford to tell his school friends on the chance his dad might get to them? That reminded him. He wanted Faraday to do a follow-up interview with Clemens and Suh. Find out if they remembered anything else. Ask them where they'd look for Jerell.

Gates looked at his watch, saw it was time to check in with Janochek now.

The trip wore on, the rumbling of the big truck keeping a steady rhythm. Once again it was impossible for Murray to guess how fast they were going, how far, or in what direction, but this trip felt like it was taking an hour or more. He glanced at Pearl from time to time as she continued to minister to her father, whispering to him, holding him as best she could to minimize the jiggling.

Murray thought again about what a . . . well, good wasn't exactly the word . . . uh, determined? . . . what a remarkable girl she was. She didn't take tough breaks lying down. She stood up, fought back. Maybe losing her mom, maybe the years of teasing she'd gotten for being a cemetery kid. Or maybe she was just born tough. *Janochek doesn't make a big deal of it but he's tough. Nobody pushes him around.*

Whatever it was that had contributed to Pearl's resilience amazed Murray. He didn't like to admit it, but she was sort of teaching him how to face life. She didn't do things the easiest way. If she made a mistake, she took the consequences. And even for all that, she could be gentle and kind, like the way she was taking care of her father.

But what about Sandray? She was so pretty. Prettier than Pearl. And lively and fun and graceful. Pearl was a jock, but Sandray was a dancer! No. Pearl *is* a jock. Sandray *was* a dancer. Pearl was flesh and blood and she'd hugged him. Sandray might like him, but she'd never hold him . . . or fight beside him either. Was that the deal breaker?

Murray felt a rush of guilt. He felt like he hadn't kept up with Blessed or Dearly or Edwin or even Feathers. He imagined sitting on their graves, touching their stones. Blessed would be cheering for him, telling him he did good, getting away from the first kidnapper. She'd say, *Do it again. Think. Turn the tables.*

Dearly would be calm, kind of philosophical. Probably say nobody can predict or control what life brings so you have to be ready. Prepare for opportunity. Seize the moment. Do what you have to.

Edwin? His buddy had hated the polio so bad, hated being paralyzed in that iron lung. He'd be saying, *Punch 'em in the pie! Go for it! Don't take this crap lying down.*

Although Murray wasn't trying, he found himself imagining Feathers. All wound up. *This here's serious shit, yo! You got to look right to feel right! Go Armageddon on their ass!* Scared as Murray was, those words made him smile. Count on Feathers to have a strong opinion even if Murray wasn't sure he got the translation. Something like fake it till you make it? Maybe.

Murray didn't know if he was inventing their words. He didn't care. Thinking about his friends made him feel better, and their advice made sense. He couldn't sit around waiting for something to happen. He hadn't earlier when he'd been handcuffed. He got busy, did things he probably couldn't or wouldn't have done if he'd thought much. So now wasn't the time to wait and see. They needed to make a plan and do it.

He told Pearl, "We have to be ready whether your dad wakes up or not."

Gates had just crossed Pine Street less than ten blocks from the cemetery when a call from Faraday changed his plans. Okay, he'd let Janochek and the kids rest a little longer. Mrs. Barker wanted to see him.

She was sitting up in bed, set expression on her face like she was ready to get this unpleasant task over with.

Gates stood at the foot and Faraday stationed herself close enough to the door to keep people from entering and disrupting the conversation. Neither Gates nor Faraday had spoken since entering the room.

"You want me to give information about my husband," she said, holding her blanket tight to her waist with both hands. "I am strong. Stubborn like your mula. I will not talk for you." Mrs. Barker gave the blanket an irritated jerk making the fold sharper.

"My husband can hit but he cannot make me. No more." She took a deep breath. "No more." She released the blanket with one hand, looked on her tray, found a small cup of water, took a sip.

A toast to herself? To her newfound will? Gates wondered.

"I will not see my family. I know. My home. My country. I will not see them." She looked to both Gates and the female deputy, apparently to emphasize her resolve.

"No more speaking. Worse than you have tried."

Gates realized she was doing exactly that. Speaking to

him. Perhaps with patience her resistance would run its course and she would talk, first of the dog, then of the boy.

"You can arrest me." She gestured toward the nursing station. "A nurse told."

Gates kept his eyes on her face, trying to ignore the woman's transformation: the shiny unruly wisps of hair now flat and lifeless, lined with gray. The smooth face, sculpted cheeks now sunken, teeth no longer bright. The beautiful gardener with large dark eyes had been replaced by a refugee, grim and exhausted. Broken, Gates believed, by a violence she had never anticipated and could not fully comprehend.

"What would I care?" She resumed her thoughts. "Jail? It does not matter." She picked up a Kleenex and wiped an errant drop of water from the side of her mouth. "Go now, please."

Gates didn't move. Waited. Hoping for more. "I love gardening," he said. "I have one. Flowers, vegetables."

Faraday shot him a look.

Mrs. Barker laboriously turned her body to face the bank of monitors. Pulled the covers higher.

In the parking lot Faraday stood outside the cruiser, made no effort to enter. "That attempt at rapport was pathetic."

"Maybe if you showed her your quilting she'd have opened right up." Gates was irritated by Mrs. Barker's intransigence and the deputy's censure, but Faraday was right.

"End result, no information," she said, brushing at the arms of her uniform shirt as if the hospital ward had left germ dust.

Gates rested his hands on the cruiser top. "Here's pot or bust," he said, looked away to organize his thoughts. "Barker killed her dog and either badly hurt or killed his boy. The only reason she's still alive is timing." He didn't seem to notice he'd begun tapping on the car's roof.

Continued. "I think Barker and possibly his brother have squirreled away a lot of money. Enough to live fat for the rest of their lives. I think Payne tried to put the finger on one or both of them and got disappeared for his trouble. Somehow the other homeless are just a cover or they're implicated in the blackmail. But what I think doesn't mean squat since I don't have enough evidence to get a search warrant, let alone an arrest and conviction. And I've lost a Dumpster the size of Paul Bunyan's bread box."

"We," Faraday said.

Gates gave the top a hard knock, and, embarrassed when he saw the small dent he'd made, dropped his hands to his sides. He walked around the nose of the cruiser to Faraday. "You can't hide a bright blue Dumpster behind a barn or in a grove of trees. Somebody will eventually wonder about it and make a phone call, so long-term, you've got to sink it or bury it. The best place to sink something that size is Sierra Lake, but you'd have to push it off a bluff into very deep water or barge it out to the middle and tip it in. Easily observed, too complicated."

She nodded, thinking along with him.

"Bury it? To dig a hole that big, you'd need a Caterpillar or earthmoving equipment."

"Trask again. At their compound? They have enough to dig to Singapore," Faraday said, remembering the idle dozers, loaders, and carriers. "But they wouldn't put the thing any-place that could be tied to them." She absentmindedly ran her fingers over the shells in her gun belt. "We need to find it before the trail gets too cold."

Gates moved past Faraday and gave the front tire a hard kick with his steel-toed boot. Swore. "Anything else?" he asked her.

"Just my chips," Faraday said, no longer frowning. "I'm all in. Hey, don't you have a psychiatrist girlfriend?"

Gates, a reluctant smile. "And you call yourself a detec-tive. One, she's a licensed clinical social worker. Two, I'm pretty sure she doesn't think she's my girl." Gates thought for a moment. "We're friendly associates."

"Then you probably shouldn't moon over her in public restaurants," Faraday said. "Get a grip." She shook her head. "Why don't you ask her if she thinks a woman might do bet-ter with Mrs. Barker. Ask her if there's a lever we're missing that might pry her loose."

"And you'll?"

"I'll grow a longer nose and sniff out that Dumpster."

Murray slipped out the pickup door again, climbed on the hood and shone the flashlight at the box roof. Were there holes? Seams? Rust? A hatch or an air vent? The area in front of the pickup looked solid. No breaks, no trap doors. He shone the light on the roof all the way to the back. Checked out the rails that guided the rear door when it rolled up. Was there enough room to hide on top of the rails and get on the door once it was opened? No way. But there was a thin patch of some kind on the truck's ceiling, left side rear. He could reach it standing on the corner of the tailgate. Up closer, it was a stretched fabric. Murray pulled back a corner, saw what he thought was a digital camera, and ducked to the side hoping it hadn't caught his image. What was that for? They were being watched, monitored! Whoever'd taken them wanted to know what they were doing. If that person had been paying attention, he'd seen the ax.

He got off the bed and examined the floor, then the rolling door. No obvious escape routes. Murray remembered the last moment as they'd bounced into the back of the truck. Had anyone been standing and watching? He hadn't seen anybody, so how would whoever took them know for sure there were three people in the pickup? They wouldn't. Pearl had been on the floor beneath Murray's feet. Nobody could have seen her.

He and Pearl were discussing possibilities when they felt the big truck go even slower and make a lumbering turn onto a much bumpier road. Pearl had leaned her dad over on a pillow she'd made from rolling up her robe. He was seat-belted in. He'd be okay. Meanwhile, though they'd been riding for what seemed like hours, he and Pearl might not have much time left to get ready.

Their ideas? Murray would stand next to the door when someone began to open it, and as soon as it was high enough he'd jam a screwdriver into the base of the guide rail on his side so if they pulled the door down again it wouldn't close all the way. When whoever it was made Murray and Janochek get out, Pearl would stay hidden for a minute or two, then use the ax as a lever to reopen the door, slide out, and follow them. The ax and surprise would be her weapons. Murray would take advantage of that and grab a gun or whatever the kidnappers had. The plan was ridiculously dangerous and full of gaps, but at the very least it might free Pearl to go for help. Better than nothing.

They were talking about how to prevent the roof camera from revealing their preparations when the cargo truck stopped, then backed a short way before the vibration ceased. The driver had turned off the engine.

Murray stationed himself at the rear on the left, lying flat against the side ready to stick the screwdriver in the rail track. He heard a fumbling at the latch: the door was opening. At a foot's gap he shoved the screwdriver in place.

"STOP! Put the gate down! NOW!"

The door scrunched back to the bottom. Murray couldn't tell if the screwdriver had worked or not.

"Get away from the truck!"

Murray heard a brief muffled conversation, a pause, a vehicle door slamming, an engine start, a sharp report like a car backfire, and then silence. In his mind's eye he imagined another man off to the side where the truck was parked, upset, yelling at the driver, making him leave. He'd only heard two voices. Two men. That was good news.

The bad news? In the brief space the rear door had opened, Murray had gotten a glimpse outside in the morning light. The truck had backed up to the edge of a pit. A deep hole the size of a two-story house had been carved into the side of a wooded hill. He saw torn roots at the upper edges, reddish dirt and boulders in the walls and floor. The pit stood empty except for a large metal container sitting all the way to the back of the cut. A blue Dumpster.

Murray had never expected to see it again. Absolutely did not expect to join it. He was jolted out of his daze by the sound of the pickup engine cranking, grinding. Good god! Was Pearl going to ram her way out? The fall out of the truck and into the hole would kill them all—and Murray was vaulting the tailgate racing to stop her.

"TURN OFF THE ENGINE!"

Where did that come from? Was there a speaker up there with the camera? Murray reached the driver's door and yanked it open, lunged to hold the gearshift lever. "Wait!" He fought with her hand trying to put the pickup in gear. "We'll crash!"

Pearl released her grip and Murray looked up to find Janochek awake, wide-eyed, practically hyperventilating.

"It's me!" Murray, so out of breath he could hardly speak. "Pearl's okay. Hold on a minute."

"STOP! NOW!"

Though the engine had never caught, had never actually started, Janochek reached over and turned the key off.

Murray collapsed to the floor beside the truck, wondering what was happening. Whose voice was that?

"I can see you," the voice said. "I can also hear you."

The patch!

"Stop," Janochek disengaged from Pearl. "We have to do what he says."

Murray wanted to argue, but he knew he was missing important information. The voice had to be the person Janochek had spoken with at the cottage and again in the pickup before driving into the cargo truck. Okay, Murrray and Pearl's plan was still in place. He could wait.

"You mentioned a negotiation," Janochek said.

Didn't that mean a compromise? Murray couldn't believe what he was hearing. Had the head injury knocked Janochek senseless? This voice had to be the same person who'd handcuffed Murray, who would have killed him. The same person who had probably killed the people on the hill. He was going to kill the three of them. Murray was a kid but even he knew you can't bargain with a murderer. No matter what the person said, if they didn't escape or attack, they were as good as dead. More bones for the pit.

"Pearl, take your foot off the brakes and turn off the flash," Murray whispered as he shut off the truck lights before climbing over the bed and into the passenger side. He needed to let Janochek know what he'd seen without alerting the voice. He turned to whisper, but the sight of Janochek's still-bleeding head wound knocked the thought from his mind. *Is he going to die?*

Gates called Janochek again. Still no answer. Maybe he was out working and the kids were still sleeping or gone to school. Gates would drive over in a few minutes and look for the man. First, one more call. He was put on hold while the operator paged. Faraday's suggestion had been a good one. Duheen, savvy resource. When she answered, Gates got right to business.

"Can I talk to you about Chuck Barker's wife? Quick?"

"I might think better in front of a plate."

"We'll do that. Soon. But I'm running out of time with this homeless thing. Mrs. Barker's in Mercy Acute Care. I saw her this morning and if the doc rules suicide attempt, you could get her on the unit."

"Not going to happen if she has any insurance. We send patients with coverage to private hospitals. Sacramento. We're full, all fifteen beds. They'll probably send her home unless she re-ups the suicide thing."

"Meaning?"

"Verbalizes intent with a workable plan."

"She wouldn't say that to a doc, but she's going to kill herself, one way or another. Alone. Definitely doesn't want therapy."

"What's she mad about? What's the bind?"

Gates liked that Duheen would always go to the heart of the matter. She'd seen it all in twelve years with the locked unit and outpatient. "I know her husband's abusive," he said. "I think he killed her dog, may have injured or killed her stepson. I think she believes she's next, as soon as the timing's right. Her family of origin's somewhere in Europe. Pretty sure her husband controls the money. No close family here, functionally penniless, I think she's decided to die her way, not by her husband's hand."

Duheen paused, looked down at the fountain's pool, pennies glinting underwater on the tiled floor. "Okay. Furious with no options is a good recipe for suicide. Can you offer her anything she wants?"

"A trip back to her homeland?"

"Maybe, maybe not. Might be embarrassed about her marriage, how her decisions turned sour. May not want to face her family."

"If I jailed her husband?"

"Likely she'd see that as temporary, just postponing the inevitable."

"Can you think of any carrot that would lead her to talk about what's been happening?"

"Is she taking antidepressant medication?"

"Yeah, and benzos too, unless the paramedics confiscated them."

"The doc should probably pull the Xanax and . . ."

"Klonopin."

"Right. Too easy. Too lethal. Keep the antidepressants, probably switch to different one hoping for better results. That's not much use to you, because even if they work, they usually take a couple of weeks to kick in."

"What about victim witness? New ID, change of scenery, safety?"

"From what you've told me, she wouldn't qualify."

"She might if she burned her husband."

"Right now she sounds too despondent to respond positively. Maybe in a month or so, if she was feeling less morose. How about bringing a close family member stateside? Like if she had a favorite sister or brother?"

Gates had been distracted by the Duheen's mention of "close family." That triggered something, relevant to a question he'd been asking himself, but which one?

Duheen could feel the change in Gates's energy. "What's the matter?"

His desk phone rang and he put it on speaker to include Duheen.

"I bought her a dog." Faraday's voice.

"What are you talking about?" Gates, confused.

"I was out at Haven Humane last weekend, looking for one myself. Mrs. Barker had one of those fluffy tan things?"

"I didn't see it. Read it in your notes."

"Yeah. It was Lhasa or a Shih Tzu or something. Fit in her hand. Haven had a tiny black dog for adoption. Different breed, but cute. I remembered. Went out and bought it. Took it to her in the hospital. Bribed the nurses."

Gates was having trouble keeping up. "Bribed?"

"See's Candy. Fresh two-pound boxes for a month."

Gates imagined the heavyset charge nurse trying to scrub chocolate smears off her chin. "Mrs. Barker?"

"She wouldn't look at it until I set it on her chest and left the room."

"And?"

"By the time I left she was holding it."

The brilliance of the strategy left Gates speechless.

"Hey, and I had an idea about the Dumpster," Faraday

said, sounding rushed. "I have to check something. I'll see you back at the office."

Gates hadn't closed his mouth when Faraday hung up. He heard Duheen clear her throat.

"You've been holding out on me," she said.

The voice. "Have you told your children what I said in the cottage?"

"No." Janochek.

Murray interrupted. "Pearl got away. She's not here."

"She needs to hear this," the voice said.

He'd heard the two of them talking! The camera must have a mic and speaker. So much for the plan. Whatever they said or did made no difference if the delivery truck went in the pit.

Janochek squeezed out of the pickup, edged to the back of the truck, and lowered the tailgate. Sat down and motioned to Pearl and Murray to do the same. "Might as well be comfortable," he said.

Pearl moved to sit beside him.

When Murray joined the two of them, he scooted as close as he could to Janochek, pressed his elbow into the man's side to get his attention. When Janochek turned his head, Murray moved his eyes up toward the rear ceiling. Mouthed "camera and speaker," but couldn't tell whether Janochek understood.

"Listen carefully." The voice was jolting, loud and fuzzy with feedback in the enclosed box. "The negotiation . . . You can live, if you will be silent from this moment forward, about the bodies, about me . . . Agree, and you can leave, go on your way."

Murray, desperate, pushed Janochek harder in the side. Would shake his head, warn him, as soon as he looked, but the voice had Janochek's full attention. He sat eyes closed, listening, concentrating.

Pearl sat straight, hand on her father's arm. "Trust *you*?" she asked. "How do we know you won't kill us later?"

"Smart," the voice said, a tone of approval. "You have only my word. But without it, you have nothing. Of course I understand." The voice paused, as if composing the right words.

"You think I'm an evil person . . . I am not. I'm a parent. I own a business. I'm a pillar of the community like the other biggest thieves in history."

Murray could tell Pearl was as surprised as he was. Another lie?

"Life isn't sacred," the voice continued. "No one *deserves* to live or die. In the path of economic or political motives, victims are no more than by-products, unavoidable circumstance, collateral damage. Always have been. Death is the inevitable result of fate or need."

Murray struggled to understand the man's words. Could they be true? Killing was just a fact of life? Not immoral? Is that what he meant? Was everything that happened either economic or political?

"It's evolution," the man said. "Kill or be killed."

Murray could practically feel Pearl's bristling disagreement. Janochek, however, seemed calm. In a certain way, the voice was making sense, but it was twisted. If everyone lived by that principle . . . was that happening more than Murray realized? Companies dumping toxic waste near towns, political groups blowing up schools. Jeez, the Indians in this country. We killed them when we wanted their land.

The voice got louder. "Our world? It's built on wink-and-nod business, wink-and-nod politics, wink-and-nod ethics. Corporate execs go to overseas conferences to hear an ex–U.S. president advise them how to shelter their profits offshore! Offshore, so they won't have to pay legitimate taxes. You or I try to shelter our tax dollars, we're prosecuted. Wink and nod. Congressmen, priests, professional golfers—everyone with a lot of money and power—they say one thing, do another. Why? Because they can."

Murray knew this guy was just building a case to justify his own behavior, but still.

"Evil? I'm hardly a speck beside what happens everywhere every day. There's no morality. Only what we invent or what we can get away with."

Now Murray didn't know what to think. If he lived through this, he was going to ask Janochek.

The voice went on. "I'm done talking. There's a law of survival. When you take matters in your own hands, never . . . leave a witness. The loud noise you heard a few moments ago? Testimony to that creed."

"You shot somebody?" Murray, this out before he could stop it.

"Your question *should* be: Having gone this far, why would I seriously consider letting you live?"

"You tell us." This from Janochek.

"Simply? The police will look a thousand times harder if you three disappear. The homeless die and it's business as usual. Any investigation, perfunctory. But if I have to kill you, and I could—either vaporize or bury you—I run a *far* greater risk of being caught. Being embarrassed. My legacy ruined, my work meaningless."

Murray was doing his best to keep following the man's thinking. People didn't care if the homeless died? And legacy? How could this crook have a legacy?

"Enough. It couldn't be plainer. Agree and you drive away, go on with your lives. Refuse? You wi—"

A rustling noise interrupted. "What the hell are you doing?" A different man's voice, rough, panting, like this man had run from somewhere.

"Get out of here." The first voice.

Murray looked at Janochek and Pearl, both puzzled. A different voice, another partner?

"Who were you talking to?" The new voice.

"People who found the graves."

"Where?"

"The truck. Locked in. We're negotiating."

"My ass!"

"I'm keeping us out of jail."

"Did you kill the security guard?"

"Had to. How did you find me?"

"Tire tracks from Mom's driveway. You put this excavation next to her land?"

"I'll fix those on the way out. This part's state forest. Anonymous. We doze trees over the hole like a mudslide. Lasts forever."

"You brought the D-7?"

"The old one, the D-9. Quit bitching, help me, and it'll be in the compound by tomorrow."

"Why are you whispering?"

"We can't talk. They can hear."

"Jesus, Roth, do you know how you sound?"

"Don't say names. They've never seen me, can't identify us . . . They agree to shut up and drive away? Cops continue to bumble and we're gone within the week."

"You can't make a deal with kids. They'll say anything to stay alive!"

"The dad'll get it."

"Right. Dads are foolproof. Ours thought you were a CEO."

Murray heard a snap and shuffling, scuffling, like the men were wrestling. When it ceased, Murray thought he could hear hard breathing, maybe whispering.

The second voice got louder, angrier, more sarcastic. "So, Golden Boy, do you get how complicated—"

"Clever."

"Right. You're a genius . . . And the CarterGuard cruiser?"

"Goes in the pit with Gary."

"The Dumpster?"

"Already there."

Murray exchanged glances with Janochek and Pearl. Nodded. Held up one finger. Pointed to his bandaged thumb and the scabs on his wrist. Held up two fingers. Shrugged. Shook his head. They seemed to get it. He knew the first voice—the man who'd kidnapped him. Didn't know the second. Murray caught Janochek's eye and pointed to the ceiling.

Janochek noticed the patch.

"You should have let me handle this. We'd already be

done . . . You planning to get the equipment back to the compound?"

"Flatbed, behind the trees on the far side."

"We sink the truck, bury everything, load the dozer . . . we still have an extra car."

"I'll drive you back, but we don't have to do this if we negotiate. We make a deal with the man and the kids. We could take our time leaving. Make it look right."

"A deal . . ."

"They don't talk, they live."

"You try that and we'll both get the chair."

"If we run now, Lillian will find out."

"You think she won't find out anyway?"

"This is for her."

"Oh, yeah, I forgot. Your daughter wanted you to steal millions?"

"A year or two, the lawyer contacts her. Delivers her trust."

"The accounts?"

"Growing. Compound interest."

"Still both our names?"

"You signed them."

"You could have made changes."

"I'm not you. This is wasting time. Let me do what has to be done."

"Yeah? Well, Dad was wrong. What has to be done is exactly what you can't do."

"I got rid of Payne."

"You made it worse. If that wet brain figured something out, who'd listen to him? He was nothing. The investigation was closed!"

"Goddamn it, you're not boss."

"I should be."

"You know they're hearing all of this."

"What we're saying? They're forty feet away."

"I'm broadcasting to the truck."

"You . . . imbecile!"

Gates thanked Duheen and headed to the cemetery to find out what Murray had been doing when he disappeared. He dreaded what Janochek might say. "You blew him out of the water with your tragic tale. He needed time alone."

Gates rolled through the entrance and up the narrow road to the cottage, going extra slow, hoping he'd see Janochek working nearby. No one but an older couple at a grave west of the big oak. Disappointed when he got to the cottage. No pickup. He left the cruiser and knocked on the workshop door. No response. The door was unlocked. Lights off.

He walked around to the cottage. Tried that door. Also unlocked. Guess that wasn't surprising. Gates couldn't think of any robbery reports related to cemeteries. Kiefer or the girl could possibly still be sleeping after a late night, so he called out. Again, louder. Hardly an echo. Gates had never been in a cemetery caretaker's cottage before. Curiosity drew him over the threshold, past the small table by the door. He took in the tiny living room, a blanket-covered love seat, a maroon easy chair, short coffee table that might double as an otto-man, a hall leading toward the back. Bathroom and bed-rooms? He checked each and found them empty.

Back in the living area, he put a hand on the food prep counter separating living room from kitchen. Walked on around to better see the fridge, stove, sink, cupboards. In the corner by the fridge the plastic garbage can had a couple of bloody rags on top. Probably a simple explanation for those. Cooking injury.

Off to his right, an alcove by the front window for the

four-person dining table. On the table a half-full coffee cup, two nearly full bowls of cereal gone to milky mush. Gates turned a three-sixty. The rest of the kitchen was clean, so why was the dining table not cleared? On his second three-sixty he spotted a ballpoint lying beside a scrap of paper near the sink.

Read the note. TAKEN AT GUNPOINT. He gripped the counter for support. *Fool!*

He ran to the cruiser, grabbed the mic, and called an all-points on Janochek's pickup: older General Motors, probably eighties, faded red, fifty-year-old Caucasian driver with two teenagers. Made it an AMBER-Alert, California-wide, posted on freeways. Didn't take time to explain. *All those phone messages!*

He speed-dialed Faraday.

She picked up second ring.

Gates broke over whatever she'd been going to say. Tried to keep from yelling. "He's got the caretaker and the kids. Their last message"—he checked his phone—"six-forty. Probably gone a couple of hours. You got anything?"

"Got a place," Faraday said. "A maybe. You at the cemetery?" She didn't give Gates time to answer. "Meet me at Deschutes, 44 off-ramp. You do the alert. I'll scramble Highway Patrol." Dial tone.

Gates peeled down the cemetery road requesting a forensics team for the cottage. Maybe they'd see something he'd missed. Prayed he wasn't already too late. Loathed himself. The Kiefer kid, kidnapped twice in twenty-four hours, this time with Janochek and the daughter. *Inexcusable!*

He shut those thoughts off. Focused on the equipment

he carried: phone, handgun, extra clips, twelve gauge, Glock and Springfield in the trunk with extra handcuffs, first aid, flare gun . . . Might not be able to use weapons if the kids were still alive. Flipped the light bar and siren as he skidded a left on Tehama to 44 west. By the time he crossed under the 5 freeway he was wondering if he had a shovel. Made him sick to think about it.

While the men continued to argue, Janochek leaned close to Murray. "Surveillance?" He gestured toward the ceiling.

Murray nodded. Pointed to his eyes and ears.

Janochek whispered, "Any more?"

Murray did another slow sweep. Shook his head.

Janochek made a fast circling motion with his hand. *Let's get moving.* He motioned Pearl to one side, Murray to the other, so their heads were touching. Said, "Dim the camera." He looked to Pearl. "Handkerchief? Kleenex?"

She shook her head.

He tapped Murray. "Under the seat? Plastic bag?"

The boy hustled to open the passenger door as quietly as he could.

To Pearl, "Did you find the ax?"

She nodded.

"Lean it up against the dash where we can grab it quick."

She lifted it from the bed and stuck it in on the driver's side while Murray came out with a couple of used ziplocks, probably once held sandwiches.

Janochek smoothed the air out of one.

Pearl was back, ready.

"Glove box, electrical tape," he told her.

Janochek gauged where to stand to get to the patch, mouthed, "Help me," and crawled onto the pickup bed with the bag and the tape. When he stood, the hidden area was an easy reach, Pearl beside him, watching, ready to brace him.

Murray stayed at the back of the truck bed, monitored the men's argument, hoping they were too distracted to notice.

Janochek taped the plastic on one side, anchoring it, taped the rest of the perimeter until the bag made a fairly tight layer over the original communication patch. He clambered down, sat on the tailgate again.

A minute took forever. Waiting for Faraday at the off-ramp, Gates got out and inspected his trunk. Everything there, including the rifle scope in the case beside the Springfield. He mounted it and did a sight check. Close enough. Heard engine noise and turned to see Faraday slewing to a stop twenty feet behind him.

"Mine," he said, motioning her to him.

"Thought you'd say that." She grabbed the shotgun from the holder, hauled a navy canvas bag off the back seat, and ran toward him while Gates started the car. "Back on 44 east," she shouted as she plunged into the passenger side, slamming the door. "Whitmore Road."

Flashers warning people to the side, Gates was at a hundred when she tapped him for the turnoff.

"Left, then right at the T." She checked pistol clips while he blew down the narrow two-lane.

"It's curvy at the start," she said, after he'd turned again and headed east.

"I remember," he said. Got back to ninety when the road straightened at the top of the long hill. "What do you have?"

"I don't know if you said something that tipped me. Maybe it was Barker's wife. Family out of town. I began to wonder, what about Mom and Pop Trask? Vacation property? Mom's maiden name? Old man dead, she doesn't use it?"

"And . . ."

"Her family had a retreat. Forty miles east. Remote. Borders on forest land."

"Lassen National Forest?"

"Latour. State forest. Hard to reach, one road in and out. Thirty acres, cabin on a creek, pond."

"Thirty acres," Gates said. "Big enough."

The road got twisty again and he had to focus. Straightened near the town of Whitmore, and he slowed to seventy. Knew there were too many people, old cars, ranchers on all-terrains. Dart out from a driveway and everybody'd be hamburger.

"I take a left on Fern?" Gates asked, passing the post office, the general store next.

"No, stay straight, but slow down. This becomes Tamarack. Nineteen or twenty miles you hit a road called Scott Lumber, then Cutter. These are more like deer trails. We'll stay on the coordinates I pulled from the GPS. The land is just before you cross the state forest boundary."

"Never heard of Latour." Gates could see Faraday was right. The road was already treacherous.

"I asked Highway Patrol for a helicopter." Faraday was holding on to the armrest and still banging side to side. "One's on a car chase approaching Glenn County, the other's searching for climbers at Castle Crags. Riverton office couldn't give me an ETA. Valley Division's too far south to do any good. Right now, we're the nearest patrol."

The first voice must have turned back to his microphone because his voice was suddenly loud again. "So do we have an agree— What happened to the camera!"

"It's pretty hot in here," Janochek said. "Might have fogged."

"Should have brought your IT manager." The second voice.

Murray. Crystal clear—these men hated each other. So why were they partners?

"Last chance," the first voice said. "You agree, I open the door. Even if the boy locates where he was held yesterday, it's been sanitized."

"Goddamn it! You had the boy and lost him?" The second voice. Even more furious.

Uh-oh. Murray remembered he hadn't told either Pearl or Janochek about the hole right behind the truck.

"We can't agree to anything unless we trust you." Janochek.

"Trust this," the first voice went on, ignoring the other's challenge. "I do what's best for me and my daughter. You live, the investigation dies. You die, we have trouble. Kids go missing after they found the hill graves? Cops will put on a full-court press. Long run, best you drive away."

"Sheriff knows there were more bodies." This from Pearl. "They're looking for the Dumpster."

Murray wished he hadn't told her about that. Couldn't decide if she was hurting or helping.

"Goddamn it!"

Murray couldn't tell which one said that, but another struggle was on.

Janochek raced to the pickup and jumped in. Yelled "We're going!"

Pearl ran to the passenger side while Janochek turned the key. The GMC made a loud, rasping sound. Didn't start.

"The fan jammed?" Janochek opened the door and leaned out to look for grille damage.

Murray's screaming alarm was drowned out by the first voice, but he couldn't understand what it said. "Go ahead"? "The ramp's down"? He had no idea because he was still screaming at Janochek. *THERE'S A PIT!"

Murray was knocked to his knees by an explosion that reverberated through the truck like an earthquake. He saw Janochek stagger out of the pickup holding his ears, saw Pearl's arm above the cab's back window, her rear halfway out the passenger door. Still near the tailgate, Murray felt his head drumming again. Might have banged it on the truck when he toppled.

Nothing else inside the cargo area had changed. No smoke. The camera, the speaker . . . did the noise come from the mic wherever the men were talking? Murray wondered if that bang meant the end of negotiations.

He listened hard. Footsteps . . . leaving, coming back . . . A car door opening, shutting, a loud scraping like someone could be moving the sound equipment.

Several minutes later, the second voice came on. "I'm raising the door. Bust out of here before I change my mind."

Then nothing.

The thin paved roads were decent in some spots and gravel in some spots with unpredictably deep potholes. Gates had nearly broken an axle on a downed tree that he couldn't avoid. It was late morning when they reached ruts the GPS suggested led to Mrs. Trask's property. They passed signs announcing Latour State Forest to the left of the road. Trask's path took off to the right. It had been traveled recently. Quite a bit. An eighth of a mile in, big tire tracks went through a dense stand of timber. Gates would have liked to follow, but they were already late. Hours since Janochek and the kids had been taken.

Just before the patrol car crested a short rise Gates stopped the cruiser and the officers slid pistols from holsters and went forward on foot, following tread patterns. In less than a quarter mile they could see a dilapidated wooden building, green metal roof. No obvious vehicles. Gates's hope faltered, and he heard Faraday muttering. Both began jogging.

Trees had been cleared in front of the cabin to allow parking for three or four vehicles. An unattached shop stood to the right side, and Faraday crept toward that. Gates went straight to the front door. Listened. Heard nothing and turned the knob. Door was locked from the inside. When he saw Faraday exit the shop, he made a big loop behind trees around to the rear. The back wall had two windows, curtained, and a door in the center above a three-foot-square cement pad, good place to knock snow or mud off shoes before entering.

He wasn't surprised the door was unlocked. Way out here, did you want a stranger to break in or walk in? Latter left you with fewer repairs. Gates stayed against the back wall and shoved the door hard. It swung freely and cracked against a cabinet, and rebounded shut. He couldn't tell if there was someone inside. He'd wait for Faraday.

She appeared around the other corner in less than a minute, shook her head. Glided up to join him on the other side of the doorframe. Gates was surprised at her grace and agility. Thick-muscled and stocky as she was, he hadn't expected that. Imagined she played sports in high school or college but couldn't imagine which one—discus? She raised her pistol and snapped him back to the present. He knew in that moment why he was losing focus. He'd given up hope. Believed the place was empty.

Faraday held the gun with both hands above her head, ready to drop and shoot. Gave the door another hard kick, breaking it at doorknob level, and rushed in, Gates right on her heels. They swung weapons in every direction but saw no targets. Back porch, cot, cupboards, hooks holding old sweaters and coats. He kicked the kitchen door open. Again nothing. Dishes in the drainer. Everything else put away. The fridge running. No fresh food. Box of butter, couple of six packs of beer, pickles. Condiments. Maybe the family came up here from time to time. Gates imagined the brothers bringing lunch, going fishing, leaving before dark.

Faraday came back from the living room. "Bedrooms empty. Sleeping bags on mattresses. Bathroom: shampoo, toothbrushes. No one's here. No hostages."

Faraday wanted to walk the grounds. Thirty acres. Room to hide things.

Gates was restless. Kept thinking about the tire tracks leading to the left, toward the state forest. Heavy equipment. Yelled at Faraday and ran for the car.

Murray got to his feet, jumped down from the bed, and stepped over a stunned Janochek. Reached inside the pickup cab for the ax. Murray could picture it. Any moment the rear door would roll up and the shooting would start. These guys wouldn't wreck the big truck. They'd kill the three of them, stuff them in the pickup cab, and push them into the pit. Murray at least wanted to get in one swing.

Janochek, clearing, must have imagined a like scenario. He was pulling Pearl around between the passenger side and the cargo wall. Helped her to the floor behind a front wheel. Pushed her flat and squeezed down in front of her.

Murray guessed the odds were the killer would be right-handed. He wedged himself in the back corner of the box where he could swing or throw the ax into the door opening before the man could bring his gun around. He put his bad hand above the other on the handle, made sure he had a strong grip in spite of the thumb.

All they could hear was their own breathing. Okay, maybe the noise had been the microphone being slammed down. That would be really loud, make a sharp bang. So there could be at least two men out there. Good thing the camera had been covered. At least he and Janochek were free to move, had the element of surprise. Murray realized he still had the knife in his jeans pocket. He should give that to Pearl. When he ran to the side of the truck he was stunned to see Janochek holding a pistol, aiming at the door. "What . . . you—"

Janochek cut him off. "My dad's. I got it out last night, grabbed it when we left." He rolled his eyes toward the hood.

"Maybe you ought to hide up front," he said. "Behind the engine, kneel by the bumper."

Pearl had risen to see what the two of them were talking about.

Janochek reached behind him to push her down again.

"Toss me my knife," she said, "just in case."

Murray handed it to Janochek who passed it on.

"Go on," Janochek told him, "before they get here."

Murray couldn't decide. If he went up in front of the pickup, yeah, the engine block would probably stop bullets, but he'd be useless. Couldn't swing the ax. His consideration was interrupted by the sound of an outside car starting, revving a couple of times, getting farther away, and then coming back. Stopping. A few seconds passed and then another rev and a whine and a crash, metal rolling and bending, slamming the ground and finally stopping.

The pit?

"What the hell?" Janochek, peering over the bed, looking at the rear door. Had it moved during all that racket?

Murray figured the three of them would be next. "I think they're coming."

"Why now?" Janochek asked, but Murray didn't know and didn't answer. Just got in the right position to use his ax. He had the image in his mind. Some guy would begin opening the rear door, maybe the guy who'd driven the truck, but maybe not. Things had gotten so confusing. *Never leave a witness.* Anyway, Murray was hoping for the first voice. Let him open it. Murray hated that guy.

He heard the rear lock snick, scrape, stop. Saw the door jostle. Watched as it began to inch up. Slow, it didn't make much noise. Murray wondered if Janochek could hear it, but he couldn't yell and give himself away.

When the door was opened about a foot, Murray had a better idea. The guy doing it, didn't he have to stand right there to raise it? What if Murray waited till the door was a little higher so he could see the guy's body before the guy saw him. Swung the ax as hard as he could right into the center of the man's stomach.

Would the guy still shoot and kill Murray? Would his partner? Okay. Would Murray die to save Pearl and Janochek? He'd never thought about that but it sounded fair.

Could he swing the damn ax? Would he? He didn't know. But the door was getting higher. It wasn't really a choice. Get the blade right! Make sure it was going straight! Fast. Hard. FAST! and he swung with everything he had and the ax hit something and the handle hit the bottom of the door and broke in half leaving him holding a piece of wood when the rest disappeared. Did he connect? The breaking made too much noise. He was afraid to look and bolted for the pickup, dived behind the front bumper.

In a moment he realized he couldn't hear anything over the thudding of his heart and he was crying, damn it, and that made him even deafer. Nothing seemed to be moving. The box was still as rock. And Murray clamped his wrist over his mouth and slowly quieted. He felt a touch on his ankle. Pearl. Reaching as far back as she could. Holding him. And in spite of everything that made the crying worse . . . if he could hold her just one more time before . . . She didn't let go and in a minute or so the tears ceased.

Everyone waited. No one spoke. Murray couldn't tell if

the enormously loud noise a few minutes ago had actually damaged his ears, but he didn't want to say anything in case the men were still listening.

Pearl jiggled his foot and he thought he knew why. He was starting to hear something, too. A fan? A hum . . . an engine . . . his stomach rolled.

A heavy patrol car bounces side to side when you gun it over a bumpy dirt track. It spins out on carpets of pine needles. Joining the path of the deep tire tracks, a wide sweeping turn nearly cost Gates a fender.

Faraday put her hand on his arm. "You bust in there, we might have another Waco."

Right. Gates took his foot off the accelerator. Branch Davidians, law enforcement's long-lasting black eye. No matter that the crazy guru had set fire to his own people, federal officers' haste and indecisive planning helped exacerbate what was already a tragedy.

"Roll your window," Gates said, doing his own. "Hear what we can."

Faraday boosted herself partway out for a few seconds before slapping branches forced her back inside. "Quiet as far as I can tell."

Gates crossed a cattle guard. Sign beside it: ENTERING LATOUR STATE FOREST. They continued, gradually edging south, came to a small creek.

"Atkins," Faraday reported, GPS in hand.

Since the bottom was rocky and the creek not too swollen, they drove through slowly enough to keep water from splashing the engine block. Saw the tire gouges on the far bank.

"Been some weight here," Faraday noted.

Gates made himself lay off the accelerator.

Not far, perhaps less than a half mile, the trees began to thin toward what looked like a small meadow at the foot of an abrupt hill. Gates stopped the car, searched the console for his binoculars. Faraday found them crammed in her side's storage bin. They left the doors open and walked to the perimeter of the clearing. Two hundred yards away, a gray van sat parallel to a large box truck. The van's driver's side and back doors were standing open.

The department-issue 10x50s helped him see all the way to the van's dash. The carry area had a standing card table, a folding chair beside. Jumbled paraphernalia on the floor: coils of rope, tool boxes. No people, unless they were huddled on the floor in front of the seats.

At the large cargo truck, it looked like both doors were closed. No people visible. The vehicle's cab was facing them so they couldn't see the rear. Behind the truck a new excavation, the side of the hill scraped maybe forty feet in, showing a dirt wall at least fifteen feet high with leaning, partially uprooted trees at the top.

When Gates refocused the nocs, he could see big tire tracks leading past the clearing into the woods on the far side. A slash of yellow, the color of road-building equipment, the rest of the shape hidden by foliage. Felt a tap on his shoulder.

Faraday pointed to his right. Maybe fifty yards farther around the perimeter a large white SUV. When they approached they found it unoccupied, the hood barely warm. Been here an hour? From this angle they could see more of the van, but still not the back of the big truck.

Gates was out of patience, afraid he was already too late.

"You walk in," he told Faraday. "Use the van for cover." That earned him a scowl. He knew if there was time she would have scolded, hated it when he told her things she already knew. "My bad," he whispered after her but she was already moving low across the meadow.

Gates ran back to the cruiser, cranked the ignition, flipped the lights and siren and barreled in. Maybe the hoopla would freeze everybody and they wouldn't make anything worse. He was planning to race past the cargo truck and one-eighty spin to a stop, facing the back. Figured that's where everybody was. *Be alive!*

Realized too late his plan was a bad miscalculation.

The shaved area wasn't flat. It was a pit. No way he was going to stop in time. He bailed and shoulder-rolled, praying the car would miss him. Tumbled, kept his arms in, head covered, legs tucked. If the bad guys were watching they'd shoot him the minute they stopped laughing. Even badly shaken, dazed, he heard the cruiser hit the excavation's bottom like a train collision.

He wobbled to his feet, reached for his pistol. Gone. Probably in the grass near one of his cartwheels. Gates balanced his weight and glanced up, ready to juke either direction depending on how the bastards were holding their weapons. Saw no gunmen, but the truck's rear door stood partially open. Barely visible inside, the tailgate and bumper of a pickup. He dropped to the ground, rolled right a few feet to make a poorer target, and risked another glance. There was something on the ground in front of the truck door.

Faraday jogged to join him, helped him to his feet. Said, "Clear," and then pointed to the bundle at the back of the truck. "What's that?"

Gates shrugged.

She handed him his nine-millimeter. "You were probably looking for this." She was already moving a step at a time toward the truck, two-handed grip on her pistol leading the way.

Gates jogged to the right making a broader target spread before joining her advance. Closer, he could see the lump on the ground was a man in fetal position. Matched the SUV. Chuck Barker.

"Drop your weapons! We're coming in!"

Murray knew that voice. He thought he saw two shadows enter the back at either side. The sound of crawling. Janochek saying, "It's just us." He heard Janochek grunt as he got to his feet. A person Gates's size stood, then another, smaller. "Come on out," the woman said, lowering her pistol. Everyone started leaving the truck. Was Pearl okay?

A week after school had started last August, Murray's history class was studying twenty-first-century cultural mores and using a pick-a-question-from-a-basket game to increase class participation. If he could have avoided picking one, he would have, but that wasn't an option. His turn. The question was "Where were you when you had your first kiss?" Murray did everything he could think of to quell the blush that began at his feet and feathered its way toward his face. The answer Murray hoped no one else could see was "nowhere." Somewhere on the walls of his blank mind he found the words "at the movies," and the game moved on to the next person.

Now, finally, he had a real answer to that question. Under a pickup bumper on the floor of a cargo truck. And he would never have guessed Pearl could deliver such a thriller. Pearl. When it was over she crawled away to join her dad, and Murray was weak. Had to drag himself up using the pickup grille. He was . . . there were no words for it. But blissed out beyond the boundaries of the known universe might be a start. He knew one more thing for certain. He'd never get that from Sandray.

His shivery pleasure lasted until Deputy Gates called him by name.

Murray knew what he'd done. He'd fulfilled the pinnacle of his mother's dreams, didn't need a high school graduation to succeed. He'd gone straight to the top. Become an ax murderer. Killed a man he did not see and did not know. The man's name? Not a clue. Whether the man had done anything wrong, Murray had no idea. Murray had killed him for opening a truck door. That wouldn't sit well with the jury.

Gates was waiting just outside at the back of the truck. "Don't touch the door," he said as Murray came close. "Slide under and touch as little as possible."

Murray complied, hoping they'd talk for a while before he had to put on any handcuffs again. He hated those things. Imagining a pair made his thumb ache. He inched out and shot a quick look into the pit. The Dumpster had been joined by two wrecked patrol cars. Two? Police cars? That didn't make sense. For a second Murray pictured Janochek's pickup burning rubber, racing backward out of the cargo box, and flying tailgate-first into the hole. Probably would have dived right into one of the cars and if the three of them weren't already dead, the crash would have broken their necks.

He shook off an involuntary shudder and concentrated instead on Pearl and Janochek several feet away, also looking into the pit. Both smiling. Well, they hadn't killed anybody. Which reminded him, where was the man he'd struck? He jumped to find him not a foot away, on the ground almost beneath the truck. He saw the blood. A big pool of it under the truck's door below the loading plate. A woman deputy knelt beside the man, hands together, pressing on his stomach. Meant he wasn't dead, didn't it? So the charge would be just something like ax with intent to kill. With any luck Murray'd eventually get out of prison. He should ask.

"I don't know that guy," Murray said, pointing to the man on the ground.

"Chuck Barker," Gates said. "His brother around here?"

"Somebody was." Murray looked around though he knew it wouldn't do any good. He'd never seen the man with the first voice. "Somebody else talked to us . . . There was an explosion. I don't know what happened."

"That was entirely too close," Gates said, stepping between Murray and the body on the ground. "I . . . uh, I haven't done right by you. I'm . . . relieved. Glad you're safe. Finally."

Murray couldn't look at the man. He believed Gates had kind of liked him. Had told him some personal things that you don't tell just anybody. Somehow the deputy who'd accused and doubted had changed his mind. That felt surprising, and good, and it was a shame Murray had let him down. He'd hurt or killed the person who must have kidnapped him. You weren't allowed to do that, not even for political or economic motives, and Murray didn't have either one. He'd just been trying to save his friends.

"There is probably a bomb inside the pickup," Murray said, amazed he'd been able to guess what it might be and then put it out of his mind.

"Then we better move a lot farther away," Gates said, bending to help the deputy he'd called Faraday drag Barker from the cargo truck all the way over to the edge of the meadow closest to the pit. They found a shady area with a flat spot for the injured man, who was still breathing but making a lot of noise doing it.

"Is he going to be okay?" Murray asked.

"If dragging him didn't put him out of his misery I guess he'll make it till the medevac arrives," Faraday answered.

Gates's hip radio squawked and he walked a few paces away to answer. Murray returned to the near edge of the pit for one more look . . . *No tombstone.* If they'd covered him with all that dirt could he have ever talked to anyone again? Probably not. Dearly had told him the friendship depended on the living person. No one would even try to connect. Nobody would guess he was buried down there.

Murray knew he'd never been this close to death. Maybe dying wasn't such a top choice. Making breakfast for Janochek and Pearl . . . that had been pretty good. Maybe he needed to pay more attention to it. Living. That reminded him of Pearl, and he was glad to see her and Janochek walking toward him, with Faraday not far behind. He could see Gates taking over care of the wounded man.

When she got close, the woman deputy pointed at something in the pit.

"Recognize the markings on the bottom car? That's a CarterGuard."

Pearl nodded. "Like the one that caught us near the stables."

"What I don't get is," the deputy said, "I think I see two bodies in it."

Murray chimed in. Might as well say what he knew before they arrested him. "There were two of those guys in the junkyard I escaped from."

"Junkyard?" the deputy asked.

"Fenced. Shipping containers, a trailer, tractor-type things, a whole bunch of stuff."

"Probably Trask's equipment yard. Gates and I were there earlier looking for this Dumpster."

"Who's down there in the sheriff's patrol car?" Janochek asked.

The deputy looked at him and smiled. "Nobody."

Gates joined them. "FBI out of Riverton's sending two teams. Kidnapping and a demo squad. We need to wait for them. I've got some bottled water in the trunk."

Faraday moved her eyes from his face to the pit.

"Yeah. Right." Gates tapped his forehead. "Maybe later."

"We can wait," Janochek said. "We're still breathing. Thanks."

"I'm sorry about the missed calls," Gates said.

Janochek waved him off. "You're here."

"How'd you find us?" Pearl asked.

"Let's sit," Faraday suggested. "Put this thing together." She turned away from the pit, returning to check on Barker. Motioned to a spot near him, where medium-size boulders had collected, maybe from Lassen's volcanic eruption nearly a hundred years ago.

When they were reasonably settled, Janochek began. "One of these guys called an hour or so after Murray got home. I'd just sawed off the handcuffs."

That raised the officers' eyebrows.

"They put a sack over my head." Murray looked at Gates. "I got jammed into a car . . . a van, on the other side of the lake where we'd been talking. They took me to this . . . construction place." He nodded at Faraday. "She said you guys were there earlier today. When I got away, it was still dark."

Janochek resumed. "I got a call early this morning. Thought it was you. A guy said he knew Murray was with us and he'd blow up the cottage if we didn't take off in the truck."

"How?" This from Faraday.

"He'd taped . . . somebody had taped a bomb to the gas pipe entering the house."

Gates looked skeptical.

"I saw it," Janochek explained. "Don't know if it was real. Couldn't risk it."

"That was when you were looking out our window?" Pearl asked. "You were acting so weird."

"You left a note," Gates said. "Otherwise we wouldn't be here."

Janochek nodded. "The guy or a partner left a phone in my truck. Told me what to do. Drive over a few streets, ramp into the back of that big truck. Soon as we did, door closed and he, they, took off, I guess. I was out of it for a while."

"So they drove us here and the voice wouldn't let some guy open the rear door," Pearl continued.

"The voice?" Faraday.

"They'd rigged a camera and speaker with a mic on the truck ceiling," Janochek said. "Could see us, hear us, talk to us without showing themselves."

"Why?" Gates.

"Negotiate," Janochek explained. "One guy said if we'd shut up about everything, they wouldn't kill us. The other guy thought letting us go was crazy."

"No disrespect," Faraday said, "but why didn't they

simply kill you as soon as they got here? They'd already murdered several. Can't hang twice."

"This guy, the voice, thought—he had these creepy ideas," Murray said. "Killing was okay, uh, economical. He said he didn't want to bury us 'cause that would bring on a bigger investigation—"

Janochek broke in, "The voice, whoever it was, rationalized it was okay to murder people if they got in your way. Said everybody with money or power did it. Said mainly he didn't want to get caught—embarrassed, he put it."

"And the second voice came in," Pearl said, "it was like two men working together who couldn't stand each other. Always arguing.

"I guess both wanted to kill us no matter what," Pearl added, talking as she pieced things together. "I think the first guy wanted to fool us and the second guy didn't get it. The first wanted us to drive ourselves into the pit, thinking we were getting away. If we did that, they wouldn't have to come in the cargo truck after us, risk getting hurt by whatever we were going to do."

"They didn't know you had a gun?" Gates asked.

"I don't see how. The first guy knew we had an ax but they couldn't be sure what else. And if we fought, even if they won, there might be blood or bullet holes. The company truck wouldn't be clean anymore."

"Mr. Janochek covered their camera so they couldn't watch us," Murray said, "and we made a plan."

"You guys are commandos," Gates said, shaking his head.

"Yeah, but something happened between them," Pearl said. "Remember that incredible noise?"

"Possible the second man shot the first," Janochek said. "The first had been running things. After that big noise, we never heard him again."

Gates thought the cemetery made a pretty good spot for a picnic. Green and shady, flowers, birds, squirrels, quiet enough to talk.

Janochek had set up a dining area under the trees behind the cottage. No one seemed to be buried there yet. At least Murray hadn't heard anyone when he checked it out. Pearl and her dad put chairs and benches around a large rough-wood table with tablecloth, silverware, napkins, and a couple of bowls filled with wild flowers. Nearby, a grill and a cooler full of sparkling juices and sodas.

Murray paused outside the lawnmower shed. He should go and say hello to Edwin and Dearly and Blessed. Even Feathers and Sandray. Let them know what was going on. How incredible it was. They'd enjoy the wild story and it had been a while since he'd visited their graves.

The picnic was supposed to begin in a couple of minutes. Murray gazed up the hill toward the graves, momentarily frozen with indecision. He should tell them. Real quick. But he didn't. He didn't move. Why? Maybe it was pretty simple. The dead were still going to be right there after the picnic. They stayed in place. The living didn't.

He headed toward the cottage, wondering if Janochek had thought to buy hot links.

*   *   *

Faraday tapped on the table with her ballpoint. "Let's share news so we can get on with some serious celebrating. And are those Scoops behind the macaroni salad? We should probably get those going around."

"Speaking of scoops," Pearl said, "give it up."

Faraday gestured to Gates. "It was his case."

"She graciously anticipated me most of the way," Gates said, nodding to Faraday, who saluted him in return.

"Okay," he began, "according to the Feds, it started with big-time tax fraud, a theft from both the company and the federal government. The rest was a cover-up. Probably would have worked if it hadn't been for Kiefer." He lifted his can of ginger ale and raised it to Murray, who blushed but didn't turn away.

"One slight glitch," Gates went on. "To move the money originally, everything had to pass through a guy named David Payne, Trask Engineering Research and Development accountant at that time. Payne suspects something, knows nothing, and when the Feds investigate him in the summer of 2008, he's afraid he'll be implicated if he speaks up. Later the firm fires him and he winds up homeless and hopeless. Before long, realizes he possesses information Trask and Barker will pay to keep hidden. He underestimates their ruthlessness and, according to the coroner's report, Roth kills him with a golf club at the stable. Barker stashes the body up the hill behind the cemetery.

"We haven't confirmed this because Chuck's still in critical condition, but we're pretty sure Payne had bragged about his great idea to other members of the mission, which led to their murders. A man named Rex said Payne believed he would be coming into a big chunk of money soon. Extortion.

"These particular homeless people were killed to freeze the investigation of Payne's murder. Chuck Barker went to the mission posing as a software marketer to get a roster so they'd have the information they needed to tie up the loose ends.

"We're pretty sure Chuck took over the killing, stashed the bodies with Payne's. He and his half brother were sometimes rodeo volunteers and convention center board members. Both of them were around the center complex often enough that their presence wouldn't be unusual. Chuck could come and go as he needed. We're pretty sure he always planned to move the bodies to a more secure location. It was his unimagined error to temporarily put them near enough where Kiefer could sense them. Otherwise, his leave-the-woman idea would have been a perfect subterfuge. Rape her, kill her, leave her body on the hill where animals could eventually uncover it. That "decoy" strategy probably would have led us to conclude that the others missing weren't connected, just coincidental disappearances for a variety of reasons. The lifestyle—pick up stakes without telling anyone."

"We know," Pearl said. "We still have the cap, coat, and sleeping bag to prove it."

Gates looked to Faraday for an explanation. She shrugged.

"That reminds me, Dad, what did you find out?" Pearl sat up straighter, possibly glad to have a larger audience for this line of inquiry. "Who did you ask about the, uh, electrostain, the remainder stuff that might be transmitted by people who are terrified or hurt?"

Janochek cleared his throat. Seemed like he might be a little embarrassed to talk about this in front of Gates and Faraday. "Yes. The something-or-other, energy possibly, that clairvoyant people might be picking up on. Secretions or some kind of remnants from traumatic situations."

Did Faraday's eyes widen? Janochek couldn't imagine what she and the others might be thinking. He soldiered on. "Well, uh, okay. I called my best friend from high school. The physicist? Steve Billings? He said such electro-chemical information could conceivably be generated in the brain during particularly traumatic experiences. That an extremely small amount of energy might possibly be transmitted to and through a person's skin leaving an almost infinitesimal residue on the skin's surface or possibly on something the person touched. Told me the human eye can detect a single photon, the incredibly small elementary particle of light. An absolute miracle, but true. So who knows what kind of information a particularly sensitive brain might apprehend? But he said, as of now, this idea is guesswork. There's no way to study the theory just like we don't currently have a mechanism to experiment with String Theory."

Pearl smiled. That was good enough for her. She was on the right track. Who knew what she might discover one of these days.

Murray didn't know what to make of the discussion. Was there some basis in reality for what he could do? He scarcely dared to hope.

Gates had listened. Nonjudgmental. Faraday looked a little skeptical.

After a moment Gates went on with the crime story.

"When Murray led you all to the hill, the killers thought you were getting too close. Roth grabbed Murray in a company van and botched it. At least according to the argument between the two that you all overheard, because Roth tried to make it right with the bombs and the Trojan truck plan. It was Roth who seemed to want to negotiate. Chuck who wanted to bury every witness and run."

"I figure Pearl was right," Faraday said. "Makes sense Roth wanted to fool you. That would juice his ego another notch. Trick you into driving yourselves into the hole."

"He didn't bother to set up the ramp," Gates added. "He couldn't risk a witness no matter what he said. Alive, you could find the equipment yard and the burial pit once you got to safety and got yourselves oriented. There was a seriously big bulldozer and a transport eighteen-wheeler in the trees on the far side of the pit."

Faraday took over again. "We believe Roth could have done the whole thing by himself. According to your testimony, Barker's arrival was unexpected. Roth probably went off the grid at some point and Barker had to find him to protect his investment. Finally had only one place to look. His dad's old place. He figured it out and showed up uninvited. After Barker shot his half brother, he put him in the Carter-Guard cruiser and sent it over the rim."

"My bet, he beat Roth to the punch, pulled the trigger before his brother could," Gates said. "Fits Chuck's profile. Act first, think later. According to his mother, neither man could stand the other. Those two weren't going to split all that money. One was going in the pit. Count on it."

Faraday momentarily grimaced. Shook her head. When

she spoke her voice had grown serious. "Our consulting contractors tell us either man could have completely filled the pit, covered the Dumpster, cars, van, pickup. Pushed and leveled the dirt and left for home in under four hours."

She looked at Janochek, Pearl, and Murray one by one. "If they'd been able to pull that off, I don't think anyone would have ever found you." She swallowed. "Barker hauls the dozer back to the compound. Hitches a ride to the dead father's cabin, which was less than a half mile from the SUV, and he's gone. Chuck had tickets in the SUV for Caracas leaving tomorrow."

Gates stood. "Crimestoppers," he said, doffing his Stetson.

Murray raised his hand like he absolutely never did in class. It got everybody's immediate attention. "I think it was Pearl," he said. "I hate to say it. I don't want to encourage her, but if she hadn't kept pushing, those guys might have gotten away with the whole thing. Her stubborness brought Carter-Guard into the mix."

Pearl blushed. Didn't deny her pivotal role.

"Speaking of family," Pearl said, "didn't somebody say that one guy, Trask, had a daughter? And the other guy has a son, both around our age. What's going to happen to them?"

"Hard to imagine how the girl will react when the news breaks," Gates said. "Maybe she'll go back with her mother. Maybe she'll move. Could bring a civil suit against Barker if he lives."

"As of right now," Faraday added, "the son's missing."

"Anyway," Gates broke in, changing the subject, "the entire sheriff's office, and especially Faraday and I, are honored to have your expert assistance with uncleared cases." He and

Faraday smiled. "Makes me wonder if I can ask you all for one more favor . . . actually two more, but that's for another day. Today, we party."

"That's what I like to hear," Duheen said, walking around the back of the cottage to join them. "Who brought the lobster?"

As the meal wound down, Janochek and Gates, Faraday and Duheen got in an animated discussion about rising crime, full jails, homeless support services, and interagency cooperation. Murray quickly lost interest and slipped away.

Pearl followed, found him standing in front of a fairly recent grave. "There's still food left," she said.

Murray nodded. Didn't turn. It had only been a couple of days since they kissed. He wasn't sure if or how that moment had changed things. Wasn't sure he wanted any change at all. No matter what, he had a memory he'd never forget.

"This a new friend?" Pearl asked.

"Used to be on the dance team at Endeavor High. Came to a couple of Sierra pep assemblies. I don't know if you saw her."

"Probably before I transferred," Pearl said. "Car accident?"

"Shot. By mistake."

"I've been thinking," Pearl said. "We're lucky."

Murray turned to her. Reached out. Touched her shoulder for a second and let his hand fall. "I guess I was thinking the same thing," he said. "This girl, Sandray, was so pretty and lively and . . ." He looked up at the sky, at high thin clouds pushed by winds that never reached the earth. "She's gone. Really gone. Can't be part of things anymore."

"Well, yeah," Pearl said, "but you two can still be friends, right? Like Dearly and Blessed?"

This conversation was making Murray sad. "Hey!" He was surprised at the stupid idea that had popped into his mind from absolutely nowhere. "Uh, want to see where I go when I'm mad at you?"

Pearl frowned. "Why would you be mad at me?" She knew she could be a little bit assertive sometimes, but really, shouldn't he be grateful? She was sure she brought out the best in him.

"Never mind. Feel like a short walk?"

"I get mad at you, too," she said. "Really really mad." She stepped to him and took his arm. "You want to know what I do when I'm mad at you?"

Murray ignored her question and began leading her down the path, out to Continental Street and over toward the river-bank beach where he occasionally went to throw rocks and curse her bullheadedness.

Her arm felt wonderful linked through his. He couldn't explain it.

Gates sat in the parent pickup zone at Sierra High wondering if he was acting unprofessionally. Several officers in the Major Crimes unit had more than one confidential informant, but he couldn't think of anybody who used a high school student for such a dangerous assignment. And honestly, Gates had to admit this was just the tip of the iceberg. He would happily pay Kiefer a stipend to help with a number of the kinds of cases he regularly encountered. Asking a dead victim to name his or her murderer was the first one that came to mind. Another, searching for a body. And his own secret wish, that Murray would speak with his son.

Now that it was a slightly more likely possibility, Gates wondered if he had the courage to go through with it even if Murray agreed. What if his son said, "Yes. I committed suicide. Dad drove me to it." What then? How would Gates handle that? He couldn't imagine, but the range of possibilities terrified him.

Today, thank god, didn't require a soul-searching decision. If Kiefer said okay, a serious question might be answered.

Chuck Barker was still critical, under guard at Mercy, but it looked like he would pull through. A lot depended on whether the ax wound developed a staph infection that couldn't be treated successfully. Murray's blow had damaged the man's liver and intestines, grazed the spine. The organs would never be right, but they might eventually heal. In fact, it was possible that within a couple of months Chuck would be well enough to stand trial.

*   *   *

Gates hadn't gone inside the high school to get the boy this time, though he understood his reporter friend Doni had been able to make Kiefer a hero without alluding to his paranormal skills. If he wasn't careful, Kiefer could become a go-to item with the coeds.

This time Gates had phoned the principal's office. Asked that a note be delivered to Kiefer in seventh period. Sure enough, in the throng of students heading for the buses and cars in the parking lot, there was Kiefer craning his neck, looking this way and that before spotting the cruiser.

"I appreciate you being willing to give me a hand," Gates said, heading up Eureka Way before taking Buenaventura to Placer. "You agreed, but do you have any idea what this is about?"

Murray nodded.

"And you're still willing?"

Murray decided to tell him. "A while ago Pearl and I had kind of an argument about the way I lived my life, the choices I was making," he said, looking out the window. "She said I had something really different and that I should use it to help people." He looked at Gates, shrugged.

"You have any idea where we're headed?" Gates asked.

Murray turned to look through the windshield at the gray wall of fog standing north above Whiskeytown Lake straight ahead against the western hills. "Maybe," he said. "Newspaper had it that the second voice, the older guy, what's his name?"

"Chuck Barker."

"Yeah. His son's missing."

Gates looked at Kiefer, looked back at the road. Said, "He is."

"Guess we're gonna look for him," Kiefer said.

Gates nodded. Said, "We are."

"Got any ideas?" Murray asked.

Gates smiled. "I do," he said. "That's why I need you. Mrs. Barker and her new dog won't want me disturbing those big rocks in the driveway without a good reason."

ACKNOWLEDGMENTS

I had an opportunity to study with psychotherapist and parapsychologist Lawrence LeShan, PhD. He thrilled me with unexplainable stories of ghosts, mediums, and mystics. Years later, my first book, *Dead Connection*, reflected that association. Since writing it in 2006, I found that the clairvoyant boy Murray, his nemesis girlfriend Pearl, and the cast of cemetery characters stayed with me, often surfacing in the quiet of long drives or emerging whenever I passed a rural graveyard. Gradually the idea of a sequel materialized. I was able to complete most of the book as writer-in-residence at the Fairhope Center for the Writing Arts in Fairhope, Alabama.

I especially appreciate Mr. Skip Jones for his tireless shepherding of the Fairhope Writing Arts Program, and Teen Siener along with the many volunteers for their diligent work in bringing the writing cottage to full bloom.

I am most grateful to my editor, Wesley Adams, for the savvy and humor that makes each literary project a pleasurable collaboration. Also to the people at Farrar Straus Giroux and Macmillan whose care and quality in publishing operations make this a beautiful book inside and out.

Thanks to my agents, Tracey and Josh Adams at Adams Literary, whose support and advocacy I hold dear.

I receive finely tuned feedback from my comrades in two marvelous writing groups: Jim Dowling, Kathryn Gessner, Carla Jackson, Melinda Kashuba, and Robb Lightfoot in California; and Skip Jones, Don Sawyer, and Teen Siener in Fairhope. I'm very lucky to have ongoing encouragement from long-time friends Kit Anderton, Chris Crutcher, Tony D'Souza, and artist Chris Knight, my fellow inspiration student.

Further thanks to Dr. Paul Swinderman for relevant medical consultations, to Manuel J. Garcia, Esq., for advice pertinent to the story's legal areas, and to physicist Dr. Steve Hudgens for perspective on the theories presented herein.

Finally, I'm forever grateful and deeply in debt to the loves of my life. My magnificent psychotherapist/artist wife, Joanie, is always my first reader, and my radiant daughter, Jessica Rose, edits from afar in Portland.